JUDE

Book Cover by Y'all. That Graphic

Edited by Sandy Ebel, Personal Touch Editing

CHECK YOUR TRIGGERS

Your mental health and emotional well-being matters to me. You can find a list of possible triggers on the book's page on my website here or by scanning the QR code below.

Xoxo

To Matt. Thank you for being just as excited about the unhinged antics I wrote about as I am. Love you, babe.

Contents

Prologue
Lucy

"Lucinda, it's time to come in," Mama calls from our rundown house in the middle of Nowhere, Nevada. Well, some people know where it is, but they're not the kind of people you want knocking on your door. At least, I don't. Someday soon, I plan on leaving this shithole behind. I know there are places out there where you don't have to worry about an explosion in your backyard because someone is cooking meth and had an accident. I'm certain other girls get to go to school and aren't betrothed to some creepy elder's son from the time they took their first steps.

"Lucinda, get in here," Mama hollers again.

"She sounds pissed, Lu. We should head back," my sister says next to me. It's amazing how different Cecilia and I are, seeing as we came from the same parents. Cece is the rule follower, never wanting to disappoint our parents or the elders. I, on the other hand, can't wait for the day to tell them all to shove their rules and beliefs straight up where the sun don't shine.

"She just wants us in because those creeps from that motorcycle club are here," I tell Cece from behind the giant decaying barn a few hundred feet from our home.

It's hot as hell in the desert, and this is the best place to find some shade in the afternoon. Especially considering the last place I want to be is in my stuffy room in our little house. From back here, there's nothing but flat lands and open desert as far as the eye can see. There's a fence that surrounds the perimeter of the compound I was born on and if my family had it their way, would die on. Guards patrol all day and all night, whether it's to keep people in or unwanted people out, who knows? Probably a little of both.

My sister is sending me nervous glances, her eyes darting between me and the direction of the house as she worries her bottom lip between her teeth.

"Fine," I say, rolling my eyes at her obvious discomfort. "Let's go in."

Cece's shoulders sag in relief as we make our way back to the house.

"Sorry, Lucinda. I just don't like making Mama or Daddy mad. The last time we defied them..." Her voice trails off.

I'm certain she's reliving the memory of the last time we were late coming in for dinner. Elder Otto decided the only suitable punishment was to go without dinner. Instead of eating, we were made to recite bible verses on our knees until four in the morning in the little chapel at our town's center.

It may sound a bit hypocritical of our elders, cooking meth while supposedly being so devoted to God and believing we're his chosen disciples. They justify it as supplying the weak with drugs to get addicted to, and in turn, we get weapons supplied to us for the inevitable war that's coming. I haven't been around many people who take the kind of drugs our compound supplies. The few times I've seen what it does to a person was enough to scare the hell out of me. The men who come to make trades are more than enough proof of what happens to the people who use what we make. The elders strictly forbid any use of drugs or alcohol on the compound. One of the many rules we must follow to be considered worthy in the eyes of the Lord.

There have been a few times I've accompanied my mama to town to pick up supplies, and every single time, she made sure to impress upon us the importance of our rules. Don't talk to anyone, especially if they wear a badge. The police are evil in her eyes, trying to enforce the laws of man, not God.

The men who came to the exchange meetings weren't much more inclined to be friendly with the police, either. They called them pigs, but the ones I saw around the nearest tiny town didn't look anything like the animals we raised and slaughtered for food. The men who visit were more akin to pigs, at least in the way they smelled.

The last day I was allowed to go to town with my mama and sister, I stole a magazine from the rack in front of the checkout at the store. The cashier was busy bagging the few items we bought while trying not to ogle us. I saw the stares and heard the snickers when we walked around. It was uncomfortable, and I'd silently cry on the way home. I know what people think. We're freaks. At least that's the term thrown around most often. When I got home with the magazine, I read through it at least a hundred times. The pages were curled and worn at the edges, bound to fall out any second. It showed pictures of cute boys, not the dirty ones around here, with anger hidden behind their eyes. The girls wore makeup and clothes much nicer than the shapeless dresses I was forced to don every day.

Daddy found me one day hiding behind the barn with my magazine after losing track of time. I thought his head was going to shoot right off his neck. I'd never seen his face so red when he ripped the magazine from my hands and grabbed me by the arm, dragging me to the chapel. Elder Otto was holding a meeting inside, and my father threw me on the floor in front of him with my crumpled magazine. Let's just say I would have rather recited bible verses for three days straight than endure the punishment Elder Otto doled out that day.

I was twelve then and knew this wasn't what life was supposed to look like. Five years later and I haven't changed my mind. Now, at seventeen, I'm looking for any opportunity to free myself from this place. I would have last year, but the idea of leaving my sister is what keeps me here. She's two years younger and a statuesque blonde beauty. I see the way most of the elders look at her, like they're sizing her up for their sons or maybe even themselves. Women don't have a long life expectancy around here, and it never fails that as soon as one of the wives passes, the man is married to a younger version of the one before. It makes my stomach turn to think that could be Cece's fate.

"Well, it's about time," Mama says with her hands on her hips, shooting my sister and me a disapproving glare. "Your father is going to be here any minute with Elder Otto and Jasper."

Mama turns, and I roll my eyes behind her back. There's no way in hell I'd do it in front of her.

Jasper is supposed to be my husband next year. He's not much older than me, two years to be exact, but he has the same evil gleam in his eyes that his daddy, Elder Otto, has. And every time he smiles at me, I think of a shark with big white teeth ready to tear into my flesh. It's unnerving, and the idea of having to be married to him turns my stomach sour. Not that I was ever given a voice in their choice of husband or allowed an opinion on the matter. Mama wasn't, and I hate the idea of what I know happens to her happening to me. I hear her cries at night and see the bruises in the morning. She doesn't speak of them, so neither do any of us.

Cecilia and I make our way to the kitchen to get cleaned up and help with dinner.

The sound of the front door opening and three men speaking loudly as they shed their coats in the small entryway instantly has me on edge. Cece senses my tension and rubs a reassuring hand over my back for a brief moment.

"Hello, Lucinda," Jasper calls from the entrance to the kitchen.

I turn and do my best to give him a welcoming smile. There's no doubt in my mind it looks as forced as it feels.

Before Mama or Cecilia turn to greet our guests, Jasper's eyes run the length of my body in a lascivious manner. While my sister is tall and willowy, I'm about five inches shorter and cursed with curves that the men at the compound have been leering at since I was thirteen.

"Hello, Jasper. We're so glad you could make it tonight. Dinner will be ready in just a few minutes. Can I offer you something to drink?" Mama asks politely. I can't tell how she feels about the idea of me marrying Jasper. Not that her opinion would matter one way or another.

"Thank you. I'll have a glass of water."

Mama nudges me in the arm, which is her way of telling me to tend to him.

I fill a glass and bring it to him. When he takes it, his fingers brush mine, sending icicles down my spine. *Gross.*

"Thank you, Lucinda."

Why do I feel like after a few words and no more than two minutes in his company, I need a scalding hot shower?

Jasper turns and leaves the kitchen, shooting me a lecherous grin over his shoulder. Mama starts bringing plates of bread and the roast she made to the dining room. Out of the corner of my eye, I see my sister staring at me. I ignore it. What can she possibly say that would make the situation any better? I'm going to be forced into marriage with Jasper, and there's nothing either of us can do about it.

At the dinner table, Elder Otto leads us in prayer before we start eating. I swear he drones on for so long, there's no way the meat isn't cold at this point. Conversation is boring as my father and Elder Otto discuss the particulars of the exchange happening after dinner. They speak in code, but it's a well-known open secret that the elders trade meth for guns.

"On to happier news," Elder Otto says, looking pointedly at my father.

"Ah, yes." The smile on my father's face is so out of character for him, I immediately know whatever he says won't be good. "Lucinda, we've decided the time has come for you and Jasper to be married."

My eyes dart between him and Mama, who is busy scrutinizing the piece of dried out roast on her plate and not meeting my confused gaze.

"Right. Next year. As far as I knew, it was already decided." Desperation claws at me, hoping against hope he isn't about to say what he's alluding to.

"Yes, but your father and I agreed the marriage should come sooner rather than later," Elder Otto replied.

"Next week, to be exact," Jasper supplies.

My eyes shoot between my parents, my mother still refusing to look at me.

"Why?" I ask my father, who irritably dabs the corner of his mouth with his napkin.

"Honestly, Lucinda, you have been a willful child since you were in diapers. It seems no matter how much your mother and I have prayed for guidance or talked with the elders about how best to handle your blatant disrespect of our rules, nothing has helped."

My father and the elders have tried to beat my "rebellious" streak out of me since my father found the magazine I stole, claiming they were doing what was best for a stubborn girl who needed to learn her place.

"As such," he continues. "We feel it's in the best interest of Cecilia for you not to be here influencing her."

I look toward my sister, who is staring at her plate, tears streaming down her face.

"Having a household and children of your own will tame your willful ways and bring you closer to your purpose in life."

In their eyes, the only purpose any woman has is to keep her husband "satisfied" and bear his offspring. A shudder rolls through me at the thought of Jasper touching me that way.

Fear and rage violently run through my body as the men stare silently at me as though I should be thanking them. There's no doubt in my mind what's waiting for me after I marry Jasper. How can my mother and father sit here and act as though this is what's best for me or my sister? Knowing I have no choice in the matter and feeling trapped in this horrible existence has me so damn angry. Angry at my parents, angry at myself for not being braver and leaving, and angry at every person on this damn compound who allows their daughters to be sold off like cattle.

The plate of food in front of me is fuzzy as rage builds inside me, clouding my vision. I sit in silence as my parents, Elder Otto, and Jasper drone on about the goings on around the compound as if they haven't just shattered my world. Swallowing a couple more bites of food takes monumental effort since the roast has turned to ash on my tongue. The only thing that registers is the voice in my head repeating the same thing over and over—I can't do this, I can't do this, I can't do this.

My mother pinches the back of my arm roughly when Jasper and Elder Otto get up to leave, shocking me out of my stupor.

"Come say goodbye," she hisses in my ear.

I go through the motions of fake smiling but don't feel anything. My anger has turned into numbness, and there is no doubt in my mind this is how I'll feel for the rest of my life if I stay.

After doing the dishes and saying our evening prayers, which consisted of my father thanking the Lord that I'm to be married to such a great and honorable man, we're sent to our room.

As Cecilia braids her long blonde hair, I pace the small bedroom.

"I can't do it, Cece. I can't marry him."

"You don't have a choice, Lu. Daddy and Elder Otto have decided. No one has ever gone against the elder's wishes, especially when it comes to marriage."

It's true. No one has, but that doesn't mean there isn't a first time for everything.

Stopping in the middle of our bedroom, I look my sister in the eye.

"I'm leaving."

She abruptly stops braiding her hair and looks at me with wide eyes.

"What are you talking about, Lucinda? Where are you going to go?"

I turn to our shared closet and grab a small sack and begin filling it with a few simple dresses and the one pair of loose pants and t-shirt I own.

"I don't know, Cece. Anywhere but here. If I marry Jasper, I may as well kill myself now. I'll be as good as dead if I have to live the kind of life he'd subject me to." The thought of his evil smile runs through my mind.

"Come with me," I tell her, not wanting her to suffer the same fate as every other woman on the compound.

"You know I can't. You don't even know what waits for *you* out there."

It's true, anytime we would daydream about our lives, our futures, I would tell her my dreams of running away. She never shared those fantasies with me, insisting she loved our family and loved the Lord too much to abandon either.

"You're right, Cece, I don't, but I know what waits for me here. I have to leave tonight, or I'll never get away. Please, come with me." I implore her with my eyes as I stand in front of the open window in our bedroom.

My sister walks over to me, pulling me into a hug, and we clutch tightly to one another. At that moment, I know she won't come, and she knows this is the last time she'll see me.

"I love you, Lucinda. Always remember that."

"I love you too, Cecilia."

Never in any of my fantasies growing up did I think I would truly escape. Or that years later, I would find myself back in this hell. I certainly never imagined the next time I left, it would be in a truck with a bunch of bikers as flames destroyed my nightmare.

Chapter One
Lucy

The clubhouse is packed tonight, which is usual for any party thrown by the club. Of course, my best friend Charlie disappeared a little while ago with her man, Linc. I swear, those two can't keep their hands off each other, and every chance he gets, he has to whisk her away under the guise of needing to show her "something." It's no secret what he needs to show her is inside his pants.

That leaves me to my own devices in a room full of bikers. The last few months, these guys have become more like brothers to me and Charlie, with one exception—Jude. The six-foot-three British biker may be hot as fuck to look at, with that thick blond hair hanging just past his shoulders and piercing blue eyes that always seem to have a storm brewing within, but the man is a total pain in my ass.

The moment I met him, he rubbed me the wrong way. From the way he spoke to Charlie when Linc found her and me in a bar all those months ago, to the way he constantly looked at my best friend with suspicion while her crazy-ass ex and the Italian mafia were on the hunt for her, as though she had something to do with them coming after the club. I mean, technically, she did since she was hiding some important information, but she was never going to use it against Linc or the club. But the way he looked at her like she was the cause of all their problems set my teeth on edge. It reminded me too much of how I grew up. When you lived a life like mine and were constantly blamed for all the ails of mankind because of what's between your legs, and the fact that you didn't conform to some asshole's demands, anyone even hinting at that kind of attitude makes me see red right off the bat.

"No work tonight?" the prospect behind the bar asks as I take a seat on one of the old barstools.

"No, my slave driver of a boss finally gave me the night off," I answer with a wink.

Since Charlie moved in with Linc and decided to plant roots in this little town, I figured Shine was as good a town as any to settle in... at least for the time being.

The Black Roses own a couple businesses around here, one of them being a bar where Ozzy, the club president, offered me a job. Charlie works there, too, much to Linc's dismay. He'd rather she concentrate on getting her degree. Living here has given her a sense of security she's never had before, and she's started taking some online classes to get a degree to become a therapist. I'm happy as hell my best friend has figured out what she wants to do. On the other hand, I don't have that option. One, I have no records to show for myself, so college is out of the question. And two, there's no way in hell I can find a birth certificate or anything the government needs to prove I am who I say I am. The only place those things might exist is a place I'll never go back to.

Cooper hands me a beer, and I tip the neck to him in thanks.

"There's another club coming in tonight," he comments.

"Yeah, I know," I reply, wondering why he's reminding me. It's not like I haven't been here when other clubs come for a night or two.

"Just making sure we don't have a repeat of last time."

I roll my eyes and turn toward the large open room that's congested with bikers and strippers from one of the club's other businesses.

The last time a club came through a few weeks ago, I was in the middle of having a nice, friendly game of pool with one of the guys from said club. Jude decided it would be a good time to challenge me in a game of darts.

The broody asshole tries to best me at every turn. Little does he know I spent long hours in pool halls during my first couple of years on the run and found I had an affinity for anything that requires hand-eye coordination. Pool, darts, shooting, you name it.

Well, the big baby didn't take too kindly to me beating him, and after a few games when the guy I was playing pool with made a comment about him being a sore loser and wanting to get back to pool, Jude hauled off and punched the guy in the face. Thank God Ozzy was around and smoothed things over with the other guys. Jude showed absolutely no remorse before storming out, grumbling about me being a demon incarnate.

Ozzy was none too happy about the situation, and the look he gave me told me I needed to watch myself. I still don't see how it's my fault his brother can't control himself when he was the one who thought he could beat me, then discovered, once again, he can't. Honestly, if it wasn't for Charlie, I would have left after all the shit with her ex and the Italians got settled, but I can't leave my girl. She's the closest thing I have to a family anymore.

I wander to the pool tables where a couple of the other brothers are in the middle of a game and slap a quarter down.

"I got winner," I announce, and they all groan.

"Oh, can it, ya big babies."

"Listen babe," Wyatt starts. "It's not that we don't love you. It's just that we hate losing every time you have a pool cue in your hand."

"Or a dart," Cash interjects.

"God, for a group of big bad bikers, you guys sure whine a lot. Ever think that it's a good thing to lose every once in a while? It keeps you on your toes and makes you try harder. Or is it because I'm a woman?" I don't believe for one second these guys are this soft.

"No, babe. If there was any woman in here we wouldn't mind losing to, it would be you, seeing as you are such a graceful winner and all," Wyatt says, sarcasm dripping from his words.

Okay, so there may have been a few times I jumped up and down, screaming "winner, winner, chicken dinner," but it was a joke, goddamnit. You think these guys would have a better sense of humor.

"Cash, you can't possibly be afraid to play me. Look how good you're doing." He's beating Wyatt, but barely. I already see three different shots Wyatt could take to end the game, but from where he's standing at the table, I can tell he's not paying that close attention. Wyatt is too easy of a target. He isn't as terrible as Charlie is at pool but close.

"I'll play you, Lucifer."

Now it's my turn to groan. I turn around and see the one guy in here who is capable of ruining any fun I was planning on having tonight. If I ever accused these guys of being big babies, Jude is the worst of the bunch. I've seen him storm off more times than I can count when I beat him at any game. I can't blame him too much. It must be demoralizing for a man like him to lose to me at every turn, but this guy is the sorest loser I've ever met in my life. It's not my fault he thought he was top shit at just about everything and gets proven wrong time and time again. Guess I have to prove, yet again, he isn't the only one with a few tricks up his sleeve.

"Fine by me," I tell him as Cash and Wyatt shoot each other nervous glances. That's fair. Our games usually end up in a little gloating from me and a lot of stomping off from Mr. British Smashole himself. Charlie once asked what smashole means, and I explained it was a hot guy I would totally smash, but he's such an asshole, I wouldn't ever dream of going there. Truth be told, I've had plenty of dreams of going there with Jude, but I'd never admit that to her or anyone else.

Wyatt and Cash finish their game, and Cash wins, like I knew he would. I learned a while back not to give the guys pointers when they're in the middle of a game. Apparently, some of them think it's cheating. Whatever.

When Jude grabs a cue and chalks it in his irritatingly cocky way, as though he thinks this is the time he'll finally prove he's better than me, little flutters start low in my belly. His arrogance is an unfortunate turn-on I've learned to ignore. Mostly. Watching him go through his routine of picking the right cue and seeing the determination in his steely blue eyes makes me think about the dreams I've had of him with the same determination in his gaze. Only in my dreams, he's transfixed on anything other than pool. Even in my sex dreams about the man, he has this look of aloof resolve to make me come over and over. He's absolutely maddening and frustrating as hell, even in my sleep.

Grabbing a stick, I ignore the butterflies in my stomach as I rack the balls.

"Ladies first," he says, motioning for me to break.

When I do, he walks around the table and studies it intently, chewing on the side of his thumb. There's no reason it should be so hot to watch him look at the table with the concentration I've seen on his face all the times I've dreamed of him, but it is what it is at this point. When his eyes flick to mine, I try my damndest to school my features, sure he'll be able to tell where my thoughts have wandered.

Jude bends and lines up his shot. Before he takes it, his gaze meets mine again, and he tosses a little wink at me. When two balls go in the pocket, the self-satisfied smirk is enough to make my blood boil and all the flutters and memories of dreams fly right out of my head. I see someone brought their A game today. Time to crush this poor man's ego. Again.

We play three games. He wins the first and I win the last two.

"You're getting better," I tell him in an encouraging tone. Okay, maybe there was a hint of sarcasm there, too. Sue me.

"Darts. Now," he demands.

This is how it goes every time the man loses. He has to order me to play another game of his choosing, thinking it's going to make a difference. I should be the bigger person and not gloat when I beat him, but there's something so infuriating about the man. He's so used to winning and is cocky as hell about it when he plays against the other guys. It's simply impossible for me *not* to rub it in his face.

"Are you going to run away and cry into your pillow again when I beat you?"

"First of all, Lucifer, I don't 'run away,' and I certainly don't cry."

"Sorry. Stomp away and sulk?"

"You just have to test my patience at every turn, don't you?"

I shrug and give him a wide-eyed stare, silently batting my lashes. I mean, he's not wrong.

Jude shakes his head and grabs the darts from the bar. He grabs two boxes he keeps back there. He's the only one allowed to use those particular darts. When I got here, there was only one set, but when he realized I could play as well, if not better than him, he bought another set, claiming we needed to be evenly matched so I wouldn't be able to say my crappy darts had me at a disadvantage when he beat me. Never mind the fact he has yet to beat me.

Jude returns with the darts and a couple of beers as I'm looking around the clubhouse for my best friend. She still hasn't returned from Linc's room. No shocker there.

"Who you looking for, Lucifer? Another soul to take with you to hell?"

The man has jokes, I see.

"No," I reply, grabbing a beer from his hand. "Just wondering when the other club is going to get here. Maybe I want to have a little fun tonight."

If the look on his face could turn a person into salt, I'd be blowing away in the wind.

What the hell?

Jude moves closer to me, studying the dart in his hand.

"Let me tell you something, Lucifer. No one in this clubhouse, brother or visitor, is going to be touching you tonight." He looks me straight in the eye and smirks—fucking smirks at me. When he raises his hand, he throws the dart at the board and makes a fucking bullseye without taking his eyes off me.

Scratch every thought about being nice or feeling bad about the man in front of me feeling emasculated. If he thinks he gets to tell me what I can or can't do or what other people can or can't do, I have no problem wiping this damn floor with the tattered shreds of his ego.

I grab a dart, look at the board, and return his smirk with a downright evil one of my own, then throw, hitting the board right next to his dart.

"I guess we'll see about that."

The hour passes, and we've played two rounds of the angriest dart game I've ever participated in. Every time I throw one, I imagine his face on the board. If the waves of anger rolling off of him are anything to go by, he's most likely doing the same. This could quite possibly be his new strategy, making me so mad that he has some advantage. It's working. I'm still beating him, but only by a point. The brothers wander over and watch here and there, but anytime they speak to either of us, Jude gives them a scowl. When Ozzy watches the scene and Jude gives him the same look he's been throwing at everyone else, I think for a moment his prez is going to tell him where to shove it. Instead, the man glances at me and chuckles, mumbling "idiot" under his breath before walking away.

Naturally, I win the last game. Jude stares intently at the scoreboard as though he can't believe what he's seeing. I don't know why. It's not like this is the first time and surely won't be the last I beat him at darts.

"It must be pretty hard losing to me again, seeing as you grew up playing. Aren't darts some sort of British pastime?" So, I may be rubbing a little salt in the wound. Ask me if I care.

Jude nods. "Where did you learn to play so well?"

I don't want to divulge my past to him. There're parts even Charlie doesn't know, and he hasn't earned the right to know my history, especially before my best friend.

"I worked in a couple pool halls on my way to New Orleans. Pool, darts, poker. I learned all kinds of things in those places." Vague, but not secretive.

"Is that where you learned to shoot the way you do?"

He asks the question as though he's simply trying to get to know me better, but the fact I can shoot so well has been grating on him for months, ever since I showed him up at the range my first week here.

"Nope," I reply, taking a sip of my beer, staring Jude directly in the eye.

I'm on to you, pal.

Jude quirks his lip, but not in a smile. Oh no, it's more of a challenging look that says I'll get it out of you eventually.

"How are you at board games?"

The question throws me for a moment. In a clubhouse full of bikers, the last thing I'd expect to find would be a bunch of board games.

"Fine, I guess," I reply, still confused by the question.

A wide smile spreads across Jude's face.

"Backgammon it is, then."

Is this guy for real?

Chapter Two
Jude

A long ride is exactly what I need to clear my head. It's been full of nothing but bullshit and images of a short girl with long black hair and curves in all the right places who's made it her mission in life to annoy me for the last three months. It seems as though every time I turn around, Lucy is there, ready to show me up. I'm happy as hell my brother found a woman he's wholly committed to and that they have a cute little house together, complete with a white picket fence. The only thing I wish was different is the blue-eyed demon who lives next door.

She's always around. Every time I go to Linc's to work on our bikes or shoot the shit, she's there. To top it off, Ozzy gave her a job at my favorite bar, Thorn and Thistle. There's not a single doubt in my mind he wasn't well aware of what he did. My president loves to fuck with me, especially if it involves Lucy.

I can't wait any longer to get back to the clubhouse. We have another club coming tonight from Nevada. The Irish want Ozzy to check them out and get a feel for them, wanting to have a stronger foothold in the West with their gun business. We've been more than happy to accommodate deliveries out there, but our club doesn't have the connections a local one would, which is fine by us. We make plenty from the work we do on the East Coast, and none of us feel the need to spread ourselves thin. That's how mistakes happen, and brothers get sent away or dead.

Turning my bike around, I head back, taking a more direct route. Ozzy will have my balls if we aren't all there on time. The years I spent in the Royal Marines made me appreciate the importance of punctuality and resent it at the same time. You would think being in a club like ours, there would be few rules and nothing but booze, women, and the open road. That isn't the case, though. Sure, we aren't in short supply of any of those things, but there is much more that goes into being a part of the Black Roses. Loyalty, respect, and brotherhood are held in a higher regard in this motorcycle club than I ever found serving Her Majesty. I respect the hell out of my president and my brothers, which is why when Ozzy gives an order, even something as simple as showing up to a party on time, I follow.

I park my bike next to Linc's and head to my room to take a hot-ass shower. The water does fuck all to calm my racing mind. Lucy's out there, waiting to goad me into another game of some sort. That's what she does, then revels in my irritation every time she bests me. The thought of the smirk that forms on her pillowy pink lips every time she beats me ratchets up my irritation and other feelings I try not to look too deeply into.

Before I realize what I'm doing, my hand is wrapped around my stone hard cock, and I'm pumping while the images of bending Lucy over the pool table and sinking into her assault my mind. The thought of grabbing, squeezing, and biting her round ass as I pump in and out of her has me blowing my load as quickly as a goddamn teenager. The last thing that races through my sick brain right before I blow is that fucking smirk. What the hell is wrong with me? I can't stand the little harpy, let alone want to fuck her. I like my women tall and not so... opinionated. Not the short curvy hellcat who never shuts the hell up.

I step out of the shower and stare at myself for a long moment in the mirror, swearing not to have another self-pleasuring session to thoughts of her... like I did the last dozen or so times. *Yeah, I'm definitely making headway there.*

After dressing in my usual attire of jeans, t-shirt, my cut, and boots, I make my way out to the main room. The party is already livening up with the brothers and hang-arounds filling the space. Ozzy is sitting at the bar, nursing a glass of whiskey and nods. I head toward him, saying hello to a few brothers on the way, and toss a wink at a couple of the scantily clad girls milling about. Some entertainment later may be in order to erase my thoughts from the shower.

I saddle up next to Oz, and the prospect sets a cold beer in front of me. After taking a sip, I turn to face the room, resting my elbows on the edge of the bar. Ozzy takes a similar position, eyeing the crowd as a king would gaze upon his kingdom—if his subjects were a bunch of fucked-up bikers and various women in all stages of undress.

"What do you know about the club coming in tonight?"

Ozzy sips his whiskey and tilts his head in my direction. "The Bone Breakers. A club from Nevada. Met a few of the guys on a run I did for the Irish out that way." I nod, remembering the ride about a year or so ago. "I didn't get the feeling they were used to dealing with anyone like the Irish. They deal with small timers, nothing on this scale, but Finn needs a firmer hold out there, and these guys seemed up to the task. At least that's what they told Finn."

A lot of clubs will try to talk a big game but fall short when push comes to shove.

"What's your impression? Can they handle what the Irish are willing to offer?"

Ozzy tilts his head back and forth, considering the question. "I think time will tell. They're hungry, that's for sure, and I don't want to see any blowback come to the Irish if shit goes sideways out there. I think I'll have a better idea at the end of the night."

I nod and sip my beer. Ozzy has always had a knack for sniffing out bullshit.

"Seen Linc and Charlie yet?"

Ozzy laughs and takes a drink of whiskey. "Yup, they got here about ten minutes ago, and Linc needed to show Charlie 'something.'"

Ozzy and I chuckle at the same time, neither of us doubting for a second what that "something" is.

Just then, I hear a familiar laugh from the direction of the pool table. The hairs on the back of my neck rise instantly, along with my frustration. Seems someone has a night off from the bar. Damn, too bad I have to be here. I could have visited my favorite hole in the wall in peace for once.

I look over and find Lucy leaning against Barrett with her arm resting on his shoulder as they watch Cash and Wyatt play a game of pool.

Ozzy must see where my gaze has traveled, and I catch his smirk from the corner of my eye.

"There's going to be a full house tonight. You good with that?"

My gaze swings back to my president and I give him a questioning look. "Yeah, why?"

He clears his throat. "Well, all of us look at Lucy and Charlie as sisters, but new guys from a different club aren't going to. That gonna be a problem for you?"

The sudden and intense rage that boils to the surface at the idea of any man other than a brother—except Barrett because I'm about to smack the ever-loving shite out of the fucker—takes me by surprise. Thankfully, I'm able to school my features before Ozzy has a chance to notice.

"That." He points to my face. "That look right there is why I'm asking."

Okay, so maybe I didn't tamp down my expression fast enough.

"What the hell is going on with you two?"

"Absolutely nothing. She gets off on getting under my skin—"

"And you get off on letting her," he interrupts.

"Hardly. We're oil and water, that's all there is to it." I take another sip of my beer before setting it on the bar and motioning for a new one. "Besides, don't you think it's a little strange that she came here, and we have yet to learn anything about her?" Maybe if I put the heat on her, it will take it off me for a minute, at least in Ozzy's eyes.

"No, not really. Not everyone who comes to the clubhouse is an open book. I don't expect her to share her life story with a bunch of guys she's only known for a few months. Besides, nothing has seemed to follow her here like it did with Charlie."

Ozzy makes a good point. When Charlie showed up here, it was on the heels of a fuckton of shit involving a deranged ex and the Italian mafia.

"Now, if I'm wrong about that and there are some deep dark secrets she's hiding, I have no doubt the brothers will handle it. She's like the little sister we've never had."

Looking back at Lucy, I catch her laugh at something Barrett says, and it grates on my nerves.

"Tell that to your road captain."

"Maybe I should be telling it to you."

I shake my head and accept another beer from the prospect.

"Nothing is happening. She's Charlie's best friend and a pain in the ass I've resigned myself to putting up with."

Ozzy's lips purse in that annoying know-it-all way. "Whatever you say." He grabs another whiskey from the prospect and stands. "I'm going to go grab some grub. Tanya made a shitton of food."

Gotta love Linc and Knox's mom, Tanya. Every time Gramps and Trick go on any sort of overnight camping trip, she comes over to the clubhouse and cooks up a feast fit for kings.

A red-headed bunny saunters over to the seat Ozzy just vacated and perches herself next to me.

"Hey, Cassie," I greet and clink the neck of my bottle to hers.

"Hey, Jude. It's been a minute. How come you never have time for me anymore?"

The pout she gives me is supposed to be cute, but I find it annoying. Normally, it would have me grabbing her hand to take her back to my room and give her all the attention she so obviously craves, but I'm anything but interested tonight. What the hell is wrong with me?

"Oh, Cassie, I'm sure you've found plenty of other brothers to entertain you in my absence."

Her tinkling laugh is her confirmation. There's no shortage of brothers in this clubhouse to give her what she wants from me tonight. Another laugh reaches my ear, and I stand, bidding Cassie goodbye, and make my way over to the pool table.

Lucy sets a quarter on the table, signaling she wants next game. Cash and Wyatt don't seem particularly enthused with the idea, considering this girl wipes the floor with them when it comes to just about any game they play with her.

"I'll play you, Lucifer."

Lucy stands stock-still with her back to me for a beat before she turns to face me. When she does, it's not exactly a look of glee on her face. Quite the opposite, with a little twinkle in her eye saying she's ready to kick my ass, yet again. Well, we'll see about that.

"Fine by me," she replies in the saucy tone she seems to reserve solely for me.

I rack the balls and offer to let her break. None make it in as I walk around the table, seeing what she's set up. Chewing my thumb as I study the balls, my eyes meet hers and before she has a chance to hide it, I catch something in her gaze. Something that looked awfully close to desire. Huh, interesting. I spot my shot, but before taking it, I look at Lucy and give her a wink. If anyone considers that playing dirty, they can fuck right off. I have a score to settle with this one.

Though I win the first round, the next two go to her. It is absolutely infuriating that this woman is so damn good at every game. Until she came around, I beat everyone at pool or darts. You name it, I won. Call it ego or whatever you want, but I simply can't let it go.

"Darts. Now." My demand comes out in a clipped tone.

"Are you going to run away and cry into your pillow again when I beat you?"

Oh, this cheeky woman.

"First of all, Lucifer, I don't 'run away,' and I certainly don't cry."

We exchange a few more barbs before I grab my personal dart set and the extra one I bought. There isn't a whole lot that can get under my skin, present company excluded, but people whining about me winning because I have a superior set of darts is one of them. There's no way in hell Lucy is going to be able to use that excuse when I beat her.

I return with the darts and a couple beers. She's looking around like she's searching for someone in particular. I can't help but give her a hard time. Seems I never can, which also irritates the hell out of me.

"Who you looking for, Lucifer? Another soul to take with you to hell?"

When she replies that she's looking for a little fun in the form of another biker, my skin feels too tight over my body, flames of possession licking up my neck. My reasons for feeling the sudden urge to kill every single man she's ever given a passing glance to is not something I'm ready to look at, but it's there. It's so intense the only thing in my head is the image of my fist pounding the skulls of nameless faces.

"Let me tell you something, Lucifer, no one in this clubhouse, brother or visitor, is going to be touching you tonight."

I throw the dart in my hand, and I know it hits the bullseye from the look in Lucy's eyes. Her look of surprise morphs into one of angry determination. For the game or because she's intent on proving me wrong about no one touching her is yet to be determined.

Through two of the most intense rounds of darts I've ever played with the little demon next to me, my brothers come and watch the carnage. And by carnage, I mean Lucy beating me at every turn. The last game is neck and neck, with Lucy up by only one point. Goddamn this woman. Anger is fueling every throw, and it seems to be working against me, especially with her standing so close while I'm trying to concentrate. I feel the heat from her skin soaking into mine, and it's distracting as hell. She's doing it on purpose; there's no doubt in my mind. This woman is full of piss, vinegar, and fucking mind games. Knowing all this still doesn't stop me from rising to the occasion each and every time she baits me, though.

Ozzy wanders over and watches us at one point. The memory of our conversation from the bar rolls through my head. How could he possibly think there's anything more going on here than the obvious need for Lucy to get under my skin every time I turn around?

Ozzy mumbles something under his breath, then wanders off, and Lucy wins the fucking game. Again. Where the hell did she learn to play like that? She's been so damn tight-lipped about her past, but she plays pool and darts like a fucking pro, has the aim of an expert marksman, yet the girl can't be more than twenty-five.

"Where did you learn to play so well?" I ask, trying not to sound suspicious. If there's one thing I've learned about her, it's if you dig too deep, too fast, she clams up.

She gives me a vague answer about working in pool halls or some such shite. Of course, she doesn't divulge where any of these pool halls were. The only thing I actually know about her is she lived in New Orleans, where she met Charlie but wasn't from there originally. Then they moved to Texas because Charlie got spooked, and Lucy wouldn't let her leave without her. The loyal bond between them I can respect, but the secrets are another story entirely.

"Is that where you learned to shoot the way you do?" I don't expect her to answer the question with anything other than the attitude and short one-word answer she gives me.

Deciding to let her keep her secrets—for now—a brilliant idea comes to mind.

"How are you at board games?"

"Fine." Her confused expression is the exact reaction I expected. Not many people can say they're board game aficionados. But I can.

"Backgammon it is, then."

Lucy's eyes widen in surprise before she doubles over in laughter.

"Are you fucking kidding me?" she exclaims, laughing uncontrollably. Not the exact reaction I was going for, but I think throwing her off will work to my advantage.

Chapter Three
Lucy

"Oh my God. You're serious about playing backgammon." I pretend to choke on the word.

I peer at Jude, studying him while I take another drink of my beer.

"What?" he asks.

"Sorry, I just thought I was talking to my eighty-seven-year-old grandma for a minute." Another chuckle escapes me.

"I'll have you know it was my grandmother, God rest her soul,"—he makes a sign of the cross and looks toward the ceiling—"who taught me to play many board games."

Now, there's no containing my laughter, and I double over once again. Standing straight with one hand on my chest, trying to catch my breath, I wipe the tears from my eyes as Jude looks on with a stony expression on his face.

"Are you okay?" he asks. "Or did me crossing myself have the demon that obviously resides in you try to make a break for it?"

This fucking guy.

I look toward the hallway and see Charlie and Linc finally emerge into the already packed main room of the clubhouse.

"As entertaining as this has been, Jude, Charlie just showed up."

My hand pats his chest, and in no way, shape, or form do I notice how toned and hard his muscles are before making my way past him. It's not like I haven't had a front-row seat for what lies under his cut. A few months ago, we went to his brother's lakefront hideaway. We spent a couple days at the lake before… well, everything else. I did my damndest not to ogle the delicious specimen of a man in front of me. Of course, as soon as Jude opens his mouth, all thoughts of lust and images of him writhing over me disappear to be replaced with irritation.

"You're just scared of losing, Lucifer. That's your problem," he calls to me.

Case and point.

"Whatever you say, Jude," I reply, throwing a two-finger salute over my head.

I refuse to take the bait. There's no need to look back to see the expression on his face. I feel his angry stare boring into the back of my head.

Bounding up to Charlie and Linc, still high from my wins and chuckling at Jude's ridiculous idea of trying to beat me in board games, I catch the blissed-out look in Charlie's eyes. Listen, if I had a hot-as-hell biker who was obsessed with me the way Linc is with Charlie, we wouldn't make it out of the bedroom much, either.

"Get this," I say, a little out of breath. "Jude wants to try to beat me in backgammon. Backgammon!" My laughter is coming back in full force. The idea is just that absurd to me. "Apparently, he played it all the time growing up and thinks he'll wipe the floor with me." A thought comes to mind, and I turn to Linc. "Shouldn't he lose his patch for being an old lady or something?"

Linc laughs, used to the antics between Jude and me.

"Nah, we all know about his penchant for board games." He turns to Charlie and mumbles something in her ear before kissing the top of her head. There's something about the easy interaction between those two that sends a sudden pang of sadness through me. It isn't likely there will come a day when I'll get to feel that. Not as long as I have to pick up and leave at a moment's notice. It's possible no one is looking for me at this point, but there were times in the beginning, I would get this feeling in my gut that wherever I was wasn't safe anymore. It's been a while, but there will always be a chance I have to run.

Before leaving, Linc turns to me and tells me to behave.

"Scout's honor," I reply, holding up three fingers.

Linc chuckles and shakes his head before leaving. Yeah, he's not buying what I'm selling.

"So, you guys staying all night?" I ask Charlie.

Linc still has a room at the clubhouse, and by extension, so do I. It comes in handy from time to time after a night of drinking. Or a night when I don't want to be in my house by myself.

"Probably, but you don't have to."

I tell her there could be some fun to be had for me with some new bikers. I actually wasn't serious about it when I said the same thing to Jude, but his reaction is still playing through my mind. It was almost as though he was claiming me, which is weird on every level. First, because we can hardly tolerate each other. He's hot, there's no denying that, but there has to be way more going on there than just physical attraction. Second, I don't have any desire to be claimed by any biker. I remember the bikers that used to come to my family's compound. They were so far from anyone I'd ever consider taking to bed. Obviously, these guys are different, or there wouldn't be a snowball's chance in hell I'd be here, but the whole biker thing is still a no-go for me.

"Just stay out of Jude's way. I know you two get off on making each other miserable, but let's try to just have fun tonight," Charlie pleads.

Oops, might be a little late for that. Looking over to where the biker in question is, I see him scowling in my direction before he turns and disappears into the crowd. Soon after, we hear more people making their way into the clubhouse.

"Oh, those must be the guys from Nevada," Charlie says, trying to get a look at who just walked in.

Craning my neck to try to see for myself, I'm hit with a sight I never wanted to see again in my life. The new guys are wearing Bone Breakers patches on their cuts.

Shit.

It's been seven years since I've seen that cut. I can't believe how stupid I was, but come on, what are the fucking chances? They're the same club the elders from my old home did business with. My family supplied them with meth, and they supplied us with guns. Never in my life would I have thought they'd be this far east or have any business with the Black Roses.

"Lucy, what's wrong?"

I shake myself out of my stupor when Charlie's hand grabs mine, as though she had been trying to get my attention.

"Nothing." I bring my beer to my lips and realize my hands are shaking. "Just thought I saw someone I recognized. Hey, let's go get another drink." I put a fake-as-hell smile on my face but can't seem to muster the wherewithal to try to make it any more believable. The way Charlie's eyes narrow in a scrutinizing stare tells me she doesn't buy it.

"Are you sure you're okay? If this is about Jude, I've told you a million times—"

"No, it has nothing to do with Jude." I cut her off before she finishes the sentence. I don't need the distraction of thinking about him. I need to get my head clear.

"But it has to do with someone?"

The thing about Charlie is she's never tried to delve into my past. She understood there were things I wouldn't talk about and left it at that. Unfortunately, it looks like my past just walked through the front door.

"I'm fine, Charlie," I attempt to reassure. "Promise."

My eyes wander back to the new group of bikers. There isn't anyone I recognize, but a couple still have their backs to us. One of the bikers turns around, and recognition instantly slams into me. He was there the night I ran from the compound. Badger, I think is what they called him. When I turn back around toward the bar, my stare zeros in on the condensation on my bottle.

Think Lucy.

What are the chances he recognizes me? There's nothing particularly special about me. My hair is black instead of the light brown I used to have, and I'm wearing makeup, something that was strictly forbidden on the compound. The large, boxy dresses have also disappeared from my wardrobe, replaced with much tighter-fitting clothes. Plus, it's been seven years. That's a long time for him to remember the girl he may have seen all of once.

Out of the corner of my eye, I see him approach and ask the prospect for a beer.

"Ladies," he says, tipping the neck of the bottle toward Charlie and me. "Nice night."

Charlie stiffens next to me when he speaks, but I don't take my eyes off the peeling label of my beer. The foul man leans an inch closer to me, even though I've yet to acknowledge his presence.

"You look an awful lot like a girl I used to know back in Nevada. Ever been?"

His rank breath hits me in the side of the face, and it's all I can do not to run out the door and leave everything behind.

This is bad. Very, very bad.

"Nope," I reply, taking a sip of my beer.

"Huh, that's pretty weird. A little older and you have black hair, but you're the spitting image of a girl I met there."

I want to scream in his face that he has the wrong girl. I want him to leave me the hell alone and let me live in the small slice of happiness I've found here. Instead, I shrug my shoulders and grab my friend's hand.

"Hey, Charlie. Let's play some pool."

Charlie starts to follow me when Badger calls out to me. "They're still looking for you, Lucinda."

I don't respond, but my grasp on Charlie's hand tightens without conscious thought.

Fuckity, fuck, fuck.

When she feels my reaction to the man calling me by my given name, she detours from the pool table and pulls me into the hall leading to the bedrooms and the back exit. Charlie whirls around on me and looks me dead in the eye.

"Okay, you need to tell me what the hell is going on right now. Why did he call you Lucinda?"

"I don't know. The guy is probably drunk. I look like a lot of people." The excuse sounds weak to my ears, so there's no doubt in my mind Charlie doesn't believe me.

Her features soften. The girl was never very good at playing the tough-as-nails best friend role. That's always been my job.

"You know I'll never make you share anything with me you aren't comfortable with, but I think it's time you started talking. If there's something I can help with, or the club—"

"It's nothing Charlie. I've never seen that guy before in my life." The lies taste bitter on my tongue, but there's too much swirling in my brain at the moment to come up with a story, and I'm not ready to tell her, or anyone, my truth. "Like I said, he's probably just drunk, and he's definitely mistaken." More bitter lies.

"Okay," she replies, still not fully buying what I'm desperately trying to sell. "But I'm here for you if there's anything—"

"There's not."

Charlie is one of the best people with the biggest hearts I've ever met, yet I can't bring myself to put the weight of my problems on her shoulders, not when she's so damn happy here.

"Listen, I'm pretty tired. I'm gonna head home."

I pull her in for a hug. Closing my eyes, I commit her warmth to memory. There will come a day when I can plant roots, but today is not that day. If I tell Charlie anything, she'll put herself and the club in the line of fire of my family and all the crazy that comes with them. There's only one choice I have, and it breaks my fucking heart.

"Why don't you go lie down in our old room? You've been drinking."

"I've only had two. Besides, I kinda want my own pillow, not those cheap ass ones on a twin bed."

Charlie and I laugh at the memory of when that bitch-bunny Stacia gave us those damn pillows and set us up in a room with the smallest beds. God, what I wouldn't give to have bunny drama be the only trouble to worry about.

"Okay, call me when you get home."

Charlie gives me a big smile before I turn to leave.

"Will do," I reply with a wave, blowing her a kiss as I open the back door that locks from the inside.

What Charlie doesn't know is I won't be calling her, at least not for a while. She'll only try to convince me to stay and let the club handle whatever may come from Badger recognizing me. They don't know how insane the elders and my father are, though. I'd never heard of anyone successfully leaving the compound, but I do remember one girl trying. The whispers about what happened to her when they caught her in the middle of the desert were enough to make anyone thinking about running reconsider after that. It worked on me until my last dinner in the home I grew up in and was told about my upcoming nuptials to a sadistic asshole in less than a week's time. More than once, I've wondered if that's what they told the girl. Is that what gave her the courage to try to escape? Maybe she saw her own mother powerless and unwilling to help her like I did.

I'm shaking like a leaf when I get to my little car. Charlie and I were so excited when I found an ad in the paper for my little beater. Knowing the guys were stellar at fixing up old bikes, Linc assured me they would have this thing purring like a kitten in no time. Between Linc and Jude, they had it running top notch in a week.

A sad smile stretches across my face when I slide behind the wheel. It's going to be a long while before I come back to Shine, if ever. Thankfully, me and Charlie have keys to each other's houses. I'll slip in before taking off and leave her a letter. Then I'm going to have to grab a new phone and leave my new old life behind. Starting the car, a half plan forms in my mind.

You can do this, Lucy. It won't be any harder than any of the other times.

I'm so focused on my internal pep talk, I miss the large figure walking up to my car and nearly jump out of my damn seat when they knock on my window.

Chapter Four
Jude

When Lucy spots Charlie and Linc coming from their room, I can't take my eyes off her animated face as I'm sure she's regaling them with the story of me suggesting we play a game of backgammon. What the hell was I thinking? There's me wanting to finally beat her at something, then there's suggesting the stupidest thing I possibly could and making her laugh her arse off.

But fuck, what a fine arse it is.

Stop that.

I don't need to entertain visions of her arse or any other part of her. The memory of when I threatened to turn her perfect backside red with my palm a few months ago springs to my mind. I've never seen Lucy blush so furiously, and she spends loads of time in a clubhouse full of bikers. Nope. Not again. My brain is quickly traveling to forbidden territory. There's no way in hell I'd have patience for a girl like that. Way too mouthy and way too opinionated. As far as I'm concerned, the only thing I need at present from a woman's mouth is somewhere warm and wet to put my dick. Not to tell me every infuriating comment that forms in her brain. Am I an arsehole for that? Perhaps. Do I care? Not particularly.

I grab another beer and sit on the couch next to Cash, who has a girl dancing over his lap. This is more my speed. Not dealing with a mouthy black-haired demon. When the girl on Cash's lap stands then bends all the way over, shaking her arse in his face, both of our heads tilt to the side. Yup, red lace thong barely covering her pussy. The sight has me half-mast. Fuck, I need to get laid. I'm about to suggest she slide the panties down her legs, so we have a better view, when out of the corner of my eye I spot three men walking in. Dammit. The fun will have to wait. I smack the girl's arse, and she yelps, then I turn to Cash.

"Nevada's here."

He nods and sends the girl away. Linc meets us just before we get to the newcomers and smirks in my direction.

"What?" I ask, already knowing he's going to have some cheeky remark for me.

"Backgammon, Jude? You know she's going to hold this against you, right?"

"Fuck off, you prat." He's not telling me anything I don't already know.

Ozzy gives us the side eye, effectively shutting us up when we're in front of the Bone Breakers. They didn't send any officers to meet with us, which doesn't bode well for whatever new alliance the Irish were hoping to achieve. It's a matter of respect, or disrespect, as the case may be.

"Welcome to Shine. I'm Ozzy." My prez holds out his hand to the man in front who takes it with an air of superiority. What the fuck is this bullshit about?

"Badger. This is Chop and Graze. Thanks for having us." He doesn't sound happy about being here in the least.

Ozzy gives the man a tight smile and nods at the other two. He's picking up on same cagey-as-fuck vibes I'm getting.

"Make yourselves comfortable. The bar is right over there," he says pointing to where the prospect is filling several shot glasses. "And we have plenty to keep you entertained. You boys relax, and we'll talk business in a bit."

"Or tomorrow," Chop answers, eyeing the stripper putting on a show in the middle of the room.

Ozzy pulls his ringing phone from his pocket, and I see the name on the screen. Tanya.

"Sorry, I have to take this," he tells Badger and the other two who are more focused on watching the show than anything my prez has to say.

"Better answer the old lady's call," Badger replies with a snarky chuckle.

Ozzy doesn't say anything before walking away to answer his mum's call.

Badger watches him go, and I get an uneasy feeling about this guy. Makes me wonder if he's here to work out routes for the Irish or to work out what his club would be up against if they challenged us. Seems more like he's casing the place and the club like a greedy motherfucker.

Deciding to keep my distance, but also keeping an eye on these gits, I wander back to the pool table where I have a view of Badger posting up next to Lucy. If there's one thing I know about the woman, it's that she has no time to suffer fools and seems to love nothing more than putting one in his place. Since that's what she considers me, I know first-hand how biting her tongue can be. This should be interesting to watch.

Lucy is staring at her beer as Badger tries to engage her in conversation, not saying a damn thing. Not what I expected at all. Instead of handing the man his ass, she grabs Charlie's hand, who's watching the exchange like a ping-pong match, and gets up. Badger calls after her, but she either doesn't hear him in the loud-as-hell clubhouse, or she's choosing to ignore him. Lucy and Charlie change course and disappear down the hallway as I make my way to the bar.

"Hey, Coop," I call to the prospect. He walks over, placing his hands on the bar.

"Hey, Jude. Another beer?" he asks like a good prospect does.

"Nah. Did you hear what the prick from the Bone Breakers and Lucy were talking about?"

Coop shakes his head with an apologetic frown. "It sounded like something about her looking like someone he used to know, but I'm not sure. She wasn't paying him any mind, and it's loud as fuck in here tonight. Everything okay?"

I nod at the kid. "No worries. I think I will take another beer."

Coop leaves to grab me one, obviously relieved his lack of knowledge about the conversation isn't being held against him.

Charlie returns from the hallway, sans Lucy, and finds Linc. Where the hell did she run off to? Instead of asking Charlie, I make my way down the hallway and out the back door into the cool night looking to see where the little hell-beast ran off to.

I scan the parking lot and spot Lucy standing by her car, having a hard time getting the door unlocked. That car may be a beater, but it gets her from point A to point B with only some minor engine work from me and Linc.

As I approach the car, Lucy gets behind the wheel, but she's not moving. It's too dark to see the expression on her face, but it's obvious she's taking several long breaths before starting the engine. She's so wrapped up in whatever is going on in her head, she doesn't see me approach. Knocking on her window, the girl almost jumps through the roof of the damn thing. When she rolls down her window, I expect a glare or a biting remark. Instead my gaze is met with watery eyes.

"Hey, what's wrong? Are you so scared I'm going to kick your arse at backgammon that you're running away?"

Lucy lets out a humorless laugh. “What do you want, Jude?”

“Why are you leaving all of a sudden? And what was Badger saying to you?”

Lucy visibly clams up, her jaw tensing and her grip on the steering wheel tightening to the point her knuckles turn white.

“Who?” she asks, attempting to look confused.

“Oh, no, Lucifer. I don’t buy it. That fuckwit said something to you, and I want to know what it was.”

Lucy rolls her eyes in typical fashion when it comes to pretty much any conversation that involves me making demands.

“Well, too bad for you, we don’t always get what we want.” Her sass is back full force.

“Too bad for you, I usually do. Now spill.”

If that asshole said anything to upset Lucy, I’ll have his fucking balls. Yes, it’s usually me trash talking her, but I’m allowed. Jesus, that sounds stupid and supremely hypocritical when I think about it. But like most things that have no rhyme or reason, I don’t give a fuck.

“No,” she states with an edge to her voice. “I’m not telling you shit. It’s none of your fucking business.”

“It is my business if it’s in my clubhouse.”

“Well, good thing I was just leaving then.”

Lucy throws her car in reverse and backs out of her spot like her fucking tailgate is on fire. When she gets to the gate, I nod at the prospect manning it to let her through. We haven’t had to be too cautious when it comes to security for the last few years, but after everything that went down with the Italians, Ozzy has been quite strict about having someone on the front gate at all times.

The prospect opens the gate, and she speeds out, throwing me the bird for good measure. I shake my head and chuckle.

Fucking Lucifer.

The bright cherry of a lit cigarette catches my eye in the otherwise dark night. I look over to the source and see the three Bone Breakers watching Lucy's car. There's nothing particularly sinister in the way they're all standing around smoking, but I've had a bad feeling about them all night.

They stub out their smokes and head inside the clubhouse. I follow them back inside but lose them in the crowd. No matter. The clubhouse isn't so big that it won't take more than a few moments to find them again if I want to. With Lucy gone and a roomful of Black Roses, I'm inclined to let myself relax and enjoy the party. After I get some answers.

I walk over to Linc with his arm draped over Charlie as they talk to Ozzy at the bar.

"What was wrong with Lucy tonight?" I interrupt.

Charlie looks a bit surprised at my question, but it doesn't stop her from answering. "I'm not sure, to be honest, but something did seem off with her."

"What was Badger saying to her at the bar?" I ask, hoping she isn't going to be as pig-headed as her friend when it comes to giving me information.

"He kept comparing her to some girl he knew in Nevada. Like, wouldn't leave it alone. Lucy ignored him, then grabbed my hand to go play pool. When we were walking away, I heard him call to her, 'They're still looking for you, Lucinda,' but she didn't respond. That's when I pulled her into the hallway and asked her about it."

"Did it go as I would expect?"

Charlie shrugs. "Pretty much," she replies, then takes a sip from her beer bottle.

"I wouldn't worry about it too much, babe. You said she's always been cagey about her past. If there was something for us to handle, she would let you know. She knows we've all got her back," Linc reassures.

Ozzy nods but doesn't look pleased with Charlie's story. Poor guy can't catch a break. If it's not one thing, it's another these days.

"Does this strike you as something we need to worry about, Charlie?" Ozzy asks.

To her credit, Charlie doesn't cower from the big man's question.

"Honestly, I don't know, Ozzy. Lucy isn't usually one to be scared of anything, but there was a flash of true fear in her eyes when the guy mentioned Nevada."

If there's one thing I learned from my time serving in the Royal Marines, it's trust your instincts, and there's something clawing the back of my mind.

Before I have a chance to think more about it, the prospect from the gate comes to Ozzy.

"Hey, Prez, the guys from the Bone Breakers left. Said something about needing to head out and they'd be back in the morning. It struck me as a little strange, so I thought I should come tell you."

"How long ago?" I ask the prospect as I stand, getting ready to get on my bike and head to Lucy's.

"Just after Lucy left. I saw them go back in the clubhouse, then you go in, too, but right after, they came back out again."

It couldn't have been more than five minutes since Lucy and the other bikers left. If they were after her for some reason, they don't know where she lives. But they got a good look at her car, and there's only one road leading back to town. It wouldn't have taken much to catch up to her while she was on the long stretch of road between the clubhouse and town.

Not wanting to sound the alarm because I'm likely jumping to conclusions, I finish my beer and set it on the bar.

"I'm going to take off."

Ozzy and Linc look at me with matching expressions of surprise.

"What? Lucifer has the night off. I can enjoy my favorite bar in peace."

"Hmm," Ozzy grunts. "Well, if you're planning on going to check on your least favorite bartender at her house, maybe take Linc or one of the other guys with you."

"Nah," I reply. "But if there's anything amiss, I'll give one of you a call."

There's obviously no need for me to attempt to keep up the charade of going to the bar. Actually, that's not a bad idea. Once I drive to Lucy's and see that everything is fine, I'll head over there, maybe even pick up a warm and willing woman and take her back to her place. It's only fair, after all. That girl has had me in knots all night. I need someone to get her out of my damn mind.

"I'll get back to the gate and let you out," the prospect tells me.

"Jude, if anything seems off, I want a phone call immediately."

"Oz, I'm sure it's nothing. Those guys seemed like arseholes, sure, but not particularly bright."

I can tell my president is a little uneasy about me going by myself, but what are we, a bunch of ninnies who have to hold each other's hands every time one of us needs to take a piss?

"Stay and enjoy the party, Prez. At least with those guys gone, you can relax. Maybe call Monaghan in the morning and tell him you don't think they're up to the task of what the Irish need. They can fuck off back to Nevada, and we'll never have to deal with them again."

"That's the plan. Alright. I'll let you get to it. Hey, Coop," he calls to the prospect behind the bar. "Round of whiskey."

When he returns with the shots, Ozzy, Linc, and Charlie raise their glasses for a toast.

Ozzy clears his throat. "May your glass be ever full, the roof over your head always strong, and may you be in heaven a full half hour before the devil knows you're dead."

The three of them clink glasses. I opt to decline only because I'm about to get on my bike. Might not be very badass of me, but I'd rather not be roadkill.

Charlie chokes down her shot, then fixes me with a stare. "Please don't be hard on her. Whatever's going on has her freaked out."

"I promise to be on my beast behavior."

"I think you meant best," she replies.

"No, I didn't," I shoot her a wink and make my way out the door. The day I promise to take it easy on Lucy is the day I hang up my cut because I'd be too soft for this life.

On the way to Lucy's, I consider the very real chance I'm overreacting to the entire situation. Lucy would have certainly told Charlie, or even Ozzy, if anything was seriously wrong. Our club has taken the two women under our wing as honorary sisters. Well, except for Linc, for obvious reasons. Lucy may think I couldn't be arsed when it comes to any of her troubles, and she'd be mostly right. I don't give a shit about any bunny drama or skeevy men hitting on her at the bar she works at, but if it comes to a threat against her, I'd never let anything happen. That would hurt Charlie and, in turn, hurt my brother.

Yeah, we'll go with that.

Two things hit me at the same time when I pull up to Lucy's place. First, there are three motorcycles I don't recognize until I see the Bone Breakers insignia on one of the saddle bags. The second is a loud crash and the light dimming behind her curtains.

Son of a bitch.

Before I can think about it, I'm charging up the stairs, drawing my gun before I kick in the door. The scene in front of me has barely registered when I point my gun at the bastard holding Lucy's bloody head up by her hair, ready to land another blow to her face, and fire.

Chapter Five
Lucy

That British fucking asshole thinks he can demand shit from me? Well, he's got another thing coming. In true Jude fashion, he pissed me off so much, I momentarily forgot about the dread swirling in my gut about Badger recognizing me. And about the fact of what I have to do now.

I peel out of the Black Roses compound like I have the devil on my ass. Good thing the prospect manning the gate was ready to open it. Lord knows, in the state of anger I'm in, I'm liable to drive right through the chain-link. God, that man infuriates me.

The drive to my house was just about a straight shot. There's only one road leading from the clubhouse to the little street Charlie and I live on. Just a couple right turns and I'm pulling up to my house. I'm going to miss the hell out of this place. The house is adorable with its white siding and black shutters. There are even planter boxes outside the windows of my little bungalow-style home. Well, I suppose after tonight, it won't be my home any longer.

Charlie is going to be pissed that I didn't talk to her face to face. Shit, I'd be pissed, too. But here's the deal. I'll be good goddamned if the shit from my past tarnishes what she's got going on here. If there was even a question that Linc wouldn't or couldn't take care of her if I left, there's no way I'd be making this decision. We've been through a lot together, and I've had her back at every turn, but I need to lead the danger away from her. She'd stand in the way of any threat to me, I have no doubt, but I can't let her.

The club would have my back as well, but again, I can't put them in that position. Ozzy wouldn't do business with them if they knew how entrenched that club is with a meth-selling religious cult that uses young women as breeding stock. Maybe the fear of what the elders could do is permanently ingrained in me, but I don't want these guys, who I've come to care for as brothers, within a ten-mile radius. The elders and my father don't play by the same rules. There's no doubt they would do whatever's necessary to win any fight brought to their doorstep, even if that meant using the women and children on the compound as cannon fodder. I couldn't walk through life with that on my conscience.

Walking into my house, the first thing that catches my attention is the mantle above my fireplace. I wanted a white fireplace and a new mantle when I moved in. Jude and Linc took a weekend and painted the brick and built one for me. Sitting on top are a few of the framed pictures of Charlie and me we've taken throughout the years. My favorite one is when we lived in New Orleans together. It was one of the rare mornings we were up early and decided to get beignets at Cafe Du Monde. It was by far one of my favorite places in the city to get the delectable pastry. In the photo, Charlie and I are mid-laugh with powdered sugar all over our faces, like we were little kids and had no need for napkins. It captured one of many silly moments we've had over the years. I refuse to let myself believe there won't be more moments like that in our future. I'll be back. It may take a few months, or even years, before it's safe enough, but there will come a day when I'll see her again.

Grabbing the picture, I head to my room to pack. When I first escaped the compound, I didn't have much, and what little there was fit in a bag that went everywhere with me. To work, to the store, it didn't matter. I never knew when or if they would find me, but there was no doubt in my mind they were looking. Call it a gut feeling, but that fear never seemed to settle. Until New Orleans. Oh, trust me, it took a little while, but I met Charlie, and it had been two years. Plus, New Orleans was so big and busy and so far away. I finally felt like I could breathe. There was always a go-bag stashed in my closet, so I suppose the fear never completely left.

Not here, though. Maybe I got complacent, maybe I was just plain dumb, but when I moved in, everything got unpacked, even the go-bag.

I pull the old bag from the back of my closet and begin throwing clothes in it. Who knows where I'll end up this time, so a little of everything is going in. It's when I get to the winter clothes on my hangers that still have the tags on them, that the tears begin to fall. I haven't even had the chance to wear any of this yet. I thought this is where I'd finally settle. So stupid. Why the hell am I crying over a few sweaters? Shaking my head, I continue to fill the bag. No time for tears. Not when there's more important things to worry about, like getting on the road and the hell out of Shine.

When that's done, I grab a notebook and sit on the bed, tearing out a sheet of paper. One last thing to do before leaving is writing a letter to Charlie. There's so much to say and so much emotion rolling through me as I stare at the blank piece of paper. The tears that dried up only minutes before are back with a vengeance. I'm leaving a sister. Again. Different circumstances, but it's the same punch to the chest that was there when I left Cece. My sister understood all those years ago. I can only hope Charlie does, too.

Dear Charlie,

I am so sorry I'm doing this in a letter, but I know if I tried to explain to you why I had to leave, you'd try to convince me to stay. And to be honest, it probably would have worked. Please don't be mad. Know that I love you and seeing you find your happiness with Linc and witnessing how he loves and protects you tells me I'm leaving you in good hands, and you're safe. That's all I've ever wanted for you. Me leaving is my way of protecting that safety. I don't know when I'll be back, but don't be surprised when I show up on your doorstep and tackle you in a huge hug.

Love Always,

Lucy

P.S. Tell Ozzy the Bone Breakers are the exact kind of club he does not want to have any part of. I can't tell you why right now, but please let him know for me.

Blowing out a breath, I fold the letter and look toward her and Linc's place when I hear a window break.

What the hell?

Grabbing my gun from the bedside table and twisting on the silencer, I rise from the bed and turn the overhead light off. One thing about my father that I came to appreciate is, although he didn't think women were worth more than bearing and raising kids and serving their husbands, he did want us all to be proficient with a firearm. According to him and the elders, it was important for everyone to fight in the Great War they were always yammering on about. I happened to be a natural when it came to shooting, even practicing with my sister and a few of the younger boys to help them along.

Peeking my head out the darkened bedroom door, I see three men enter through the front door. Immediately, the leather vests they wear catch my attention. Bone Breakers. How the hell did they find me?

"Let's find this bitch. Her dad and that stupid elder fuck want her back, and I want the reward they promised," Badger tells the other two, who are obviously dumb enough to go along with his stupid plan.

Like fuck I'm letting these assholes take me anywhere.

The living room lights are still on, but the hallway leading to the bedroom is covered in darkness, giving me the opportunity I need. Before the last one makes it around the corner into my kitchen, I raise my gun and aim for his head. A soft pop from my gun sounds loud to my ears in the otherwise silent house. The next thing I hear is the thud of the biker's body hitting the floor.

One down.

"Fuck, that came from the hallway. Chop, you whole?"

Silence is his answer.

"This was supposed to be a quick grab, Badger. That's what you said."

"Shut up, Graze. There's one of her and two of us."

The voices are definitely coming from my living room.

"Hey, Lucinda. You hear that? You sure you have enough bullets in that gun to take us out and get out of here alive? Why don't you make it easy on everyone and come on out?"

This fucking guy. The fact he honestly expects me to cower to him because I'm a woman and couldn't possibly hold my own is almost laughable. Maybe I'll get a good chuckle out of this when the night's over.

Before I can tell exactly where they are in my living room, a large figure comes barreling toward me. I take a shot, but it goes wide when he tumbles into me, hitting the lamp in the other room and shattering the bulb as it crashes to the floor.

The heavy asshole lands on top of me. In a split second, he grabs my wrist and slams it onto the floor, causing me to lose my grip on the gun. Before I have a chance to feel around for it, Badger slams a fist into my face, and blood pours from my nose. Goddamn, that one fucking hurt. Another quick punch to the face renders me almost unconscious, and the only thing that registers is a searing pain through my skull.

A loud crash comes from my entryway as the door flies open. Badger whirls around while holding my hair in a vice grip, nearly ripping it from my scalp.

Jude takes half a second to survey the scene in front of him before firing a shot right between Badger's eyes. Dead weight falls on me, along with what seems to be brain matter. Fucking gross.

Another shot sounds, thankfully missing Jude, who whirls on his would-be murderer and shoots the man in the arm, then the knee. His gun drops, and Jude takes three long strides to the man, kicking the gun from his reach.

"A little help here," I croak, trying to move Badger's lifeless body off me.

Jude rushes to my aid and pulls the man off me while keeping his gun trained on the man in my living room, howling in pain.

"Oh, quit your caterwauling," he taunts the only man left alive.

"Fuck you, asshole. You'll pay for this," Graze grits out.

Jude helps me to my feet and over to my blood-splattered couch.

"Maybe," Jude drawls. "But not today," he says, then punches the other biker in the face, like Badger had done to me.

"Who knows you're here?" he asks, holding the man's bloody face.

"Fuck you," is the reply he gets.

"Wrong answer, areshole," Jude says, then punches the man in the face again. "I could really do this all night." Jude grabs the man by the arm, which now has a bullet hole through it, and digs his thumb into the wound before hauling him onto one of the chairs in my living room.

"What do you say we play a little game, hmm? For every moment of fear she felt"—he nods in my direction—"you feel several moments of intense, blinding pain." He squeezes the wound harder.

Graze tries to put up a good fight as I witness Jude's line of questioning from the couch after I grab his gun which is now held tightly in my grip. When Jude pulls the knife from his boot, all bravado is wiped from the man's face. It could be the bleeding wound or the fear of the hours of torture Jude is threatening, but I don't think I've seen a man go so pale so fast.

"You know," Jude says with a wicked smile. "It's been a minute since I've had the pleasure of putting my knife to good use." His tone is polite, but the way he looks at his knife is anything but. "Lucy, have you had much experience with a knife?"

I shake my head. "No, I prefer guns. Much quicker."

Jude nods and cranes his neck to see the dead biker in my kitchen.

"My girl over here is quite adept with a firearm, as your friend can attest to. Well..." Jude releases a dark chuckle. "Obviously not, since he's dead and all."

Graze swallows hard, staring at Jude like he's lost his mind. Shit, maybe he has. Or maybe this is a side of Jude he keeps well hidden from the rest of the world.

"You see, Graze, was it?" The other man nods. "Right. Well, I always preferred knives. There's control in them, ya know? Every cut I make, every place I make you bleed, I'm in complete control. How deep or how shallow depends on the pressure I use."

To demonstrate, Jude takes the sharp blade and runs a trail from the top of Graze's tight white t-shirt and cuts a perfect line down the middle. The bloody shirt falls open, exposing the shallow wound he just inflicted.

"See, look at that. Hardly a scratch."

He presses the blade harder into the man's sternum. "I'm going to ask you again. Did you tell anyone you were here?"

Graze clamps his mouth shut, but I see indecision warring in his eyes.

Jude digs the knife further in, twisting as it slides into the man's flesh. Graze lets out a howl of pain.

"Didn't I already tell you once to quit your caterwauling?" he asks as he drags the knife down a few inches.

I can't help myself as an amused chuckle rushes out of me.

"What are you laughing at over there, Lucifer?"

I'm questioning my own sanity at this moment for the simple fact I could be finding anything funny in this situation, but *come on*.

"Caterwauling. It's just a funny word. Do you know what it means, or are you just using it to sound smart? Maybe that's the reason he's still 'caterwauling.'" I reply using finger quotes around the unfamiliar word. "Who even says that?"

Jude rolls his eyes. "Do you always have to give me a hard time? Even when I'm in the middle of trying to extract a little information from our friend here?"

"Oh, he's not my friend. This one and the other two were attempting to kidnap me."

"Hmm." Jude considers what I just admitted to. I suppose now that he's gone through all the trouble of saving me from the kidnapping, or worse, I'm going to have to come clean about a few things.

Jude looks back at Graze, who's gone a little grey around the edges.

"Who sent you to take her?"

When he doesn't answer, Jude raises his knife to Graze's nose and slices through his septum, causing him to yowl in pain.

"That's caterwauling. In case you were unaware, Graze. Shall I continue?"

"No! No one sent us. It was Badger's idea. He said we'd get a reward for returning her home."

Jude gives me a look that says we'll be discussing this later. Like I didn't already have that figured out.

"Did you tell anyone you were here?"

"No. We saw her car but saw you watching her leave, so Badger had us go back inside, knowing you would follow. As soon as you slipped through the crowd, we left. Then it was just dumb luck we caught up to her on the road."

"Dumb luck, eh?"

Graze swallows again. "Yeah, man."

A sadistic smile spreads across Jude's mouth. "Not so lucky for you, I'd wager."

Before Graze can react, Jude takes his knife and slides it across his neck. I watch as the blood pours from his body all over my rug in the living room. Damn it. I've always loved this carpeting.

"Did you seriously have to kill him in the messiest way possible?" I ask, looking at the red as it spreads around his body.

Jude cocks his head to the side and stares at me. "Oh, I'm so sorry, Lucifer. How rude of me to ruin your already blood-stained carpet... with more blood."

I look around my little house and the three dead bodies scattered throughout. Jesus, what an absolute mess.

Jude walks over to where I'm sitting and takes the gun from my hand. With a gentleness that a few minutes ago I didn't think he could possess, he lifts my chin and inspects my injuries.

"Do you want to go to the hospital?"

"Does it look like I need to?"

Jude studies me for a few more beats. "Nah, but it's going to hurt like a bitch tomorrow."

I let out a humorless chuckle. "It hurts like a bitch now."

Jude releases my face and sits next to me, eyeing the destruction.

"I need to call Ozzy in on this."

I nod, figuring this is a little bigger than the two of us can clean up on our own.

"Then you're going to tell me everything. Starting with who these fucks were bringing you home to."

I nod again. "Sounds fun."

It really doesn't.

Chapter Six
Jude

"Ozzy, we have a problem."

"What are you, a fucking astronaut now?" my prez quips back with a laugh.

"Can't say that I am, but it's definitely going to be a mission to clean up this shitstorm," I reply, looking around the room.

Lucy went to her bathroom to try to clean some of the gore off her face. I hear the shower running as I survey the damage to her house. The carpet will need to be replaced, and a couple of the walls will need to be bleached and repainted to get rid of the blood evidence. I'm not particularly worried about the police coming in here and doing an investigation or anything like that. Our kind tends to handle these things without any sort of law enforcement intervention, but the idea of even a trace of these assholes' DNA being in the same house as Lucy doesn't sit right with me.

"What do you need?"

"A full clean-up."

"Shit," Ozzy breathes out. "Is she okay?"

"Not sure yet. She's washing herself up. Took a few hits to the face but doesn't seem to think she needs to go to the hospital or anything."

"Okay. We'll be right over."

I hang up and wander through the house, peering inside Lucy's bedroom. There's a large bag that's seen years of use sitting on the bed, packed to the brim with clothes. A letter sits on her nightstand addressed to Charlie, and as I'm about to open it, Lucy emerges from the bathroom.

"What the hell, Jude? That's private," she says walking toward me in nothing but a bath towel and snatches the paper from my grip.

"I should be asking you the same question, Lucifer. Looks to me like you knew trouble was about to find you, and you decided to tuck tail and run."

Lucy rummages through her packed bag, pulling out some lacy underthings, a pair of pants, and a shirt with jerky movements. She's pissed? Good. I'm none too happy myself at the moment.

"And in my estimation, privacy went through the window about twenty minutes ago, considering the three dead bodies in your house." I raise my finger along with my voice and point at her doorway. "You were going to leave and not warn anyone about those fucks."

"No, I wasn't," she exclaims. "I put in my note to Charlie to tell Ozzy not to trust that MC." She stalks back to the bathroom and slams the door.

"We aren't done talking about this," I yell through the wood.

"I know, *Dad*, but would you mind if I got dressed so we can have this conversation when I'm fully clothed."

Her snarky-as-hell tone isn't lost on me. What I also notice is her lack of, I don't know, freaking out. She was almost kidnapped, she shot and killed one of her intruders, watched as I questioned the other one, then slit his throat, yet she has no issue with mouthing off to me. That last part isn't unusual, but the circumstances we find ourselves in tonight are. It would make more sense if she was going into shock or at least something to indicate some sort of fear on her part, but throughout the entire ordeal, she was cool as a cucumber. It makes me wonder what kind of horrors she's witnessed in the life she led before coming to Shine.

Lucy walks out of the bathroom, fully clothed and with the same attitude I'm accustomed to.

"Oh, great, you're still sitting on my bed," she says, followed by her customary eye roll. "Is Ozzy on his way?"

I nod in her direction, sure that any moment she's going to break down.

"I'd prefer if Linc didn't come. I haven't told Charlie anything about my past, and I'd rather do it when there aren't bloody corpses all over my house."

"You haven't told anyone anything, and that needs to change. Tonight."

The annoyed sigh that escapes her isn't at all surprising. Lucy is locked tighter than Fort fucking Knox.

"I know, but this isn't something I want her walking in on. She would definitely not be okay if she saw this."

Lucy flops down next to me and lies on her back, staring at the ceiling. Looking over at her, it still seems odd to me how emotionless she seems.

"Why aren't you freaking out?"

I think back to the bar in Texas where we found Lucy and Charlie a few minutes before Charlie's ex piece of shit caught up to her and shot the place up. Lucy remained pretty calm through that, too.

"I don't know..." She shrugs. "The way I see it, it was them or me. Since I wasn't about to let it be me, I don't feel all that bad about what I had to do to survive."

"You had to kill someone tonight to survive," I point out. "Most people would be curled in a corner, rocking back and forth over something like that."

"What about you? I don't see you crying over some spilled blood."

"That's different." My face has been the last many people saw before they took their last breath between my time in the Royal Marines and the MC. The shock of it wore off long before I came to the States.

"Why? Because you're some badass biker," she scoffs.

"No. It just is," I reply irritably. I don't know how to explain why it should be or why I'm so bent on the fact that it's not.

"Well, hate to break it to you, but the likelihood I'll ever react as you would expect is slim to none. And slim is lying in a pool of his own blood."

The sudden bark of my laughter startles Lucy.

"You are dark as fuck, Lucifer." And I kind of like it.

"Hello?" I hear called from the entryway. I did close the door before my interrogation of Graze. Granted, the doorjamb splintered when I kicked the door open, so I'm sure it wasn't latched.

"Ghosts?" Lucy whispers with wide eyes, faking the look of surprise.

I cast a wry grin in her direction. "Ozzy."

"That was going to be my second guess," she says, rising from the bed.

When we enter the living room, we're met with Ozzy, Wyatt, Knox, and Barrett.

"Hey, girl," Barrett says when he sees Lucy next to me. "You okay?" He walks up to her and takes a long look at her face before pulling her into a hug.

I'd like to say the scene of her hugging my brother doesn't bother me in the slightest, but I'm not one to lie to myself. I may not be inclined to delve into the reasons I'm annoyed over him with his hands on her, but they're there, nonetheless. A low growl emanates from my throat before I realize the sound came from me. Barrett looks at me with surprise, and Lucy looks annoyed. No shocker there.

Barrett steps away from her and takes his place next to Ozzy. Smart man.

As the four men take in the carnage, I watch Lucy from the corner of my eye. She's not showing any sort of outward reaction to what my brothers are seeing for the first time. In fact, they seem to have more of a reaction than she does. Of course, it still isn't much, considering this isn't the first time we've had to clean something like this up.

"Did you tell Linc what's going on?" Lucy asks.

"Not yet," Knox answers. "I wanted to see what was going on before I filled him in."

Likely to see what kind of state Lucy was in before Charlie saw her. Though all the brothers have become like family to Lucy and Charlie, Knox is her old man's actual brother, so Charlie is basically his sister-in-law. Anything that hurts Charlie will inevitably hurt Linc, and Knox would do anything to protect his little brother.

"I'd rather explain all this to Charlie myself," Lucy says.

"I'd rather like an explanation myself," I grumble under my breath.

With Lucy standing so close, she hears me and rolls her eyes.

"Damn, who got the big guy in the kitchen," Wyatt asks, looking around the corner and seeing the body.

"I did," Lucy tells the impressed-looking biker.

"Nice shot. Right between the eyes," he says and lets out a whistle.

"Okay, Lucy, time to tell us what they were after and why you were targeted," Ozzy tells her.

She visibly stiffens under his command. I don't think she can help bristling at anyone's demands, even Ozzy's. She's so used to calling the shots and being closed-lipped about her past, the idea of being forced to share isn't going to sit right with her.

"How about we have this conversation outside. It's starting to stink in here," I suggest.

The six of us walk out to Lucy's back porch and take a seat around her patio table. The night air is a hell of a lot fresher out here.

"Do you want the long version or short?" Lucy asks Ozzy.

"I'll settle for short, for now, but at some point, in the near future, we're going to have to know everything. Start with how you knew Badger."

"He bought meth from my family's compound in Nevada. In exchange for cash and guns, his club got an endless supply of drugs."

If Ozzy is surprised by her admission, he doesn't let it show.

"When you say compound, exactly what do you mean?"

Lucy takes a deep breath and slowly exhales, as though she's coming to realize how much she's going to have to divulge.

"My family is part of a cult that lived in the Nevada desert. It was a doomsday religious kind of thing, heavy on the doom. And religion. Kind of like the shit you would see on the news with the FBI or whoever going in and raiding. The elders ran the place with an iron fist. Badger was one of the guys who would make exchanges."

"I know you met Charlie in New Orleans. How did you make it from point A to point B?" Ozzy asks.

"Badger and a few of the guys from his club were at the compound one day when my parents told me... well, something I had no intention of following through on."

I'm sure my president would like to know what that something was, but he doesn't comment.

"Anyway, I snuck out of my house and was trying to figure out how I was going to get out of the compound when I remembered they were leaving with a load. I made it to the side of the property where the exchanges took place and snuck into the back of the van. They stopped in Colorado, and I snuck out when they were getting food."

"Damn, girl, do you have any idea what would've happened if you would've been caught?" Barrett asks.

"I do, but at the time, it seemed like a risk I had to take." Her reply is so matter of fact. She truly believed she had no other option.

It makes me wonder what was said to her that night to make her leave with nothing and make the risk worth it to her.

"What did Badger say to you at the clubhouse tonight?" I ask.

"That they were still looking for me. He somehow recognized me from the compound."

Ozzy considers everything Lucy just told him, even though there's a lot more to her story, I'm sure.

"Why didn't you tell anyone?" he asks.

Lucy shrugs and takes a minute to answer.

"I've had to take care of myself for a lot of years now. The last thing I wanted to do was drag anyone into my mess. I honestly thought they would've forgotten about me by now. Never in a million years did I expect to run into anyone from my past thousands of miles away. It's not like they were going to file a missing persons. They looked at any sort of law enforcement as the enemy."

"You could have said something tonight, though. I would have kicked those pieces of shit out of my clubhouse and figured it out from there," Ozzy says.

"I didn't want to risk anyone bringing my family or the elders to Shine. I figured if they found out I was gone when they came looking, they would leave you alone."

"Listen, girl," Ozzy starts. "You've been on your own since you were a kid and obviously had to deal with a shitty family and a shitty upbringing. I don't know the specifics, and I don't need to, but whatever you think you know about this club, know this—we take care of family, and you're family." Everyone around the table nods in confirmation. "And we don't do business with anyone who thinks doing this to women"—he points at Lucy's bruised face—"is ever tolerated by me or any member of the club."

"Pretty sure they got that message, Prez," Wyatt interjects.

Barrett chuckles, and even Knox lets out a rare huff of laughter.

“Alright. Let’s get this cleaned up. Barrett, go grab the van and back it up to the back porch. I’d rather not be carrying dead bodies through the front door. We’ll get the bodies out of here, then come back and start the clean-up.” Ozzy looks at me. “Why don’t you take Lucy to my cabin for the night?”

“Wait, can’t I just come back to the clubhouse?” Lucy asks, sounding anything but excited about spending a night alone with me.

“Honey, there’s still a party going on, and if you walk in there with those bruises, too many people are going to start asking questions. Plus, if anyone comes snooping around, we can tell everyone you and Jude went to the cabin for the night and weren’t in town.”

“The dead dumbfucks didn’t tell anyone they were here,” I tell Ozzy.

“I’ll have Braxton go through their phones just in case to be sure, but I don’t want Lucy seen at the clubhouse again tonight. Too many people there with loose ties to the club. Someone could let it slip that they saw a beat-up girl matching her description.”

I nod, as does Lucy, although much more reluctantly. Guess we’re having a slumber party.

The ride up to Ozzy's cabin is a mind fuck with Lucy on the back of my bike. I asked if she would rather we took one of the guys' trucks, and she looked at me like I'd sprouted another head. Fine with me. I was just trying to be a little accommodating since she's the one sporting the injuries.

This isn't the first time I've had Lucy on the back of my bike. In fact, the last time she rode with me was when we were hiding out with Linc and Charlie, kind of like tonight, only this time, it's just the two of us and a much smaller cabin.

The sun is going to be up in a couple hours, and the way Lucy is leaning into me, it's obvious she's well past exhausted. The feel of her arms wrapped tightly around me, and her ample tits pressed into my back is giving me all kinds of ideas that I absolutely shouldn't be thinking after the night we just had. I must be some sort of sick fuck to imagine what it would feel like to have her full breasts and tight nipples in my palms. When we pull off the main road to the cabin, I try to avoid all the potholes, but you pretty much feel every one of them on a bike. Feeling her tits bounce up and down against my back is doing things to my dick I'd rather not think about too hard.

See? Sick fuck.

"What is it with you guys and murder cabins in the middle of nowhere?" she asks when I park my bike.

When we had to lie low with Linc and Charlie, my brother let us use his cabin. Liam's cabin was more of an off-the-grid hideout, while Ozzy's is an actual hunting cabin that he, his dad, and Gramps sometimes stay in.

"You can't possibly be scared of a little cabin in the woods."

"Not even close. It just seems like you all tend toward the serial killer aesthetic."

Grabbing our bags off the bike, we walk up the stairs, and I open the door.

"Night's still young," I say as she walks past me.

"It's okay. I brought my gun."

"Of course, you did."

There isn't much here. It's a one-bedroom, old-as-hell cabin with a pull-out couch, a small kitchen, and an even smaller bathroom.

"Cozy," Lucy comments, taking a spin around the living room.

"Not up to your standards?"

"Oh please, you should have seen some of the places I've stayed in. This is practically a five-star resort."

Lucy has never so directly addressed her past or her time on the run. Shit, until tonight, we didn't even know she was on the run.

"How did you make it from Colorado to New Orleans?" I ask before taking a seat on the couch.

Lucy flops down on the other side of the worn-in sofa and looks me in the eye.

"No. We're not doing that," she says.

"Doing what?"

"We're not staying up all night as I tell you my whole sad story so you feel sorry for me."

"Lucifer, there has never been a day since meeting you that I felt sorry for you. I'm not about to start now." God, this woman could try the patience of a fucking saint.

"Good," she says, grabbing the TV remote from the coffee table. "How do you turn this damn thing on," she mumbles, pressing every button on the remote.

"Good God, woman, you're going to break the damn thing. Here." I grab it from her grasp and stand, using the power button on the tv then turning on the VCR with the remote. "This place is old as fuck. Trick never cared to upgrade any of this shit, so all we have are three channels and a VCR. Gramps loves old westerns," I say nodding to the stack of VHS tapes on the bookshelf next to the fireplace. "Pick one out."

Lucy grabs a movie, and I pop it in the VCR before returning to the couch.

"I hope you don't think we're sharing a bed," she says as the movie begins playing.

"Lucifer, I give you fifteen minutes before you're passed out snoring on this couch. I'll be taking the bed."

"Such a gentleman," she grumbles as she sinks into the plush cushion.

"Never claimed to be."

Chapter Seven
Lucy

The heat is the first thing that registers when I wake up. It's fucking stifling in here. The second thing is the large, tattooed arm around my middle and the hard chest at my back.

What in the actual hell?

Okay, last night I remember watching one of Gramps' old westerns and the feeling of melting into the soft couch. Not like a drugged kind of melting, but that bone-tired, can't keep your eyes open a second longer kind of feeling.

Which then begs the question... how the hell did I end up in the one bed with Jude after he specifically told me he was taking the bedroom?

"Jude," I try whispering. Not that I would usually care how I talked to the British asshole, but I don't know what kind of morning person he is. If he's the kind of person who wakes up swinging, I don't want it to be on me. My body has taken enough abuse in the last twelve hours.

"Jude," I try again, a little louder this time.

I twist my body around and get a look at the sleeping man next to me. The movement causes him to stir, but instead of opening his eyes and looking on in horror at the position we're in, a smile graces his full lips as his hand runs over the skin of my stomach before he pulls me tighter to him. From the feeling of his half-hard cock and the soft moan he lets out when he presses it into my hip, I would wager Jude isn't an angry morning person. Quite the opposite, in fact.

"Jude, wake up," I say, adding a bit more bite to my voice.

Things are getting a little uncomfortable, especially because of the way my body is reacting his touch. Listen, it's been a minute, okay? I can't be too hard on myself. But this is *Jude* lying next to me—asshole manwhore extraordinaire. My lady bits don't need to be having *any* sort of reaction to him, other than complete revulsion.

"Woman, let me sleep," he mumbles into the side of my face. I'm wondering if he even realizes who he's sleeping next to.

"Do you know who you're talking to?" I mean it's entirely possible he doesn't, considering he's not jumping out of the bed from shock.

"Yes, Lucifer. I know exactly who I'm sleeping next to, and you're so warm." He pulls me tighter into his large frame. "Must be left over from the pits of hell you were created in."

"Get off me," I tell him, grabbing his arm and tossing it back to his side. Sitting up, I scrub a hand over my face before turning my eyes to the ever-relaxed biker still lying by my side, giving me a smile full of mischief.

"How did we end up in bed together," I ask as Jude stretches his arms over his head and lets out a loud yawn.

The sheet covering us slips down past his tight abs and displays that fucking V thing guys have that makes my damn mouth water every time.

"Oh my God, are you naked?" The horror on my face does nothing but make the asshole laugh.

"No, Lucifer, I kept my boxers on like a gentleman. But I sure as shit wasn't going to sleep in my jeans."

I roll my eyes.

"Are you always like this in the morning?" he asks.

"Like what?"

"Cranky as hell."

"Only when I wake up in bed next to a barely dressed, six-foot-two biker, with no recollection of getting here," I volley back.

"First of all..." He stands from the bed, bending over to grab his discarded jeans from the floor. I am not staring at his ass. Nope. No way. Not me. "I'm six foot three. Second,"—he turns to me and crosses his arms—"you fell asleep and didn't look particularly comfortable, so I figured I'd be nice—"

"For once."

His eyebrow quirks in an annoyed expression at my interruption.

"As I was saying, I thought I'd be nice and share the bed with you. We were both in need of a solid night's rest."

"That seems… reasonable." And so out of character for Jude.

The loud engine of a motorcycle roars outside the little cabin, and Jude grabs his gun sitting on the small bedroom table.

"Stay here," he instructs as he walks out of the bedroom to find out who our visitors are. I hear voices from the other side of the door before Jude comes back inside the bedroom.

"Charlie and Linc are here."

Great. Here we go, and I haven't even had coffee.

Jude walks back into the living room and calls to them that I'll be out in a second.

When I emerge from the bedroom, Charlie is standing in the middle of the small space, her mouth hanging agape as she looks back and forth between me and a shirtless Jude, who's going about brewing a pot of liquid gold.

"When Linc told me we needed to come out to Ozzy's cabin because some shit went down, this was the last thing I had in mind," she says, pointing between me and Jude.

"This isn't what I was talking about, Charlie pop, but it's definitely a new development in the story."

Jude chuckles from the kitchen, being entirely unhelpful in the situation.

"There is no new development here," I say to the room as Jude turns around to face us with his arms crossed over his chest and a half smile tilting his lips.

"It's okay," Jude starts. "Listen, we slept together and—"

"Jude!" I exclaim, cutting him off from any more insane bullshit that may spew from his mouth. "We didn't sleep together." Charlie and Linc give me a disbelieving look. "Well, we slept in the same bed, but nothing happened."

"That's what I was going to say, Lucifer, before you interrupted me."

"Yeah, sure it was, pal." I shoot him a look that tells him I don't believe that for a second. Turning back to Charlie, who obviously has no idea what the hell's going on, I give her a serious look.

"Some stuff went down last night I need to tell you."

"I knew it. It has to do with that creepy biker, doesn't it?"

"Yeah." I nod and let out a breath. "Let's get some coffee and go outside."

Charlie's concerned expression makes me wish there was a magical way to rewind the clock about twelve hours and somehow not run into Badger at the compound. If I had been at work, or anywhere else, none of this would have been happening.

We fill our cups and walk to the little lake the cabin overlooks. Someone built old wooden benches at the edge of the water. Presumably to have a peaceful place to come think and soak in the tranquility of the quiet. I hope some of that serenity somehow absorbs into my frayed nerves while I sit out here with my best friend and open up about the secrets I've kept hidden for so long.

"I lied last night. When I saw Badger, I lied about knowing who he was." Maybe not the best way to break the news, but it's all I have.

"I knew something was going on, but I know how you get about opening up, so I didn't want to push."

I take a long sip of my coffee and a deep breath of fresh, woodsy air before beginning my story.

"Badger was in an MC that used to trade guns for meth in Nevada. He got the meth from a compound run by a doomsday religious cult. That's where I grew up. And that's how he recognized me."

Charlie's face remains fairly stoic. Sure, I see a bit of surprise in her eyes—of course there would be after finding out your best friend was raised in a cult—but otherwise, she sits by, patiently waiting for me to continue.

"The elders didn't believe women played more of a role in the household other than having kids and tending to their husband's every need, including being baby-making machines to further populate the congregation. When I was little, I thought the women on the compound must be accident-prone like I was because every Sunday, they would show up in their Sunday finest with bruises on their faces and wrists. I saw it in my house, too, and Mama always said it was an accident, that she wasn't paying attention. Obviously, later, I realized it was my dad doing it to her, and the other women's husbands were doing the same."

"Did he beat you, too?"

"Not when I was little, but the older I got, the less he cared about hiding his temper. He claimed it was God's will for my sister and me to learn how to obey our husbands, so the beatings we got from him were to help us be better wives."

"Wait. You have a sister?" Charlie looks at me with wide eyes. "Where is she?"

My eyes fill with water, remembering the night I left.

"She wouldn't come with me. She was terrified of getting caught. We heard rumors about what happened to another girl who tried to run. Her name was Bea."

"What were they?"

"When the elders found her, they took her back to the church. There were eight men who took turns beating her. They branded her and continued to rail on her. Every time she cried out in pain, they would beat her more. Apparently, they were 'exorcising her demons' or something. I was friends with Bea's sister. She said she could hear her screams for hours. I guess her body gave up in the end. Her sister said she saw them carrying her naked body out of the church, and she was covered in blood. They told everyone the next day Bea's demon killed her when they were trying to save her."

Charlie covers her mouth with one hand and holds my hand with her other.

"Did anyone ever manage to get away?"

"Not to my knowledge. The boys were treated like little princes being raised to one day become kings, and the girls carried demons inside them. If they didn't pray every day and follow the teachings of the elders, their demons would take over and kill them, damning their souls to eternal hell."

"What in the actual fuck?" It's not so much a question as it is a statement of disgust. "How did the meth and that other MC come into play?"

"They believed there was going to be a great war, and evil spirits were going to rise from hell and take over people's bodies and come for the true believers. They told us some of these infected people were already here and masked as police officers and people in government. That's why we could never trust any of them." Charlie's eyes get wider the more I tell her about the crazy shit they preached to us. "We weren't a rich congregation or anything like that, but we had a lot of land to put meth labs on."

"Seems reasonable," Charlie comments.

"Right? Totally logical," I reply, injecting some humor into the extremely heavy conversation. It's how I cope when shit threatens to pull me into darkness. My best friend knows it's what I need right now. One of the many reasons I love her.

"The MC sold us guns, and the elders paid them in meth. Of course, no drugs or any kind of alcohol were allowed for any of the members. But they justified it by allowing the non-believers and sinners to die from their own wickedness."

"How magnanimous of them." Charlie rolls her eyes.

"Hmm. Quite."

"What made you try to escape if you knew what would happen if you got caught?"

"I was going to be married off." Jasper's twisted smile fills my mind. "I could tell the boy they decided for me was a sick asshole. There's just that feeling you get about people, you know? The way he'd look at me like I was already his property. His hands would wander if he got close enough to me, and they weren't gentle. There was no one I could tell who would do anything about it. I wasn't always the most obedient daughter, and they were afraid it would rub off on my sister. She was the sweet one, never wanting to cause problems."

"Yeah, that's definitely not you."

"Hey, I was a lot better about hiding my 'wicked ways' back then," I joke, using air quotes.

"Not better. Just terrified. I much prefer this version of you." Charlie squeezes my hand and gives me a soft smile.

"His dad was one of the elders, and they came to dinner one night. They told me instead of waiting another year, we were going to be married within the week. I knew my time was up. There was no way I could live my mother's life. Shit, it undoubtedly would have been worse. You wanna talk about someone with a God complex? That was Jasper." I shiver at the memory of his smarmy smile and the way he looked at me. To this day, it still gives me the creeps. "The Bone Breakers were making an exchange, and I snuck onto their van, then got out when they stopped. I was hundreds of miles away before anyone was the wiser."

"And your sister stayed?"

The idea of her still living there without me is a regret I live with every day.

"Yeah. I couldn't stay, and she was too scared to leave. So, I left Cece there." Another tear makes its way down my cheek.

"Lucy, no one could ever fault you for leaving. You had to run, or that bastard would have gotten his hands on you. She made her choice to stay. You couldn't."

Everything Charlie is telling me is what I've told myself over and over again, but it doesn't lessen the sting of not seeing Cece for the last seven years or of not knowing whether she's okay.

"What happened after you left the clubhouse last night?"

"What did Linc tell you?"

"Nothing. He said you had some things to tell me this morning and left it at that."

"I don't know how much I'm allowed to say. Ozzy usually leaves telling you about club stuff up to Linc, doesn't he? I don't want to piss him off."

She looks at me like I've grown tentacles or something.

"Don't give me that. We tell each other everything. If there's a problem, they can go fuck themselves."

Damn, she's sounding a lot like me these days.

"Sorry, forgot who I was there for a minute."

"Don't worry. I'll always be here to remind you," Charlie tells me with a slight tilt of her lips.

I relay the events of last night. She gives me the evil eye when I get to the part about going home to pack without saying anything to her but allows me to continue. When I finish, she leans back on the bench and looks out onto the water. I do the same, exhausted, yet lighter after telling her what I've kept hidden for so many years.

"I'm going to tell you right now, Lucy, if you ever leave me, I'll find you and make you see reason. And I won't be happy about it. I may even take a page out of your book and smack the sense back into you."

"No, you wouldn't."

"Okay, maybe not that last part, but I'm not going to let you run because you think you're somehow protecting me or the club. That's dumb as shit."

After last night, I realized the error in my judgment. Jude didn't waste a second coming in and taking Badger out when he saw what he was doing to me. Then Ozzy came and cleaned it up. The only thing he wanted from me was the truth. He did all that because that's the kind of man he is. It's the kind of club president he is.

"There's those lady balls. Glad to see I've been rubbing off on you."

"I mean it. You're my family, and I love you. Everyone here has your back. Especially Jude."

"I don't know about that." Even after last night, I have the feeling he wishes trouble hadn't followed me. It's a hell of a mess for him and the brothers to have to clean up.

"You didn't see him. When he came back inside from talking to you last night, then found out those other guys left right after you did, he was the first on his bike to make sure you were okay. You two fight like I've never seen, but the second he thought your safety could be in question, he was out the door. I doubt he would do that for any of the other women who hang out at the clubhouse."

I can't deny what she said is true. He was the first person there. It's no stretch to think my night would have ended up a whole hell of a lot different if he hadn't gotten there when he had, but I'm not sure what to do with everything Charlie is insinuating. Jude and I are in this weird place right now, where I don't hate him and don't think he hates me, but exactly what that means is anyone's guess.

"Alright, I'm starving and need more coffee," I say, looking down at my empty mug. "Let's go back up and see if there's anything we can make. Otherwise, these guys are taking us for a huge breakfast."

We stand, and Charlie envelops me in one of her full-body hugs.

"I mean it, sister. No more running... from me or the truth."

"No more running," I agree. I hope with everything in me, I can keep that promise.

When we get back to the cabin, Linc and Jude have already pulled out a few things. Linc is mixing batter, and Jude is beating eggs.

"Well, this is cute," I say, taking in the very domestic scene as Charlie bounds up to Linc, placing a smacking kiss on his mouth.

"I see you found your shirt." I nod toward the now-clothed biker getting ready to pour eggs into a pan.

"Yeah, Linc was feeling emasculated with my perfect physique on display. Said something about him not wanting his woman seeing what a real man looks like."

"Shut up, fucker. I said no such thing. Charlie is well aware of what a real man is. She sleeps next to one every night." Linc flicks a batter-covered spoon in Jude's direction.

"Lucy can attest to what it's like sleeping next to perfection, can't you, love?"

"I'm not touching that with a ten-foot pole. You both can leave me out of your dick measuring contest, thank you very much," I reply, grabbing a coffee warm up.

"Darling, if you want me to whip it out, all you had to do was ask."

This man is absolutely insufferable, but when he calls me darling… yeah, no. Not going there.

Walking over to wash my hands, I see a pack of bacon in the sink.

"I defrosted it so you could pop it in the oven," Jude says next to me, keeping his eyes on the eggs he's cooking.

"I thought you said baking ruins it."

He shrugs, still not meeting my gaze. "I may have changed my mind."

"Well, slap my ass and call me Susan. I never thought you would admit to being wrong."

Jude's heated gaze meets mine. "Lucifer, don't give me ideas. If you think I haven't imagined what my handprint would look like on your fantastic fucking backside, you'd be dead wrong," he replies softly and winks. The man fucking winks at me.

Turning away from Jude, I start searching the cabinets for a baking sheet, attempting to hide my heated cheeks.

I am so fucked.

Chapter Eight
Jude

It's been a week since everything went down at Lucy's house. So far, we haven't heard from anyone from the Bone Breakers, but that could mean any number of things. It took a few days for us to get Lucy's house back in order, but she's been staying at the clubhouse, much to Charlie's irritation.

"I just don't understand why she'd rather stay in a clubhouse full of bikers rather than getting some rest at our place. We have an extra room," Charlie complains to Linc as we stand in the kitchen this morning at the clubhouse.

"Oh, come on, Charlie. We aren't that bad. I think I heard something about Barrett giving her a pedicure the other day," I tease when the man in question walks in to refill his coffee.

"Fuck you, arsehole," he shoots back.

"How many times do I have to tell you wankers not to use my words?"

"You don't own the word, dick," Linc chimes in.

"Maybe not, but you sound like a bunch of twats when you use it."

Linc rolls his eyes and turns back to Charlie. "Maybe she didn't want to be next door to the house she almost died in while she recovered, Charlie bear."

Charlie shrugs at Linc's reasoning. I mean, it sounds logical to me, but Lucy also made sure to warn me that she would rarely react to things the way I would expect her to, so it's anyone's guess why she decided to convalesce at the clubhouse. One thing for certain is I haven't minded her being here. There was no end to my irritation before all this happened when she would always be around, giving me shit, but something's changed. There's a comfort in putting eyes on her every day and making sure she's okay. The unfamiliar emotion isn't something I've looked too hard at, that's not really my MO, but it's there, and I've come to uneasy acceptance of the fact.

Ozzy lumbers into the kitchen and heads to the coffee pot. "What are you yahoos gabbing about in here?"

"Barrett's new career," I reply with an innocent smile.

"I don't want to know," Ozzy says, then turns his gaze to me. "Meet me in my office when you're done here."

I nod before he turns and walks out.

"Why is it like being summoned to the principal's office when he says, 'Meet me in my office?'" Charlie's poor imitation of Ozzy has us chuckling.

"Don't quit your day job, love," I say before she shoots me a dirty look. "Cheers." I raise my coffee mug as I leave the kitchen and head to talk to Ozzy.

"What's up, Prez?" I ask, walking into his office and sitting in one of the chairs in front of his desk. Charlie's right. It is like being in the headmaster's office, just with more black shit and skulls decorating the space.

"How's Lucy?"

"Fine, I suppose. Did you call me in here to chit-chat about a girl?"

"No, wise ass. Braxton looked through the phones we took from the Bone Breaker fucks. He saw something that raised alarm bells. Badger sent a text to someone back in Nevada. Said he found an opportunity that was going to be good for the club, and he'd be in touch."

"Did he mention what it was?"

"No, but considering where he went right after he sent that text, I'd bet money it had to do with Lucy. You said Graze thought they'd get some sort of reward from the elders of that fucking cult."

Lucy told Charlie all about her childhood that day at the cabin. I still can't believe a woman like Lucy grew up in a cult. She's so much bigger than any box those sick fucks would have tried to put her in. Charlie didn't tell Linc the details, well not anything more than what we needed to know, but Lucy had already spoken to Ozzy about everything she remembered about the Bone Breakers, which wasn't much, and the compound she grew up on. She left out personal stories from her childhood, that's not what Ozzy needed from her, but Charlie told Linc it was bad. It doesn't take much of an imagination to fill in the blanks.

"So, someone knows Badger thought he was going to get some big score. That could have been connected to anyone. What do you think the chances are of them sniffing around here?"

Ozzy considers my question for a few moments before answering. "Pretty good, to be honest."

"Do you have a plan?" Waiting for these fuckers to randomly show up doesn't lend itself to having any sort of peace of mind for the foreseeable future.

"As far as anyone who was at the party is concerned, they were just passing through. If I get a call from their prez, the story I think we should go with is they wanted to check out a bar in Boston. We can even allude to the fact that they said they had some business there. That way it plays off the mystery text."

"Can Brax figure out who the text went to?" I'd certainly feel better knowing who was on the other end.

"He said he could try. It's not like he's some tech genius."

I scratch the five o'clock shadow I'm sporting these days and think about suggesting something I know Ozzy isn't going to like.

"We could always ask my prick brother to have one of his guys look into it."

My brother Liam is a private security specialist. If anyone assumed that simply meant he was a bodyguard for hire, they'd be very wrong. His work includes all sorts of shady shit for rich-as-hell private citizens and the occasional government coup. You know, normal nine-to-five shit.

"I'd rather not cross that bridge unless we absolutely need to."

The last time Liam did a favor for Ozzy, he ended up owing my arsehole brother a couple favors that have yet to be called in. Plus, the man is a complete pain in the arse to deal with. I love my brother and would lay down my life for him, but if anyone can burrow under my skin faster than Liam, I've yet to meet them. Well, maybe the raven-haired she-devil sleeping in one of the rooms could give him a run for his money.

"Any idea how much longer Lucy is going to be here?"

My question takes Ozzy by surprise for a moment until a wide smile stretches across his face.

"Not sure. As long as she needs to. Why do you ask?"

I shrug, trying to play off my curiosity. "Her house has been done for a few days. Figured she would have talked to you about going home. Plus, Charlie's been working a shitton, and Linc is getting irritated not having his old lady home."

Complete bullshit. Linc couldn't care less about hanging out at the bar with Charlie.

"Hmm. Interesting," Ozzy says, looking at me like the interesting thing *isn't* what I said about Linc. "She mentioned not wanting to overstay her welcome. And I know she's working tonight. Her face is healed enough to go back to work without having anyone asking questions."

"Sounds good. Alright, if there's nothing else…" I need to get out of here before Ozzy decides to dissect any other bullshit that comes from my mouth.

"Nope. All good here. Just wanted to give you an update."

I knock my knuckles on his desk and stand.

When I make it to the door, Ozzy speaks up.

"Maybe I'll come have a beer at the bar with you later."

"If I'm there, sure."

"Oh, I have a feeling you'll have your ass parked in a stool."

I toss a rude gesture over my shoulder before leaving. Fucking know-it-all prez.

The bar isn't particularly packed for a Wednesday night. Walking through the door, I spot Lucy behind the bar, talking to a group of men who are obviously admiring their bartender. It's impossible not to see Lucy as the drop-dead gorgeous woman she is. All that long black hair and those bright blue eyes. She's not tall by any stretch, but she's got curves for days and carries them well. When she first arrived at the clubhouse, there wasn't a man there who didn't salivate over her round ass and full tits. She's a pin-up model come to life.

"Well, look what the cat dragged in." she says when she sees me. "A grumpy British biker."

And then she opens her mouth, and all my fantasies die on the vine. She'd be the type to tell me everything I'm doing wrong if I ever got it in my head to take her to bed. The damn woman can't stop giving me shit. I'd have to shove my dick in her mouth to shut her up. Fuck, now I'm thinking about her lips wrapped around my cock.

Stop it, you fucking idjit.

"Dammit, I thought you had the night off. It's been so pleasant here without you." Obviously, I knew she was working tonight, that's why I'm here. I'm questioning my sanity at this point.

"Nope, back to the grindstone," she says as I have a seat at the bar. She plops a cold beer in front of me.

Raising the bottle in thanks, I take a long gulp.

Lucy returns to her customers and continues whatever conversation they were having.

"Round of shots to welcome Lucy back," one of the men yells, raising an arm and pumping his fist like a dumbass. "Glad you're feeling better, sweetheart."

Lucy laughs and begins pouring six shots of whiskey into glasses.

"Yeah, that was a killer bug," she tells the group, shooting me a subtle wink.

I huff out a quiet laugh, and the four men at the bar remain oblivious to our silent conversation.

Lucy walks over to me and sets one of the shot glasses next to my beer.

"I don't think they meant me, Lucifer," I say quietly.

"I don't give a fuck. Let's do a shot." Lucy raises her glass for a toast, clearing her throat before she speaks again. "Here's to those who wish us well, and all the rest can go to hell."

After a full chorus of "Here, here," we all take the shot. When Lucy walks back over to clear away the glasses, I shoot the group of men a look. It's not menacing, per se, but there's no mistaking they take it the way it's intended. If they think any of them are going to be getting Lucy drunk and taking her home tonight, or any other night, they no longer hold such aspirations.

The rest of the night passes fairly quickly. Ozzy doesn't make an appearance like he suggested he would, much to my relief. Not that I wouldn't mind having a few beers with the man, he works too damn much and could use a night to blow off some steam, but I'm not in the mood to deal with his knowing looks every time he witnesses any interaction between me and Lucy. It's been hard enough figuring out the way my feelings have been changing for her on my own, the last thing I need is my prez breathing down my neck.

Before the night at her house, she was firmly in the 'hot but way too much trouble' box. Now, trouble isn't looking like such a terrible idea. That thought excites and unnerves me in equal measure, and it doesn't help matters that Lucy isn't razzing me to no end like she usually does. Sure, there are still the jokes at my expense, but I can't deny even those aren't as biting as they used to be. Knowing what I do now about her past sheds some light as to why she's so fucking hellbent on protecting the people she loves, namely Charlie.

That's where it all started. The night we found her and Charlie in a bar in Texas, I wasn't particularly keen on Charlie being back in Linc's life. He spent six years locked up for beating her shithead ex almost to death. Who would want their best mate involved with any part of that situation again? Lucy practically jumped down my throat when she viewed me as a threat to her best friend. Not much different than I would do or have done. Shit, I've done a whole hell of a lot more when any number of my brothers had been in the line of fire.

Come to think of it, I did a lot more for Lucy just last week. Maybe it's the understanding that she cares about those she considers family the same way I do that has me reconsidering a lot about her. I'm man enough to admit my biggest problem has to do with my ego and not necessarily the woman behind the bar. At least to myself. Never to anyone else. Certainly not Lucy.

"What's that look on your face?" Lucy asks as the last of the customers leave for the night.

"What look?"

"I don't know," she replies, turning off the open sign before she begins flipping chairs and setting them on top of tables. "You look like you're working through one of life's great mysteries or planning world domination. With you, it could be either."

I laugh at her theory. "No need for world domination, love. I'm fine right here in Shine."

"How did you end up settling here?"

Standing from my stool, I help Lucy put the chairs up.

"My grandfather knew Gramps. Back in London, they were mates. Both of them liked to ride and work on bikes. When I got out of the Royal Marines, my grandfather and I came to visit my brother and tour the East Coast on our bikes. We met Gramps at a bar in Boston, along with Trick, Ozzy, and Knox. My brother was trying to convince me to work for him at the time, but I wasn't interested in security work. The idea of having to adhere to a schedule or answering to my brother didn't appeal to me whatsoever. I was more interested in taking a break for a bit and seeing where my bike would take me. Trick was president back then and suggested we swing by Shine sometime. I doubt he thought I'd end up staying here, or maybe he did. I don't know. Me and my grandfather rode in one day and met the rest of the guys. Decided I liked it enough to stay."

"You went from being a soldier to a biker?"

"They're not as different as you would imagine."

Lucy scoffs. "It sounds like it couldn't be more different."

"The training exercises, strict schedule, and routine, sure, but then there's the brotherhood you feel toward the other men in your unit and the loyalty we all shared. That's not so different from what I found when I joined the Black Roses. I'd take a bullet and fire them just as readily for any of my brothers."

Lucy nods. "I can see that. You're all a part of this ragtag family that looks out for each other."

"That's the piece that was missing when I left England. I have my brother, sure, but he's all about following orders, only this time, he's the one calling them."

"Do you get along with him?" Lucy grabs a broom and begins sweeping under the tables.

"Depends on what you mean by get along." I pick up another broom behind the bar and start sweeping at the other end. "We give each other massive amounts of shit, but when it comes down to it, we love each other."

"What about your parents? Do you see them often?"

"They passed away in a car accident when Liam and I were kids. Our grandfather raised us. We go back to London from time to time to visit the old coot. Liam's been trying for years to get him to come here, but Grandfather is set in his ways. He has his life there and friends he sees every day for a pint at the pub."

"You must miss him."

"Sure, but I'm not about to change his mind. He came to visit once a few years ago. It was something, seeing him and Gramps working on Gramps' old bike together. I swear, it was like looking at me and Linc fifty years in the future." I chuckle at the memory. "Liam and I thought he would want to stay, but he said the lads at the pub wouldn't know what to do without him," I say, imitating my grandfather's deep timbre. "We decided to let it go. Personally, I think he has a lady friend."

Lucy laughs. "Did you ask him about that?"

"Sure did. He told me he has several and how could he deprive any of them by moving across the globe?"

"I think I'm seeing some familial traits," Lucy says as we meet in the middle of the bar with our brooms.

"It's the Ashcroft curse. How could we possibly deny the needs of all the beautiful women?" I tilt my lips up in a half smile, and Lucy rolls her bright blue eyes.

"You're ridiculous."

"You call it ridiculous. I call it my contribution to the female population."

"Should I thank you for your service?"

"Oh, darling, you have yet to appreciate the extent of my services."

Lucy stares at my lips for a heated moment, then backs away. Ah-ha. So, this uncomfortable attraction isn't one-sided.

"What are you doing tomorrow?" I ask as Lucy grabs her till from the bar and begins closing it out.

"No plans. It's my day off. I tried to cover the shift since everyone's been working for me, but Maizie wants to work."

"Perfect. I'll pick you up at ten."

"I didn't agree to spend my day off with you," she says, sounding slightly offended.

"I didn't ask." A wry grin spreads across my face.

Lucy clenches her jaw and blows out an annoyed breath. "Fine, but only because you helped me close tonight."

I would have helped regardless of whether or not she agreed, but I'll take the win.

When she finishes counting her cash drop, I follow her back to her place. I ask if she wants me to come in with her, seeing as it's her first night in her house in a week, but she insists she's fine. If there's one thing I've learned about Lucy, it's when to push and when to back off. I shouldn't be too worried. I had a friend of the club hook her place up with all kinds of security. She's as safe inside as she would be at any of my brother's safe houses. When I get the notification on my phone that the alarm has been set from the inside, I take it as my cue to ride back to the clubhouse. Yes, I had him connect the alerts to my phone. No, I don't give a shit if that sounds stalkery. I know damn good and well Lucy wouldn't check in with me if I asked, so I decided to bypass her entirely in the name of safety.

Yeah, keep telling yourself that.

Chapter Nine
Lucy

It's strange being in my house again. I stopped by before my shift with Ozzy so he could show me the new security system and how to arm it before I leave and unarm it when I get home. When I thanked him for thinking of it, he got this weird look in his eyes and told me the club wanted to make sure I felt safe being alone.

I'd been staying at the clubhouse since the attack so they could clean the house and do whatever they needed to before moving back in. It only took the guys a couple days to repaint and lay new carpeting and tile in the kitchen. After living on my own for a few months, it was comforting to be in a place where someone was always around. I loved living with Charlie before we came to Shine, but I'm not about to be the third wheel in her house. Besides, she's right next door. It's not like we don't spend a ton of time together. But it was time to get back to my routine. While I spent a few extra days at the clubhouse, I'm not about to use it as a crutch. There's no reason for me to hang around underfoot, and it's a lot less fun without Charlie there with me.

Jude coming to the bar was an unexpected surprise. He doesn't spend a lot of time there, at least not on my shifts. Maizie's told me he comes in on hers, and she could never understand why I couldn't stand his grumpy ass. She said he's always been kind to her and was a great tipper, which Maizie appreciated, considering she has a little one at home she takes care of by herself. Not that I thought he was a tightwad or anything, but to hear he was kind to her was a little bit of a surprise. Maizie is stunning, and I thought for sure Jude would have tried to get her in bed, but according to her, he's always been respectful. Still didn't change my mind about him.

At the time, I didn't think anything could, but this last week has been... different. The entire week at the clubhouse, Jude had been almost, dare I say, nice. I mean, he'd still pout like a petulant child when I kicked his ass at pool, but a certain ease had developed between us. Maybe committing triple homicide together made people closer. Who the hell knows? Regardless, I enjoyed the shit-talking and jabs we took at each other over the last week. It was more for fun than trying to piss the other one off, which is another reason to get back home. The last thing I need is to start developing any sort of stupid feelings for the man.

When we were closing the bar tonight, there was a moment when we finished sweeping that I had an urge to... well, an urge. That's all it was. A passing feeling that I'd like to have a little taste of what he was offering. Not that he was necessarily offering it, but the innuendo was there. There was a sudden and short-lived inclination to see if he lived up to his own hype. It was so dumb and better for everyone not to act on it. Then why did I agree to have him pick me up in the morning and take me on some mystery date? No, not a date. A mystery *outing*.

It may be possible I'm overthinking this entire situation.

Walking through my little house, I admire the work the guys did. When my bare feet meet the lush carpet for the first time, my eyes roll back in pleasure. They spent some money on this. I might just sleep on it tonight; that's how fucking soft and comfy it is. They even replaced the furniture in here. Good thing, too. I don't think any amount of steam cleaning would have gotten the blood out of that couch. Charlie had to have had a hand in picking out all the stuff in here. Everything is overstuffed and comfortable as hell. She'll be getting a huge hug and thank you tomorrow.

One thing I noticed when I was here earlier was the new bedroom and the giant king-sized bed that wasn't what was there before. When I laughed and told Ozzy that Charlie was looking out for my imaginary boyfriend, he got that weird look on his face again. Maybe it's a little awkward hearing his honorary little sister talk about having a man in her bed. And that's what Charlie and I have become to these guys. Aside from the light flirting that's always done as a joke, these guys have taken us under their wing. Most of them are regulars at the bar when Charlie or I are on shift, and they have never been inappropriate with us in the least. They would answer to Linc if they were.

After brushing my teeth, I slip under the covers, exhausted from being on my feet all night. While I assumed sleep would find me in no time, that doesn't seem to be the case. Am I thinking of last week and having to defend myself from being kidnapped? No. What's on my mind is much worse. It's the idea that some inconvenient feelings are developing for a particular biker with a British accent. Most of the shit that comes out of that man's mouth irritates me, but the one thing that never fails to give me those damn flutters is when he calls me darling in that sexy-as-hell voice. Sweet Jesus, that shit is panty-destroying. I'm having a hard time with the idea that just one week ago, I was cursing the day he was born, and now, I'm making plans to spend time with him. Alone. Just the two of us. What in the fresh hell was going through my mind when I said yes? Oh, yeah, nothing because of those damn flutters.

Son of a bitch, I'm fucked.

"Good morning, Lucifer. How'd you sleep?" Jude greets with a smile when I open the door this morning. "Doesn't look like much."

"Fuck you, asshole. I closed a bar, then had to get up and be ready this morning. What did you have to do, roll over and throw on a pair of the least dirty jeans you could find?"

It's possible I'm a little cranky from lack of sleep, but anyone who's ever had to work a job that requires you to be there until after two in the morning understands mornings can be tough. The truth is Jude looks perfectly put together as far as biker attire goes. The way that man fills out a white t-shirt and a pair of worn-in jeans is sinful and unfair to just about every other man on the planet. Fucking prick.

"Nice to see you're as pleasant as always in the morning."

Jude walks into my house, pushing past me with two cups of coffee and a bag with a heavenly smell emanating from it.

"Whatcha got there," I ask, shutting the door and following him into the kitchen.

"This is for nice girls who don't scream at me like angry harpies."

"I promise to be a good girl if you let me have whatever's in there." I flutter my lashes and smile pretty at the man bearing treats.

"I said nice, but good girl works, too."

His wicked smile makes me realize how that sounded. I pretend those flutters aren't making an untimely appearance again and grab the bag from his grip. Opening it, I inhale the delicious smell of what I'm guessing are lemon blueberry scones with a cream cheese glaze. My favorite.

"How did you know?" I take one out of the bag and bite into it, a loud moan escaping around the bite.

"Your reaction right there. It's not the first time I've heard it. I rather like the sound," he replies with heat in his gaze.

My heart seems to have decided now would be a good time to gallop like a fucking horse as I swallow the baked deliciousness.

"Thank you." I take a sip of coffee and polish off the rest of the scone. "So where are we going?" I ask when both of us have finished our breakfast.

"Not far," is the only response he gives me.

We head to his bike, and I throw my leg over the machine, wrapping my arms around Jude's middle. I never thought I'd be one for motorcycles—considering the only bikers I'd had any direct dealings with were the type to beat and kidnap a woman—but I've come to appreciate the freedom and downright fun of riding with Jude. The way he handles the bike with effortless ease, as if it's an extension of himself, allows me to enjoy the time I've spent on the back of it. There's something so different about not being stuck in a car when we're winding through the sleepy town to the outskirts. It's easy to understand why people consider riding addictive.

We pull in front of a two-story brick building surrounded by a tall wrought-iron fence. There's a small playground in the back, making the property look like some sort of school.

"Where are we?" I ask after Jude parks the bike inside the gate, and we get off.

"It's a women's shelter. I come here every Thursday to teach self-defense."

Someone knock me over with a fucking feather.

Jude sees the look on my face and chuckles.

"Not what you were expecting?"

"Umm, not even close. You come here every week?" I'm stunned with this new information and still haven't moved from my spot next to his motorcycle.

"Yeah. Figured I have all this training courtesy of Her Majesty, might as well put it to some good use." Jude shrugs as if it's the most natural conclusion to come to after retiring from active duty.

"Come on. Matilda is surely wondering why the hell I'm standing out here with a woman who's liable to catch flies if she doesn't pick up her jaw from the ground." He presses a finger to my chin and pushes my mouth closed. Cheeky bastard.

We walk up the stone stairs to the giant, wooden double-sided door.

"What did this place used to be?"

"It was an old elementary school. Matilda, the director here, bought it years ago and completely refurbished it. Trick's mom used to do a lot of volunteer work for the shelter. She roped Gramps and, by extension, the entire club to help with the remodel. Tanya spends a lot of time here, too, and even makes Thanksgiving dinner for them every year. Anytime there's an issue with anything around here, Matilda calls Tanya, and she gets one of us to come down and fix it. It's an old building, so it's pretty common for one of us to be here at least once a week."

"I'm surprised the women here are okay with a bunch of bikers traipsing through the place." If it were me, I'd be a little apprehensive.

"Sometimes, the newer residents are nervous, but Matilda and the other women reassure them that we're the good guys. Matilda thinks it does them good to get used to the idea that not every man they meet is some piece of shit who's going to put hands on them or worse. That's all some of these women have known for a lot of years."

I nod, understanding exactly what he means.

The reception area is blocked off from the rest of the building, and by the looks of it, the only way in is with a keycard or code of some kind. Jude walks up to the glass window, and a woman with glasses and long gray hair pulled into a messy bun looks up from her computer.

"It's Thursday, I take it," the woman greets with a warm smile.

"Got you pulling desk duty today?" Jude asks as he signs in on the clipboard she hands him.

"Yeah, the lady who runs this place is a real pain in my ass," she jokes.

"Matilda, what happened to telling yourself affirmations? You know that negative self-talk doesn't help," Jude quips back.

"Smartass," she says, sending him a faux scowl.

Matilda reaches her hand through the open glass window and introduces herself.

"I'm Lucy," I reply. "It's great to meet you."

"I'm happy to finally meet you. Tanya has told me so much about you and Charlie, I feel like I know you both already."

"Lucy's going to help me teach class today. From what Linc tells me, she and Charlie are some kind of self-defense experts," Jude states.

"That's great. I'm sure the ladies will love to see it," she replies, laughing. "Alright, get in there. I have a shitton of paperwork."

"Language, ma'am," Jude jokes, pretending to clutch his imaginary pearls.

"Oh, fuck off," she replies on a laugh and presses a button that unlocks the door heading into the interior of the center.

"So, Linc told you about the time Charlie kicked his ass?" I ask as we walk through the long corridor.

"I don't think he used those exact words, but he did say you and she spent some time training."

"Hmm, interesting. And you thought you'd want to try me out?"

"Oh, love," he says, stopping in front of another set of large double doors. "I'd love to try you out." He winks—because of course he would—and opens the door to a gymnasium with a group of women ready for class. This will be fun.

"I think we found the one thing you're better than me at," I say breathlessly as Jude pins me again.

Class cleared out about twenty minutes ago. It was great watching the large biker be so gentle and encouraging with the women here. I could definitely tell who was new and who had been in his class a few times. The women who were new seemed to get more comfortable the more times I was able to get out of a hold. He didn't ask them to practice with him, but a couple of the women asked me to. I get it. After leaving an abusive situation, it makes sense they wouldn't want a man touching them, even in an environment where they're perfectly safe. Jude would watch and give pointers when I was with the other ladies, but he never tried to physically show them. God, the last thing I need is more fuzzy feelings toward him, but it is what it is.

When class ended, Jude and I decided to really spar. Charlie and I had been fixtures at one of the gyms in New Orleans that taught Jiu Jitsu. Of course, I opened my big mouth and bragged about it, and now here I am, pinned under this giant.

"Oh, now, Lucifer, I've had more training and have at least a hundred pounds on you. If I couldn't pin you, I'd never hear the end of it."

"Hey, I got you a couple times," I say, indignation lacing my words.

"That you did, love," he says sweetly, helping me to my feet.

"Do not tell me you let me win. I will punch you in the dick."

The asshole laughs, grabbing a towel and wiping the sweat from his brow.

"As much as I love the idea of you touching my cock, no, you won those two rounds fair and square. I would never dream of throwing a match to soothe your ego."

I'm not sure if I believe him, but him saying 'cock' is so fucking hot, I don't care right now. And for the millionth time today, I question what the hell is wrong with me.

"Do you have time for lunch? I'm starved." Jude runs his hand over his taut stomach, the motion causing his shirt to ride up, displaying his rock-hard abs under the sweaty t-shirt. My mouth goes dry, and I think I nod in affirmation.

Okay, Lucy, this is getting ridiculous.

"Great. Let's go sign out, then I'll take you to my favorite little diner up the road."

We head back to the office, and Matilda is still at the front desk.

"What did you think, Lucy? Pretty fun beating up a biker, huh?" Matilda asks me.

"I loved it, actually. If you wouldn't mind, I usually have Thursdays off and would love to come back. I think it was good for some of the women to have another woman to practice with."

Matilda beams. "Of course, honey. I'll take all the help I can get."

"Great, see you next week, then." I wave goodbye as we make our way out the door and back to Jude's bike.

"That's kind of you to offer your time. There isn't much funding, and what Matilda does have is mostly used for utilities and general housing costs. I'm glad you volunteered."

"Well, it wasn't entirely selfless. I plan on making you teach me some of those fancy military moves you were using on me."

Jude lets out a bellowing laugh as I slide behind him.

"Anytime, Lucifer. All you have to do is ask."

He revs the motor, and we take off back into town.

For being a manwhore biker, Jude has been showing me sides of himself I didn't expect, and I'm not quite sure what to do with this new information.

Chapter Ten
Jude

Lucy and I eat our weight in burgers and fries. One thing I've always appreciated about both her and Charlie is they're not afraid of shoveling large amounts of meat into their cute-as-hell faces. And when in the actual hell did I start considering Lucy cute?

It's still early when we finish lunch, so I suggest we go for a ride. The way her face lights up tells me my little demon is turning into a bit of a riding addict, which is fine with me. I've not had many women on the back of my bike. In fact, I can only think of maybe two who thought it would be fun to take a walk on the wild side for a night and be game for a little cruise before I took them back to their place and gave them another ride entirely. Riding with Lucy, on the other hand, is a completely different experience. I've never been so aware of a woman's body pressed against my back and the way she lets out little peals of laughter every time I go a bit faster than necessary.

When we return to her house, there's still plenty of daylight left, but I can't come up with any other ideas to stick around. I've come to realize I like being around the girl, not just to give her a hard time but to hear her laugh or whatever silly bullshit comes out of her mouth. She has a sense of humor that matches mine. I especially appreciate it when her rude jokes aren't directed at me, but I'm beginning to come to terms with the fact I actually like the girl.

Don't get me wrong, there's been plenty of women I've liked in the past. And not in that "I like them enough to have some fun for a night" way, either. I love Knox and Linc's mum, Tanya, and I enjoy chatting up Matilda when I come in on Thursdays. I enjoy Maizie's company when I go into the bar on nights when Charlie and Lucy aren't there. I even find myself caring about Charlie, but that has a lot to do with how important she is to my best mate. Granted, my feelings for Lucy are a bit different, considering I'd jump at the chance to sleep with her. That's *not* something I feel for the other women. Sex and actually liking someone have always been kept in separate headspaces for me. No need to muddy the waters and all that.

"Thanks for today," Lucy says after I've parked my bike in her driveway and walked her to her door. "It's been a minute since I've had a chance to spar with anyone. If there's one thing that's lacking in Shine, it's a martial arts gym."

"Yeah. I thought of opening one but haven't had the time. Maybe you should," I suggest.

"Really?" Lucy laughs and rolls her eyes. "Me and what money? No bank is going to give a loan to a girl with no social security number or credit history of any kind."

I suppose when you live life moving from town to town with a fake ID, banks or investors wouldn't be too keen to fork over their money.

"But I liked working with the girls today. I'm looking forward to next week."

"It's a date," I say and watch the blush cover her cheeks.

Fuck it. She's too damn adorable not to kiss. Leaning in, I take her lips in a small, barely there kiss. I don't wait for her to reciprocate, pulling back and giving her a soft smile. Lucy's eyes are wide with surprise but not anger. I'll take that as a good sign.

"See ya later, Lucifer." I step off her porch and head back to my bike while Lucy is still staring at me with a deer-in-headlights expression. That one simple touch of our lips has me fucking harder than any messy wet kiss I've ever shared with another woman. I sit on my bike for a moment, trying to think of anything that will kill this raging hard-on, when Lucy comes storming down her stairs and stops right next to my bike with fire—and not the good kind—blazing in her eyes. *Well, shit.*

"What the hell was that?" she yells, pointing to her porch. "You're going to do that, then just walk away?"

I have a feeling this isn't an actual question.

"I'm sorry?" I have no idea what she wants me to say, but this delayed anger isn't something I'm used to dealing with from women.

"You're sorry? That's all you've got? You sure know how to make it worse."

"What do you want me to say?" I ask, getting off my bike and standing in front of the hellion giving me quite the dressing down. "I wanted to kiss you, so I did. It seemed like a good idea. Obviously, I was wrong."

"You call that a kiss? That was a mindfuck." She holds up one hand. "Is Jude attracted to me?" She holds up her other hand. "Was he just giving me a quick goodbye kiss like he would any girl he's friends with?" She moves her hands as if she's weighing both questions. "Do you see where the confusion is? We've been at each other's throats since we met, then all of the sudden, you're staking some claim on me at parties and threatening to spank me. Then we *are* actually getting along, and you plant one on me."

"Do you like being spanked, darling?" I ask, arching a brow.

"Ugh! Then you call me darling, and I can barely think straight," she exclaims. "Fucking British asshole."

"Lucy?"

"What?" She plants her angry fists on her hips and glares at me.

"Shut up." I grab her by the back of the neck and yank her to me, taking her mouth in an anger-fueled kiss. Though this kiss shouldn't be described as such. It's more a war we're fighting, using our lips, tongues, and teeth. She yanks me closer by the back of my long hair, and I do the same, tilting her head up so I have better access to her hot-as-fuck mouth. Our height difference is to our disadvantage, so I run my hands down her back, over her ass, and grab her by the back of her thighs, hoisting her around my waist.

I pull my head back slightly and remove my lips from hers, panting with the restraint it takes not to shove her pants down and fuck her bent over my bike.

"Jesus Christ, woman, you have to turn everything into a goddamned fight."

"Well, kissing me is definitely one way to shut me up."

"It was either that or shove my dick in your mouth."

Lucy narrows her eyes. "I'd like to see you try."

"Is that a challenge, Lucifer?"

"Fuck you." She slams her mouth to mine again. This time, with her in my arms, the kiss is wilder somehow, deeper.

I take several long strides up to her door and punch in the key code to disarm the alarm.

Lucy breaks the kiss. "How do you know my alarm code?"

"I had a hand in setting it up," I reply, trailing my teeth down the soft skin of her throat.

"We'll be discussing this later."

I nod in agreement. "Much later."

The door slams shut with some assistance from my booted foot before I use one hand to reset the alarm.

"If this is all that's going to happen, you'd better tell me now," I say, pushing her back against the door. There has always been a clear plan whenever I've taken a woman to bed. Whether it be a bunny or a woman I met in a bar, it was always known where the night was going to lead. With Lucy, the waters tend to be as clear as a Louisiana swamp.

"You backing out?" she asks with challenge in her tone but insecurity in her eyes.

"Hell no, love. Just wanted to make sure we're on the same page."

"If the page includes hours of orgasms, then yes, we're on it."

"Oh, darling, you have no idea," I growl in her ear while grinding into her.

"So far, there's a lot of talk and not a lot of orgasms happening."

I chuckle and angle my hips just so, rubbing her clit through her pants with the hard bulge of my jeans.

"Fuck, yes," she moans out, pressing firmly into me.

"Nuh-uh. I want to see that wet pussy while I make you come for the first time." Whirling us around, I stomp toward the bedroom. Her bed is still unmade from this morning, and I throw her down on the mess of blankets and sheets.

"Good thing I got you a bigger mattress." I crawl up her body until we're nose to nose at the head of the bed.

"That was you?"

My long hair hangs down around our faces, which are nearly touching. Lucy runs her hands through it, pulling it away from our faces.

"Awfully presumptuous of you," she says, tugging the strands back.

"Maybe, but if my time in the Royal Marines taught me anything, it was to be prepared for anything."

"I should kick you out of my bed just for being a pompous ass."

"Your mouth says that, but the way your needy pussy is still grinding against me tells me you won't." The woman hasn't stopped squirming under me the entire time from the door to her bed. "Let's take care of that, shall we?"

I take her mouth in another kiss, loving the way she meets me. There are no tentative little licks. Lucy kisses like she fights—with everything she has.

My lips move down her neck and over the swells of her full breasts, nearly popping out of her tank top. Not being able to stand it another second, I sit up and rip the top from her body. All that soft skin on display is beckoning to me, needing me to mark it with my tongue and teeth. My shirt comes off next. I look into Lucy's eyes, and her pupils are blown out from lust as she bites her lip, appreciating what she sees in front of her.

"Unless you want that bra cut from your body, I suggest you lift up a bit so I can get it off."

She sits up and meets my mouth, yanking my head to hers. My fingers go to the clasp of her bra and snap it open, her tits spilling from the lacy fabric. Lucy lays back down and stretches her arms over her head.

"Jesus fucking Christ." The vision before me is absolutely sinful in the best possible way. I've never seen a more perfect pair of tits in my life. The way they're going to overflow in my already large hand has me salivating. I swipe a hand over my face and revel in the dumb fucking luck I must possess to be in this bed with the fucking knockout under me.

My mouth lowers to her nipple, and I taste her sweet skin, sucking it as she moans beneath me.

"How do you taste so damn sweet?" I ask, moving to the other nipple. "Fuck, I could feast on you for hours."

"I hope you plan to put that mouth somewhere a little lower within that time."

"Demanding little thing, aren't you?"

"What happened to giving my needy pussy some attention?" she sasses in a terrible fake British accent.

"Can I enjoy myself without you giving me a bunch of shit, please? Your tits need attention, too."

"Do you always have to argue with me?" she asks, still squirming under me.

It hits me then. This has been our foreplay. It was never a question of if we would get here but when. I've never been so fucking attracted to a woman I've fought so much with in my life. Shit, I don't even remember the last time I was this attracted to any woman, and considering that all the blood in my body is currently in my damn dick, I won't be figuring it out any time soon.

"Alright, Lucifer. Just for that, I'm going to give you so many fucking orgasms, you'll be begging for mercy."

"I don't think that's the threat you think it is."

"We'll see."

I lick my way down her body but stop short at the waist of her pants. Her hands go to my head, trying to push it further to where she needs my mouth so desperately. I sit up and rip the material from her legs in one fluid motion. The sight before me is one I never believed I would witness.

"You're fucking drenched," I say, gazing at her glistening pussy. My finger lightly runs up the seam of her center, and her hips buck off the mattress, a loud moan escaping her.

"Goddamn, Jude. Don't just sit there and stare. Fucking do something."

Oh, how I love teasing this woman. Making her wobble on the edge is too fucking fun.

"Like what?" I ask, swiping my finger ever so gently over her again. If I thought her tits were mouthwatering, I was wrong. I want to devour the pussy in front of my face more than I've wanted anything in my goddamned life, but torturing my little demon is worth the wait.

I dip my finger between her folds and flick her clit gently with my finger.

Lucy lets out a growl of irritation and grabs my hair, jerking my head up, so she can look me in the eye.

"If you don't do something soon, I'm going to get up from this bed and lock myself in the bathroom. Then I'm going to make myself come loudly while you sit out here and listen."

"The hell you will, Lucifer." I insert a finger into her tight channel making her back arch off the bed.

"Yes," she moans out.

My mouth latches onto her swollen clit, and I begin flicking it with my tongue over and over as I pump one finger inside her. The decadent noises coming from her throat and the wet sound of my finger and mouth working her over has me humping the mattress like a damn teenager. I look up and see Lucy pinching those perfect tight nipples, and I nearly shoot off in my jeans.

"Fuck, yes. Don't you dare stop," she commands as her walls begin to flutter around my finger. I add another, and the woman detonates like a fucking bomb. Her pussy squeezes my finger so damn hard as a rush of sweetness fills my mouth. I continue licking her as she comes down, her legs shaking around my head.

"Oh my God, stop," she says with a half moan, half giggle.

Lucy almost jumps off the bed when I kiss the crease between her pussy and her thigh.

"That fucking tickles," she says, pulling my hair again. This woman and my fucking hair.

"What?" I mumble, feathering my lips from her ticklish spot all the way down the inside of her soft thigh to behind her knee. "You don't like it?"

"I wouldn't say that."

"Then shut up and let me have my fun."

"Wow, your pillow talk needs some work," she quips.

"You're one to talk."

"Jesus Christ, would you stop fighting with me and fuck me already?"

"Greedy little thing," I tsk. "I could leave you here like this."

Lucy sits up, her hand going to my hard cock, still imprisoned in these blasted jeans.

"You could," she whispers as her tongue makes its way from my shoulder to my ear. "But you won't." The vixen bites my ear, and I let out a low growl.

"Alright. If that's how you want to play it."

I jump off the bed and hurriedly shove my jeans and boxer briefs down my legs after grabbing a condom from my pocket. Lucy is lying spread out, watching me with a slight smirk on her damp face. She's fucking beautiful lying there post-orgasm, but it's time she learned a little lesson about being so fucking demanding. After rolling on the condom, I grab her ankles and none too gently pull her forward, so her ass is on the edge of the bed. Lifting her legs, I hold them wide open and slam my cock inside her in one hard thrust.

"Fuck," she yells.

For a moment I'm worried I went too hard, but she screams for me to go deeper. Goddamn, this woman is going to be the death of me. I have to bend my knees a bit to make up for the height difference, but I piston into her as she cries out in pleasure, over and over. Holy shit, her pussy is so perfectly tight around me. The feel of being inside her is surreal as I watch her clutch the sheets in her fists.

"I'm going to come," she moans out right before she tightens around my shaft and screams as another orgasm tears through her.

I didn't get to fully appreciate the look on her face when she came the first time with my head between her legs, but the vision before me is something that will be ingrained in my memory for years to come. Her eyes are connected to mine as her entire body ripples with waves of ecstasy, mouth wide with moan after moan. This is the look of a woman fully overcome. And I'm the one responsible.

"You feel so good," she says as she catches her breath.

"I'm not fucking finished."

I pull out of her sweet heaven and grab her by the waist, tossing her up the bed. Crawling up her body, I take her mouth in another savage kiss.

"You're going to come again," I say after breaking the kiss.

"I don't think I can."

"The fuck you can't."

I flip her over and grab a pillow, shoving it under her hips and prop her arse up. When she's in the position I want, I lean over her, using one arm to hold myself up, then guide my dick back into her. We let out a groan of satisfaction at the same time. My hand moves between her body and the pillow, so my fingers can strum that pretty little clit. Resting my weight on one elbow, my body presses farther into her back.

With my mouth against her ear, I whisper. "You're going to strangle my cock as you come again, then I'll let you have a break."

My cock is hitting her at a whole new angle, and that with my finger working her clit, her walls begin to tighten again.

"Don't hold back, Lucy. I want you to fucking soak me."

"Yes." She lets out a deep moan. "Fuck yes."

I bite her earlobe, turn about being fair play and all, and she does just what I told her to, soaking my cock and fingers when she peaks for the third time. I can't hold back another minute and let out a roar as I fill the condom, my body shaking over hers.

Pulling out, I remove the latex, throwing it in the trash next to her bed. Lucy is still lying face down on the bed, sweaty, sated, and fucking perfect. Lying on my side next to her still form, I run a finger from her tailbone, along her spine, to the base of her neck. She shivers and lets out a quiet laugh.

"What are you doing," she asks.

"Making sure you're alive."

Rolling onto my back, my arms cross behind my head, and I smile toward the ceiling.

"Don't look so smug," she says. "You didn't fuck me into a coma."

"Not yet."

She rolls her eyes as her phone chimes from the bedside table.

"Ugh," she groans, rolling over to grab it. Lucy shoots up and stares at the screen. "Oh, my God. Charlie and Linc are headed here with pizza. Said she saw your bike and figured we could have dinner and beers."

"Thank God. I'm starving," I say, rubbing my hand over my stomach.

Her wide terrified eyes look toward me like I've lost my damn mind.

"You need to get dressed. They absolutely cannot find out about this."

For some reason, her statement irks the shit out of me.

"Why not? We're all adults. Who cares if I made you see God in the last hour? Three times." A smile tips my lips. I'm feeling pretty damn good about that achievement.

Lucy rolls her eyes and jumps out of bed, pulling fresh clothes from her drawers.

"Jude, I'm... not ready to have this discussion."

"Fine." I take a deep breath and let it out slowly before sitting up and grabbing my jeans from the floor. "But we will be talking about this at a later time." She doesn't respond. "Lucy?"

The distracted woman finally stops and looks at me.

"Fine, but for now can we please just have a normal dinner with our friends?"

"Great. I just adore being your dirty little secret."

"Jude…" She trails off uncomfortably.

"Don't sweat it, Lucifer. We'll talk about it later."

I'm being a little bitch about this, but the woman has me twisted inside, and I don't know what the hell to do about it.

Chapter Eleven
Jude

Lucy's bright idea is to tell Linc and Charlie that I was over fixing the pipe under her sink. She grabs a toolbox from her hall closet and opens the cabinet door under the sink, spreading random tools around the floor. Even though she ran a brush through her long hair because she looked thoroughly fucked, there was no hiding the rosiness in her cheeks from the orgasms I gave her.

My irritation wanes when I see the state she's in. At this point I find it comical she's going through such lengths to hide that we had sex. Amazing, mind-bending sex. I've barely wiped her cum off my dick before she runs to the door, opening it with a flourish.

"Hey, guys," she exclaims. "This is a nice surprise. Jude was here working on my pipes."

She waves them in, and I chuckle from under the sink where she insisted I be to make the scene more believable. Lifting my head, I catch her glaring at me. Yeah, I worked on her pipes alright.

Linc sets the beer and pizza on the counter and watches me climb out from under the sink.

"You decide to try your hand at maintenance man?" he asks as the girls walk into the living room, Charlie commenting on how great everything looks after the impromptu remodel.

"Something like that."

"So, what was wrong with her sink?" he asks casually. Too casually.

"Leaky faucet, I guess."

"Hmm. I've known you for a lot of years. Never realized you knew anything about kitchen sinks."

"What? Like I have to tell you every detail of everything I've learned throughout the years. Jesus, mate, we aren't an old married couple." My hand brushes through my hair as I attempt a look of indifference to his line of questioning.

"Awfully defensive, there, brother."

Obviously, it didn't work.

"Fuck off."

The girls come back to the kitchen, and Lucy starts setting out plates and napkins for the pizza.

"It's so nice out tonight, let's eat on the patio," she suggests.

Charlie piles several slices on her plate, then Linc does the same, grabbing the six-pack and taking it out the back slider.

"Did you show Charlie the new set up in your room?" I whisper in Lucy's ear before we walk outside.

"No, we didn't get that far."

The woman hasn't looked me in the face once since our friends came over.

"That so? Or is it because the room still smells like you had the best sex of your life?"

She turns to me with a wicked smile. "Oh, you silly, silly man. Who said that was the best of my life?"

"Your pussy seemed pretty convinced when I made you come three times," I reply as I casually take a bite of the pizza.

"Hmm. Sorry to burst your bubble, but you didn't accomplish anything I couldn't have done myself."

"You've never struck me as a liar, Lucifer. Don't start now."

"You aren't God's gift to women, Jude. Don't start thinking you are now," she sasses back before strutting her bitable arse outside.

Goddamn, I was right when I said this woman was going to be the death of me.

It's gotten dark since Lucy and I got back to her place and had the fuckfest of our lives—no matter what she says to the contrary—and dinner is wrapping up.

"I'm glad Jude was here to fix your pipe. The last thing you would've wanted was your new floor getting drenched," Charlie says.

I nearly spit out my beer, and Lucy shoots me a look, telling me to shut the hell up. Linc notices and shakes his head. My brother definitely suspects there's more going on here than sink problems, if he even believed the flimsy story to begin with.

"Yeah, so lucky," Lucy says, taking a long sip from her beer.

"Babe, it's getting late, and you need to get up for class in the morning," Linc tells his adorably clueless woman.

She's been taking classes online through the community college to become a therapist. She said she feels a pull to help women who had a similar past as hers through their traumas. Of course, the way we helped Charlie through her situation was by burying her ex six feet deep, but I suppose her way works, too.

"Yeah, I need to get some studying in before I go to sleep. Come on Lucy, I'll help clean up."

When the girls grab the plates and walk back into the house, Linc levels me with a stare.

"Be fucking careful, brother. That's my woman's best friend. You aren't used to having a woman in your life long term, so let me break it down for you. If Charlie gets wind that you're sleeping with Lucy, then you turn around and hurt her, I'm the one she'll complain to," he says, pointing at himself. "The last thing I need is to get involved with your relationship drama."

"Oh, settle down. There is no relationship, so there will be no drama." Jesus, my best mate has turned into a meddling ninny.

"But there is something?"

Dammit, I walked right into that one.

"Calm your tits. Nothing is going to come back to you. Jesus, you are a pain in my arse."

"Just as long as none of whatever this is"—he swirls his index finger in circles—"becomes a pain in mine."

Charlie sticks her head out the door. "Ready?"

"Yup," Linc replies before giving me one of his looks.

I roll my eyes. I'm not a fucking child, for chrissake.

"Thanks for bringing dinner guys," Lucy says, opening the front door when Linc and I walk back inside.

Charlie is the first out and gives Lucy a long hug before Linc follows her.

"You sure you don't need me to stay just in case that pipe leaks," I ask quietly.

"No thanks. I'm sure if there's any more problems, I can take care of it myself," she replies, still holding the door open.

I lean in like I'm going to give her a hug just in case Charlie and Linc are slowly meandering back to their house.

"As I said before, Lucifer, like hell you will. Your orgasms are mine." I bite the side of her neck, and she lets out a quiet yelp of surprise. Pulling away, I shoot her a meaningful glare.

"Goodnight, Jude."

I bound down her stairs toward my bike and throw a hand in the air.

"Night, Lucifer."

After starting my bike, I see she's shut the door. Instead of taking off right away, my bike idles in her driveway until the notification chimes that she's set her alarm. There's no way to wipe the smile off my face as I make my way back to the clubhouse. That little demon has her claws in me, and I can't say it upsets me.

It's a few days before I have a chance to see Lucy again. We had to do a run for the Irish, so me and a few brothers have been on the road since the morning after leaving Lucy's place. The temptation to go back to her house that night was strong, stronger than I've had before with any other woman. That fact alone is why this run was a good idea. Wyatt stayed behind this time around, so I may have asked him to keep an eye on things for me.

"What's good, brother?" he asks when I walk into the clubhouse and see him sitting at the bar with Cooper. He reaches out to shake my hand, and Cooper jumps up to grab me a beer.

"Thanks, mate," I tell the prospect and take a long swig from the bottle. "Glad to be back. How were things while I was gone?"

"Nothing out of the ordinary. Ozzy still hasn't heard shit from those Bone Breaker fucks."

"Usually, I would say no news is good news, but I can't say that applies in this situation. Seems odd they haven't reached out at all."

Wyatt shrugs. "Seems odd to me, too. Maybe this isn't unusual for them. They deal in meth. It's not as though guys like that are particularly reliable. Maybe his prez thinks they're holed up in a motel somewhere on a bender."

"Pretty long bender," I reply.

"You never know with tweakers."

"Maybe." I'm still not convinced. It's strange as hell, but I don't know much about the other club, apart from what I saw of them that night at Lucy's and what she's told us. None of it good.

"You going to the bar tonight? Lucy's working."

I grab my bottle and stand from the stool. "I know. Gonna shower and change."

Of course, I know she's working. I've been looking forward to this reunion all damn day.

After showering the road grime from my body, I head to the bar. It's Sunday night, so the place isn't packed, but of course there's another group of men at the bar with fucking hearts in their eyes as Lucy pours drinks and laughs with everyone. For being the prickly wench I thought she was when I first met her, she definitely seems to have a way with people. Ozzy's even mentioned since she and Charlie started working here revenue has gone up. There's something to be said for having a hot-as-hell woman behind the bar serving drinks, but it's more than that. She has the kind of personality that seems to draw people in, men and women alike.

"Hey, stranger," she greets when I have a seat a few spots down from the group of men.

"Lucifer." I shoot her a half smile, and when she sets a beer in front of me, I wink. "Thank you, darling."

Lucy inhales a sharp breath and narrows her eyes at me before shaking her head. She really shouldn't have told me what me calling her that does. I plan on using it to my advantage every chance I get.

"Just get back?" she asks, tossing a towel over her shoulder.

"Yup." I take a sip of my beer, all the while giving her a knowing look.

"Did you at least take time for a shower before you got here?"

"You don't like me dirty, Lucifer?" My voice remains low and even as I stare into her intoxicating blue eyes. *Jesus, get a grip, man.*

Lucy narrows her eyes. "Why would it make a difference to me?"

"Love, I think we both know the answer to that." I quirk a brow, a small smile playing on my lips.

"You're pretty sure of yourself, biker boy."

My eyes widen in mock offense. "Boy? Darling, I think the other day proved I'm no boy."

"Oh, I'm sorry, biker man. Is that better?" Her sarcastic tone and the challenging look in her eyes are giving me a fucking hard-on. Lucy's smartass mouth used to irritate the shit out of me, but these last few days, every time I think about her comments or she gives me a ration, like now, I spring a boner like a thirteen-year-old boy. My, how the tables have turned, and I was the last one to expect it.

The door opens, and a couple guys I don't recognize walk in. They have a seat at one of the tables, and Lucy walks over to greet them. I'm not too keen on the way they're ogling my girl's arse when she walks away from the table to get their drinks. Wait... *my* girl? The sudden urge to pop one of the guys comes out of left field. It's been grating on my nerves for a couple weeks when men flirt with Lucy and try to talk her up in the clubhouse or here, but this possessive impulse wasn't part of the equation before. Or maybe it was, and I was too stubborn to give it any consideration. Lucy would throw an absolute fit if I tried to tie her down in any way, shape, or form, but the idea isn't scaring the ever-loving hell out of me, which is concerning as fuck.

When Lucy returns from giving the two new customers their drinks, she comes to check on me.

"Have you ever seen those guys before?" I ask after declining another beer. I don't know these two, but I know they aren't local.

Lucy shakes her head. "Never seen them before. Why?"

"Just wondering."

She goes back to her other customers and doesn't seem particularly concerned.

"Hey, friend," one of the guys says, having a seat next to me at the bar. "You in the Black Roses?"

"That's what the patch on my back says," I reply dryly.

The guy laughs but doesn't move.

"Something I can help you with?" I take a sip of my beer and look the guy dead in the eye.

"Well, my cousin was up here about a week ago. Told me he was meeting with a club up here."

"Your cousin got a name?" I know what he's going to say before the words leave his mouth, but like hell I'm going to act like it.

"Badger. He came up with a couple buddies from the Bone Breakers."

"Yeah, they were here. Stayed for a couple hours then said they had some business in Boston."

The guy's smile is amiable enough, but I see something else lurking behind his eyes, and I don't like it.

"Well, seems no one's heard from any of them since they were here. Phone's dead, too."

That's not all that's dead.

"Don't know what to tell you. I haven't seen him or the other two since they left the clubhouse."

"Thanks, man. Can I buy you a beer?"

"Nope," I reply with a tight, not-so-friendly smile.

The man nods and goes back to his friend at the table. My fingers are itching to call Ozzy, but like hell that's going to happen while they're still sitting in the bar, nor is walking outside and leaving Lucy alone an option.

"What'd that guy want?" Lucy asks quietly and hands me a new beer, even though I didn't ask for one.

"Nothing." I shoot her a look that says we'll talk about it later, not wanting to tip her off. There's a very real chance she'll get spooked, and it's better if no one is around for that.

The guys pay for their drinks and leave a few minutes later. Pulling out my phone, I text Ozzy.

Me: *Badger's cousin was here looking for him.*

Ozzy: *Was he wearing a patch?*

Me: No. *Not sure if he's a Bone Breaker, though. Stuck with the Boston story.*

Ozzy: *You think he bought it.*

Me: No.

Ozzy: *Fuck. Stay with Lucy. I don't like this.*

Me: *Already planned on it.*

"Okay. What the hell is going on?" Lucy asks as I pocket my phone.

"Those guys, are you sure you didn't recognize them?" They looked a little young to have been around when Lucy was still living in that shithole, but what the hell do I know? That club could very well have been using kids to do their dirty work.

"I've never seen them before. Why are you asking me that again?"

"They were looking for Badger. That was his cousin."

Lucy lets out a long breath. "Shit."

"Listen, love. We knew someone was going to ask about him at some point. As far as anyone knew, this was the last place they were. We stick to the story about them taking off for Boston, and no one will be the wiser."

"Yeah," Lucy responds distractedly, not meeting my eyes.

"Look at me, Lucy." Her eyes swing to mine, but I can't read them. "It's going to blow over. They didn't recognize you, and you said you've never seen them. That means they were never at your compound, and as far as Brax has been able to tell, no one that night sent a text from their phone saying you were here. This probably doesn't have anything to do with that fucking place. Just someone looking for them."

"You're right." Lucy pastes a smile on her face, but it doesn't take a genius to tell it's fake. "Want another beer?"

"You just gave me one. Are you trying to get me drunk?" My tone is teasing, and she barks out a sharp laugh.

"Like I want to deal with your drunk ass."

She walks away, putting some extra sway in her full hips. God, what I wouldn't give to close this bar right now and spank her round arse for sassing me.

My phone buzzes in my pocket. Pulling it out and looking at the screen, I see Ozzy's name.

Ozzy: *Church in the morning.*

I send him a thumbs-up. Apparently, my plan of giving Lucy orgasms until the sun comes up will have to wait.

Chapter Twelve
Lucy

Jude and I close the bar together when the last customer leaves. I've been trying to play the whole situation that happened earlier off like it's no big deal. The last thing I want to do is worry that those guys somehow knew me from my old life. Is there a possibility? Maybe, but I've wracked my brain for the last two hours and for the life of me can't remember ever seeing them. The likelihood is pretty slim, considering I rarely had anything to do with the Bone Breakers, but I'd seen them around the compound when they'd make exchanges.

"Come on, love, I'll follow you home. You look dead on your feet," Jude says as I scan the bar one more time making sure everything's done. Closing when you're distracted fucking sucks, and I don't want to leave anything unfinished for the other girls.

I nod. "Yeah, I'm pretty beat." Grabbing my things, I head out the back door to where Jude's bike is parked next to my car.

"You don't have to follow me. I think I know the way," I say, opening the door and throwing my things on the seat. Turning back to him, I watch as he stretches a long leg over his bike.

"Get in the car, Lucifer."

Ugh, this man. Always bossing me around. I mean, I get in because I'm tired and want to get the hell home, but still. He doesn't need to command me like some petulant child.

When we pull up to my house, Jude pulls in behind me in the driveway. The entire drive over, I was a worried about how this was going to play out. Obviously, I want him to come in and give me all the orgasms I can handle, but at the same time, I'm tired and still somewhat freaked out by what happened. The urge to invite him in to distract me from my worries is strong, so fucking strong, but I've never been the type of girl to fall into the habit of having a man be any sort of distraction, and I'm not about to start now. Especially this man.

There's no doubt in my mind the second I start depending on him for anything more than a few orgasms, he'll hightail it right on out of my life. Only he can't. Not in any real sense. When he decides he's through, we're still going to have to see each other. His best friend is practically married to mine, plus, since coming to Shine, most of the club has become like a big extended family to me. Jude and I don't exist together in a vacuum. We can't.

No, my mind's made up. He's not coming in.

"Okay, I'm home. You can go about your business now," I tell him as I get out of my car, slamming the door shut.

If my slightly bitchy demeanor fazes him at all, he doesn't let it show. Instead, he gives me an annoyingly sexy smirk and beckons me to him with two fingers.

"Come here, love."

I walk over to him, even though my mind is screaming at me to go inside and put the alluring biker out of my mind. When I'm standing in front of him, he cups the side of my face with his strong hand.

"Do you want me to come in?"

Yes.

"No, I'm good. I'm going to take a shower and head to bed."

A low growl emanates from his throat. "Great now I'm going to have a raging hard-on, thinking about you naked and wet in the shower."

"Typical male fantasy," I scoff.

"Maybe, but there's nothing typical about the girl I'll be fantasizing about."

Goddammit, when he says things like that it makes me question why I'm determined not to let him come in. Jude pulls me in for a kiss. This one is different from the other night. Last time, we were fighting with every swipe of our tongues. It had been a battle of wills, and I'd say we both came out the winner. This one, though, is sweet. Just as passionate—I don't think the man knows how to kiss any other way—but it's not frenzied or angry. I love it, and I hate that I love it. Son of a bitch. Leaning into him for a few moments, I allow myself to get swept away. When Jude pulls back, he touches his forehead to mine and breathes deeply.

"You better go inside before I convince you to let me come in."

"Like you could."

He straightens and releases me, giving me that damn smirk again.

"Oh, darling, we both know I could."

Of course, he could, but I'm not about to tell him that.

"Whatever. I'll let you leave with your ego intact tonight."

Jude chuckles and starts his bike. "Lock your door, Lucifer. I'll see you tomorrow."

I stand ramrod straight and salute the amused biker. "Yes, Sir."

"Careful, love," he growls loud enough for me to hear over the rumble of his motor.

Walking up to my door I unlock it and turn the alarm off. Before closing the door, I wave at Jude still sitting on his bike in my driveway. With my door closed and the alarm set again, my phone buzzes with a notification that I'm locked in tight. I look out the window and notice Jude looking at his phone, too. What are the chances he gets a text... No, that's crazy. There's no way his phone is connected to my security system.

Good Lord, Lucy, time for bed.

It's been five days since Jude was in my bed. Not that I'm counting or anything. Except for the days he spent on a run, I've seen him every night at work. And every night he follows me home, but I don't invite him in. He doesn't push the issue, just leaves me with a toe-curling kiss, then waits for me to walk in and lock the door. I've figured out that asshole has my alarm set up for notifications on his phone. Last night, I peeked out the window, and sure as shit, as soon as I got a notification on my phone, I saw him look at his. The sneaky bastard.

I hear my door open and the alarm beep when Charlie comes in.

"Lucy," she calls out. "You about ready?" Charlie disables the alarm before coming to find me in my bedroom, searching for my favorite boots.

"Wow. I haven't been in here since... before. It looks great. Love the giant bed."

The last time Charlie was here was a few days ago when she and Linc showed up unexpectedly. Like hell I was going to show her my room then.

"Found them," I say popping up from the floor, holding the black cowgirl boots up triumphantly.

"It's hot as shit out, and you're wearing boots?"

"What? I have shorts on. Besides, I'll take the extra height where I can." It may not help much, but it's something.

We head out the door, and Linc is waiting for us in his truck.

"Hey, Lucy," he says when I hop in. Charlie slides in next to him and plants a loud kiss on his cheek. Linc turns to her and shoots her a sweet smile.

The pang in my chest surprises me. It's not that I'm jealous. I would never be of my best friend. She deserves all the happiness in the world, and the man sitting next to her gives it to her. This is more wistful imaginings, wondering what it would be like to have a "Linc" of my own. The sudden image of Jude's face when he pulled me in for a goodnight kiss last night fills my head.

God, the last few days have seriously been messing with my head. It's been less than a week since we slept together, but the way Jude has been acting is the complete opposite of what I was expecting. Truthfully, I thought he would've lost interest by now. Yes, it's only been a few days, but Jude has always struck me as a hit-it-and-quit-it kind of guy. Not the 'sending texts and checking in throughout the day' or 'being perfectly content with being sent home with nothing but a kiss' kind of guy.

My phone vibrates in my bag. When I pull it out and check, low and behold, it's the man I can't stop thinking about but wish I could.

Jude: *Linc said he's taking you downtown to go shopping.*

Me: *I told you that this morning when you texted. We're picking up some stuff for Maizie's kid's birthday.*

Jude: *I didn't know you were going downtown. One of my favorite stores is there.*

Me: *Oh, Jesus. I'm pretty sure I know which one.*

Jude: *Why don't you pick up something for later? My favorite color is red.*

Me: *Of fucking course it is.*

Me: *And you're a pig.*

I shake my head and slide my phone back into my purse. There's a little lingerie shop run by one of the nicest women I've ever met. Charlie has been in there a few times, and, of course, I may have bought a few things from there as well. Not for anyone in particular, but I think a girl should feel sexy, and if lingerie does it, I'm all for it, even if there was no one seeing it.

"What's got you smiling back there," Charlie asks as we pull into a parking spot on Shine's little main street.

Huh, I didn't realize I was.

"Nothing. Just excited to be hanging out with my best friend."

"Mm-hmm," she replies, giving me a disbelieving look.

I haven't told her about Jude. When I get home from the bar, it's late. I know she's already fast asleep, so she and Linc wouldn't hear Jude's bike. The only thing holding me back from talking this through with her is I don't even know how I feel about everything yet.

The second Charlie gets word, she'll be planning double dates and couples' vacations. I love the girl like a sister, but she's *that* girl.

There's a great candy store with every delicious concoction under the sun. I thought it would be fun to get Maizie's son, Colby, a bunch of awesome candy and some toys for him to go crazy with. I'm sure Maizie will appreciate me for it.

Linc decides to check in with a few of the guys at the bike shop, which is right down the street from the candy store. He gives Charlie a very inappropriate kiss and tells her to text him when we're ready to head back home.

"Happiness looks good on you, sister," I say as she watches him walk away with that dreamy look in her eyes.

"It feels pretty amazing, too." She gives me a wide smile and links her arm through mine. "Okay, let's get that kid all the sugar his mom's going to hate us for."

We're about to walk into the candy store when a license plate on an old truck catches my eye. Nevada. I stop before we enter the store and look around. I don't see anyone I recognize, but it's unusual to see a plate that far from the state around here. My overactive imagination is most likely running wild, but the pit in my stomach from being caught off guard gnaws at me as we pick out candy. Jude said there was no indication any of the men that night called or texted anyone that they had found me.

"Hey, you okay?" Charlie asks, noticing my distraction.

"Yeah, just overwhelmed with the amount of candy surrounding me." My attempt at a smile probably misses its mark. Jude would have told me if there was anything to be worried about. And surely Linc wouldn't let us wander around Main Street if there was a threat. But this damn feeling won't go away.

We pay for our goodies, and I tell Charlie I'd like to stop at the lingerie shop.

"I'm always up for a little shopping," she says, wiggling her brows.

As we're heading to the shop, I see the backs of two very recognizable men. The older one turns to the younger one as they walk into a coffee shop, and my blood runs cold. Elder Otto. I only see his profile, but I'd put money on the younger man he's talking to being Jasper. I quickly angle my body away from them, almost running into Charlie.

"You okay? Why do you look like you've seen a ghost?"

"Yeah, I'm fine. Listen, I'm not feeling so hot. My head is killing me. Can we skip the shopping?" I begin walking back to the truck with my hair pulled to the side, attempting to hide my face from anyone who may spot me from across the street.

"Lucy?" Charlie asks, catching up to my hurried steps. "What's going on?"

I can't tell her. She doesn't deserve to be pulled into this mess, and the longer we're on the street, the better of a chance there is of Otto or Jasper spotting her with me. They can't see her. Anyone associated with me is in danger, and I'll be damned if Charlie gets caught in their crosshairs.

"I think it might be a migraine."

"Oh, no," she says, sympathy lacing her tone. "Okay, let's get you home."

She texts Linc, who meets us at the truck in less than a minute.

The entire way home, my damn knee won't stop bouncing up and down. Goddamnit. I never should have stayed when Jude told me the club could protect me. Sure, maybe if it had just been the Bone Breakers, but now Otto and Jasper are here looking for me. They're so much more insidious. They'll have everyone thinking they're the good guys who just want to spread the word of God, and I'm a wayward sheep. They'll surely make up outrageous lies to gain sympathy in their plight to bring me home. The second they get their claws in me, I'm as good as dead. There's no way in hell any other members of the compound won't come looking for them if they were to disappear, and they'll bulldoze right over anyone standing in their way.

Charlie keeps looking at me from her side mirror. The concern etched on her face absolutely guts me. I promised her never to run, but some promises have to be broken, and this is no exception.

When we pull up to my house, Charlie turns in her seat.

"Do you need anything before Linc and I take off to the clubhouse?"

They're having a party there tonight for Cooper's birthday, and I was supposed to go.

"No, thanks. I'm going to lie down. If I feel better, I'll make my way there."

"Okay, sister. Feel better."

Hearing her call me that breaks my heart even more than it already is. I know what I have to do, and she is going to be so fucking mad.

"Thanks." I force a smile on my face, but it's hard. I want to cry, to rage. Why did they have to find me? I was just getting used to the idea of staying, and now there's no way that's going to be possible. The Black Roses may be able to protect me from another club, but an entire compound full of religious zealots? That's another beast entirely.

I throw the bag of candy and toys on my sofa and head to my room, grabbing that damn bag I always kept in the closet. Time to pull it out and take off again. This time, for good. There won't be any coming back now that Otto and Jasper know where to look.

"Lucy." The deep British accent sends shivers down my spine.

I turn around and see Jude in the doorway to my bedroom.

"How did you get in here?"

"You didn't lock the door or set the alarm. What were you thinking?" he questions angrily.

"You need to leave."

Jude leans over and spots what I'm doing.

"What the hell? Linc texted and said you had a migraine. What the fuck's going on?"

Shit. A pissed-off six-foot-three biker is the last thing I have time to deal with.

Chapter Thirteen
Lucy

"I'm cleaning." *Really, Lucy? That's the best you could come up with?* "And I don't recall inviting you in, so feel free to see yourself out." I turn my back on him, hoping he'll get the hint.

Surprise, surprise, it doesn't work.

"Fuck that." He says, storming over to me and grabbing my arm to whirl me around so I'm facing him. "You're going to tell me right now what has you spooked."

I shake my head. Spooked? Try fucking terrified.

"It's time for me to go. I saw some people from the compound in town today. I have to leave, or I'll be leading them to your doorstep."

Though the elders never wanted anything to do with the government and said they were basically the devil incarnate, I wouldn't put it past them to call any of its agencies to make trouble for the club, especially if they knew the Black Roses were hiding me.

"Fuck that. You're not going anywhere," he demands, pulling the clothes I've already thrown in my bag to the floor. “I’m not scared of a bunch of assholes from a commune.”

Jesus. They’re so much more than that, and he has no idea.

“Listen up, Jude. They aren’t some random religious freaks who spend their days praying and believe in turning the other cheek. They are very much the eye for an eye type, and I refuse to put Charlie or the club in that kind of danger.”

“I appreciate that you want to protect us, but we’re big boys, and I guaran-damn-tee you we’ve handled worse. Stop fucking trying to run when you get scared.”

We’re both breathing hard as the frustration bubbles from us.

“You’re not listening. I’m doing the only thing I can to protect everyone and myself. I can’t stay.”

“I’ll protect you,” he bellows in my face. “When are you going to stop being so fucking stubborn and realize I’m here? For you, goddamnit. I will stand in the line of their fire, or anyone else’s for that matter, if it means keeping you fucking safe!”

His eyes implore me to see his truth, and I’ve never wanted to believe anything so badly in my entire life.

“I’m scared,” I say in a soft voice that’s foreign to my ears. “I’m always scared they’re going to find me, and I’ll be dragged back to that hell.”

Jude cups my cheeks and lowers his forehead to mine. “It’s your turn to listen. That won’t happen. You aren’t going anywhere. Me and the rest of the club won’t let that happen, Lucy." He gives me a soft kiss on the lips. "Never," he punctuates with a low growl.

"Kiss me," I say in a soft, pleading whisper. I need to get these thoughts out of my head, to feel something other than this clawing fear that has the power to bring me to my knees.

Jude looks at me for a moment before moving. I don't know if he's gauging where my head is at or deciding if this is the best time for what I know we both desperately want, but when he makes his decision, all hell breaks loose.

Jude smashes his mouth to mine, and a whimper escapes my throat. My arms instantly band around his waist, trying any way I can to pull him closer.

"Goddamn, love, your mouth was made for me," he says, momentarily breaking the kiss.

He dives back in, taking my mouth in a passionate frenzied kiss. Instead of using his words, he's using his mouth to tell me all the ways he needs me to understand how he feels.

Jude turns us and sits on the bed, positioning me between his legs. He roughly swipes at the bag I have sitting there, and it tumbles to the floor, the remainder of my clothes falling from the inside.

"Up you go, love."

He grabs me by the waist and lifts me so I can straddle his thighs. His hand goes to the button on my shorts, and he flicks it open before pulling the zipper down.

"I want you to come all over my fingers before I slam my cock into your tight cunt," he growls before thrusting two fingers inside me and rubbing my throbbing clit with his thumb.

"Ahh," I cry out, grinding into his palm.

"Take your shirt off. Let me see those gorgeous fucking tits."

Whipping the shirt off my body, I toss it onto the mess on my floor and grab onto Jude's shoulders for support. He lowers his mouth to my lace-covered breasts and sucks my nipple through the sheer fabric. It feels so damn good. Between his wet mouth and his long fingers, I'm riding his hand like my life depends on it, so damn close to the edge.

"I feel you getting wetter. Are you ready to come?"

"Please," I moan out.

"Take your bra off for me. I don't want anything between my mouth and your tits."

As soon as the fabric slides down, exposing me to him, his mouth latches on the other nipple, and he bites down.

"Fuck," I yell as my hands go to the back of his long hair, fisting the strands.

"That's it, Lucy. Pull my fucking hair while you ride my fingers," he commands, taking my mouth in a brutal kiss. Jude breaks the kiss and leans back a bit so he can get the full view of me half-naked on his lap, riding his hand to orgasm.

"I'm going to come," I cry out.

"Fuck, yes, you are. I feel your little pussy tightening around my fingers. Let me hear you."

My back arches as wave after wave of bliss overcomes me.

"Jude. Oh, my God, yes," I yell incoherently.

My movements slow, and I sink farther into his lap, completely wiped out and sated at the same time.

Jude removes his fingers from my core and brings them to his mouth, moaning while he sucks them clean.

"You taste divine, darling. I'm going to have to lick that cunt later and really get my fill." Jude grabs my waist and tosses me off his lap onto the bed.

"What is with you and throwing me?" I yelp.

"I like watching your tits bounce," he replies, shrugging unapologetically. He stands and stares at my topless form, rubbing a hand over the large bulge behind his denim. "The things I want to do to you, Lucy, would cement my place in hell. And you know what? It would be worth every second."

Jude tears his shirt over his head, and I get the full view of his defined six-pack and pecs. My mouth practically waters, staring at the man in front of me. If I made a list of every physical quality I'd want in a man, Jude would check every box.

"Oh, yeah?" I purr. "Like what?"

"I want to lick and bite every part of your flesh, starting here." His fingers go to my hard nipples and twist, eliciting a deep moan from me. "I want my mark all over your body." His hands move to the waist of my shorts, and he pulls them down over my boots. "I want to redden your perfect arse with my handprint. Fuck," he groans. "The thought of seeing that mark there has me so fucking hard."

"What else?" I breathe out.

Jude kneels at the foot of the bed, taking off one boot then the other. His hands run up my calves before spreading my thighs and lightly trailing the tips of his fingers over my center.

"I want you to squeeze your tits together so I can slide my dick between them, and after I come all over your neck, I want to watch you clean me off with your tongue."

I shudder, the images he's putting in my head making me a squirming mess of need.

Jude shucks his jeans then flips me over, pulling me up by the hips until I'm on all fours at the edge of the bed. I hear the foil of a condom wrapper tear open while one hand finds my clit, and he begins rubbing.

"But first, I'm going to watch your ass bounce while I fuck you." Jude slams into me and lets a loud moan escape deep from within him. "Fuck," he drawls out. "You're fucking sin wrapped up in a perfect package just for me, aren't you?"

I don't answer him right away, too overcome with the sensation of him filling me so completely.

Jude's hand comes down hard on my ass, and I let out a small shriek of surprise that ends on a moan, feeling the way my pussy tightens around his cock.

"It's even better than I imagined," he comments, rubbing his hand over the stinging flesh. Another slap and I'm ready to come.

"I think you like that just as much as I do, love. Are you going to come for me?"

"Yes, fuck, do it again."

His deep chuckle fills the room as he lands two more slaps to my ass, and I fall apart, coming so hard, my vision goes hazy around the edges. Jude roars out his release, and I feel his cock spasm inside me, drawing out my orgasm.

Jude stills inside me as we both come down, then pulls out and throws the condom in the trash. I'm lying on my stomach when he comes back from the bathroom. He lies down next to me, and a self-satisfied smirk adorns his face.

"Proud of yourself?"

His hand caresses the spot on my ass that's tingling deliciously. "I like seeing my handprint here. You redden perfectly, darling."

A small snort escapes me. "I can't believe I liked that," I say, burying my face in the pillow.

"Woah, now hold on there." He grasps my chin and pulls my face toward him. "Never, and I mean never, hide yourself or feel a bit of embarrassment for liking what I do to you. I fucking love that it got you off. And I'm going to love finding other things that get you off. What I don't love is you feeling any shame connected to that."

"I don't think it's shame, more like I'm surprised. Honestly, this whole thing surprises me."

"What are you talking about?"

"You. Me. This," I answer, waving my hand around my room. "We never exactly got along, and now we're…"

"Having the best sex of our lives?"

I roll my eyes. "Sure. That."

"Foreplay," he says, pulling me into his arms.

I lay my head on his shoulder and wrap my arm around his taut waist.

"What the hell are you talking about?"

"The fighting. It was our foreplay. Once you chilled the fuck out, you realized how amazing I am and finally let yourself give in to your feelings."

My finger finds his nipple and twists. Jude lets out a high-pitched yelp, and laughter bursts from me.

"That's what you get, asshole."

"Don't be angry with me because I speak the truth, Lucifer." Jude kisses the top of my head, chuckling when I growl at him.

"I may be rethinking this whole thing. You should really stop talking while you're ahead. And definitely before I kick you out of this bed."

"You were appreciating what was coming out of my mouth not that long ago."

"Shut up, Jude."

He chuckles and runs his hand through my long hair, the action making me sleepy as I cuddle into his warm body. Could be the orgasms, too. Those never hurt.

"Yes, ma'am."

I lay contentedly in his arms, and soon my eyelids close, and I fall into a peaceful, safe sleep.

When I wake, I'm still wrapped in Jude's arms. Instead of taking a nap with me like I would have expected, he has his phone in his hand.

"You better not be taking naked pictures of me," I say, sleep making my voice a little rougher than usual. Or it may have been all the screaming I did.

"As much as I would love to have those pictures, I would never take them while you're sleeping. But if you're up for it, I'll gladly have an impromptu photo-shoot with you now."

"Dream on, pal."

He lays his phone on the nightstand and turns to face me, pulling me close.

"I was texting Ozzy. I needed to let him know what you saw earlier today."

Well, if that isn't a bucket of cold water being dumped over my good mood.

"What did he say?"

This isn't like the shit with Charlie. No one from the compound attacked any of the guys like her ex did when they found us in that little bar in Texas. It's amazing it was only a few months ago. It feels like so much longer to me. Even though I've come to care about all the guys, the truth is, there's been no direct threat to the club.

"He's calling church in the morning. We'll get it figured out."

"I'm not sure what that means," I tell him, nervous about what Ozzy is going to say regarding my situation. "Dealing with the Bone Breakers was one thing, but this is something else, altogether."

"This is a threat against you, which means we'll handle it. It doesn't matter whether it's another club or some crazy tossers from Nevada."

"They're a bit more than crazy tossers, Jude. They're dangerous. Most of the people on that compound were practically raised with a gun in their hand. When you're talking about religious zealots, you have to understand they aren't playing with a full deck. They'll come after you because they believe it's their God-given right to take me. They won't stop."

"Lucy, they haven't found you. There's no reason to think they're doing anything more than the Bone Breakers' dirty work. That asshole's cousin made a huge mistake telling me who he was, the daft twat. These guys could be here looking for their missing partners on behalf of the Bone Breakers."

My head tilts to the ceiling. "I seriously doubt that."

Jude cups the side of my face and pulls it toward him. "Look, what I'm saying is we don't know anything for certain yet. I'm going to talk to Ozzy and the rest of the brothers, and we'll get this shit figured out. You're safe."

"For now."

"No. For always. I wasn't fucking blowing smoke up your fine arse when I told you I'd protect you." Jude shoots me a playful smile, his attempt at distracting me from the worries racing through my mind.

"Now, stop doubting me and spread your legs. I told you I wanted to get my fill off your cunt, and I'm not waiting another second."

His smile may not have been enough of a distraction, but everything else he does with his mouth for the rest of the night sure as hell is.

Chapter Fourteen
Jude

"Were you going to wake me up?" Lucy asks as she steps into the shower with me.

I wrap an arm around her naked waist and pull her flush against my wet body, dipping my head to give her a sweet good morning kiss.

"I thought you needed your sleep, love." Without breaking my hold on her, I turn us, so the steaming water hits her back.

"Mmm, that feels good," Lucy says, tipping her head back in the spray.

It didn't escape my attention that every time Lucy fell asleep last night, she tossed and turned. The little whimpers she let out in her sleep weren't from pleasure. Not that I slept great, but it had more to do with the fact it was the first time Lucy and I spent the entire night together. I couldn't help waking through the night and touching her in some way. My touch seemed to calm whatever she was dreaming about. When her blue eyes fluttered open and she looked at me, her features would soften as though she was relieved I was still there. I've never had that reaction from a woman, and I certainly never thought I'd like it, but here we are.

The idea that a woman could count on me for more than a night of fun was laughable. If someone had tried to suggest it, I would have run so fast in the opposite direction, there would have been flames trailing behind me. But not now. Not with Lucy.

Reaching over, I grab her shampoo from the bench seat in the shower. I squirt some into my hand and begin rubbing it into Lucy's long black hair.

"Oh, I get the full-service treatment?" she asks playfully, closing her eyes and enjoying the scalp massage.

"There seems to be something about you that makes me want to take care of you." That's the most honest I've ever been with anyone. It's also the only time I've wanted to say it.

Lucy's eyes flutter open, and she meets my gaze. "Jude," she whispers.

I don't know what she wants to say, but instead of letting her finish her thought, I lean down and take her mouth in a kiss. I'm not ready for her to tell me anything quite yet, good or bad. I just want to be here, in this moment, with her.

Breaking the kiss, I tilt her head back into the water and rinse the suds from her hair.

"You know there's something we never got around to doing last night. Something you said you wanted." She looks at me with lust-filled eyes and a devilish smile.

"There's a long list of ideas from last night. Which are you referring to in particular?"

She looks up at me through wet lashes and bites her lower lip. I pull it out from between her teeth with the pad of my thumb.

"Nuh-uh, love. If anyone is going to leave marks on you, it will be me."

Her eyes narrow, but she doesn't argue. That's a first.

Lucy turns us so that my back is against the water. She walks over to the shower bench and sits down, spreading her thighs and running one hand down her stomach to her gorgeous cunt while the other palms her breast as she pinches her hard nipple.

"You said you wanted to fuck my tits."

The cock that was at half-mast while I washed her hair is now a raging fucking hard-on as I watch her squirming on the seat, playing with herself.

"Fuck, Lucy. If I believed there was a God, I'd be on my fucking knees thanking Him," I tell her as I stroke my hard dick. "Put your fingers in your pussy."

She does precisely that and pumps slowly for a few beats, staring at me with hooded eyes.

I walk over to stand directly in front of her, never breaking her electrifying gaze.

"Take them out and give me your hand."

When she lifts her fingers, I see her arousal coating them, and my mouth waters. Pulling her hand to my mouth, I suck the fingers she was just using to fuck herself with and let out a deep moan as her taste explodes over my tongue. I spent a lot of time last night exploring every part of her with my hands, mouth, and tongue, but if it proved anything at all, it's that I'll never get enough of her.

Her hand grasps my cock, which is nearly eye level with her. Just the sight of her and the wicked way she plays her body, then mine, has me ready to blow this minute.

"Careful, love. This isn't going to last long if you keep doing that."

"Then you better keep your promise from last night." Lucy grabs her conditioner and spreads a handful all over her heavy breasts. "Come play with me, Jude," she moans out.

Goddamn, if she isn't the perfect woman, I don't know who is.

I lay my hard cock between her tits, and she squeezes them together, encasing me in her slick breasts. I begin pumping, and every time the nearly purple head peaks from between her breasts, she opens her mouth so she can taste me on her tongue.

"Fuck, that's it, baby. Just like that." My hands go to the side of her wet hair, and I hold her head still while I fuck her tits and mouth. When she takes me between her lips, she lets out a lewd moan.

"You like that? Do you like when I fuck your perfect tits, then let you taste my cock?" I ask, holding the head in her mouth. She moans around it, and I can't take it another second.

I pull away, and Lucy gives me an irritated look.

A chuckle escapes my throat. "Why do you look like I've just taken away your favorite toy?"

"Um, because you did?"

I palm the side of her face and smile down at her. God, she is beyond anything I could have dreamed for myself.

"I want you to take my cock down your throat, love. Think you can do that?"

Her eyes darken, and she opens wide for me.

"Such a good fucking girl you are."

I slide between her lips, and my eyes roll back in my head. God, her mouth is something else. She moans around my length as I take a few shallow pumps in and out, letting her get used to me. That's not enough for my girl, though. Oh, no. Lucy holds my hips still and moves her head forward, taking me deep until I reach the back of her throat.

"Fuck, yes," I moan when she pulls back. "Do that again." I stand stock-still as she sucks me like my dick is her favorite lolly.

"I'm close. If you don't want me to come down your throat, I suggest you move," I grind out.

Lucy looks me dead in the eye and takes me deep again, swallowing around the head. I lose it, and my cock jerks roughly in her mouth as I come long and hard.

"Ahh," I bellow and smack the shower wall when she sucks the overly sensitive head. "You little vixen."

When I pop out of her mouth, she smiles widely, scraping her nails up and down my thighs.

"Your turn," I tell her, lowering my tall body to my knees and throwing her legs over my shoulders. I open her up and take a long lick through her center. "I'm going to make this quick and fucking filthy, darling. Hang on."

My mouth latches onto her clit, licking her furiously while I pump two fingers in and out of her tight core. The wet sounds of her pussy and her loud moans are indecent and absolutely amazing. I love listening to Lucy let go as much as I love being the one doing it to her. Within moments, she's tightening around my fingers, and her walls pulse while she comes all over my mouth and hand.

"Oh, shit," she screams, yanking my hair tightly in her fist.

I follow her down with my tongue, still licking her, cleaning every last drop.

When I pull my fingers from her, she grabs my hand and licks herself off, then slams her mouth to mine.

"You're a filthy bird, Lucifer, and I love it."

"Right back at you, babe," she stands from the bench and steps out of the shower, smacking my naked ass on her way out.

This fucking girl.

When I walk into the clubhouse, it's quiet. Considering it's still early, I'm not surprised. There was a party for Cooper's birthday last night, but since I was tangled with the stunning woman I left naked in bed after fucking her one last time before leaving, we both missed it. There was no way after what Lucy saw that I was going to leave her unprotected so I could party with everyone, and she didn't seem in the best shape to be in a crowd last night. She was more relaxed after a couple orgasms, but by that point, the last thing that was going to happen was me suggesting we leave her bed.

Cooper is standing in the kitchen, pouring himself a cup of coffee when I walk in.

"Hey, prospect. Sorry I missed your party."

He turns to face me, his eyes bloodshot and looking beat to hell.

"No worries. I doubt I would've remembered you being there," he croaks out.

I chuckle at his obvious discomfort. "Good party, then?"

"Yeah. Excuse me while I go throw up for the third time this morning." Cooper walks away, looking a little green, and passes Linc on his way out.

Linc shakes his head, watching Cooper hobble back to his room. "Poor kid," he says with a grin.

"Yeah, you look real sympathetic."

Linc shrugs. "Nothing we all haven't dealt with."

He comes to stand next to me as I sip my coffee and pours himself two cups.

"I take it you and Charlie spent the night?"

He nods in affirmation. "I take it you spent the night somewhere else?"

Ozzy walks in before I have a chance to answer.

"Am I interrupting your little coffee clutch? Time for church, assholes."

Linc gives me a look that says we'll be discussing this later. *Oh, joy.*

Walking into church, we take a seat at the huge table with the Black Roses insignia carved into the center.

"Alright," Ozzy says, banging the gavel on the table. "I know we're all hungover." A chorus of groans fills the room. "Jude, tell us what you know."

"Yesterday, Lucy saw some of the guys from where she's from. Sick fucks that run some crazy cult in Nevada. The same one that has connections to the Bone Breakers. It's no coincidence they're here after those fucks went 'missing.'" My fingers make air quotes.

Every person in the room knows exactly what happened to the assholes who tried to take my girl.

"Badger told Lucy they were still looking for her, so it stands to reason that's why they're here." I finish and look at the concerned faces of my brothers.

"Or they could be looking for the three missing Bone Breakers. If they have ties to that club, maybe their prez asked for a favor. It would be obvious if a bunch of Bone Breakers were walking around Shine. Maybe he wants to try to find them on the down low," Cash suggests.

I tip my head back and forth. That thought occurred to me as well.

"That's possible. The truth is we don't know why they're here. I say we talk to a few people downtown and have a look around. Lucy said she saw an old blue pickup truck with Nevada plates."

Ozzy nods when I finish. "Sounds good. You, Linc, and Wyatt, see if you can find anything out. In the meantime, what do you think Lucy needs?"

That's a great fucking prez right there. Lucy may not be anyone's old lady, but she's family.

"I don't want her alone. Either a brother or prospect should be with her anytime she leaves the house when I'm not there."

"You plan on being there a lot?" Ozzy asks, raising a brow in my direction.

"I do." Every brother in the room knows what that means without me having to spell it out for them.

"Alright," Ozzy replies without any further fanfare. "You all have your marching orders. Someone go check on Cooper and make sure he isn't passed out face down in his own vomit. Fucking kid didn't know when to quit last night," he mumbles the last part and shakes his head.

"Don't worry, Oz, he'll learn fast enough," Knox says.

"From who? You were the one pouring booze down his gullet all night," Ozzy shoots back.

Knox laughs, a rarity for him. "Nah, that was one of the strippers. Poor kid's never been able to get the full experience of partying with us, Oz. It was only fair he got the royal treatment last night."

All the brothers around the table chuckle. Sounds like we missed quite the spectacle last night.

"Man, he's really going to be hating life when he has to clean up after his own party," Braxton comments.

"Eh, we all had to do it at one point," Cash says.

When we head out of church, Cooper is already throwing away spilled beer bottles and empty cups. The boy looks positively green, but he's doing his job, and no one had to tell him.

"Good on you," I say, walking up and slapping him on the back. Poor guy nearly falls over, and I laugh. Fucking amateur.

"Let's stop by the coffee shop first," I tell Linc and Wyatt as we head out to our bikes.

"Sounds good."

The great thing about being in a small town is everyone here knows the club. We run charity rides for the hospital and the schools, always trying to help the community where we can. It's bought us some favorable goodwill among the residents of Shine and the businesses along Main Street.

"Hey, Jude. I'm just about to ice a fresh batch of lemon blueberry scones if you have a minute," Betsy calls to me when the three of us walk into her coffee shop. Cool Beans has some of the best baked goods I've ever had in my life. And the way she makes her tea would make my grandfather weep with appreciation. You don't get that in most places in the States.

"Sounds great, Betsy." I give the woman a warm smile. "Listen, I know this is a long shot, but do you remember a couple guys who came in yesterday? One was older, and the other was his son with a blonde crew cut. They weren't from around here. Maybe they were looking for someone?"

Betsy busies herself with glazing the mouthwatering treats I plan to take to Lucy when I finish up here.

"Yeah. They came in asking after three guys. Showed me a couple pictures. I thought it was weird since the guys they showed me a picture of were a little rougher around the edges than those two. It struck me as odd that two guys who looked the way they did would be looking for guys like that. I thought maybe it had something to do with a sister or something getting mixed up with the wrong crowd. It felt off, though."

"Off how?" I ask when she hands me a bag that has my mouth salivating.

"They were just creepy. I can't put a finger on it, but they definitely had the hairs on the back of my neck standing up."

"You have a pen and paper back there?" I ask, pulling out a twenty and setting it on the counter.

"Sure." Betsy tears out a paper from her order pad and hands me a pencil.

"Here's my number. If you see them again or think of anything else, give me a call." I hand the paper back to her, and she nods.

"Oh, I did overhear them saying something about having to go back to their hotel. It's that little one off the highway a few miles out of town. The Motor Inn." Betsy shoots me a slightly worried look. "Do we need to worry about anything around here?"

I smile back, hoping it reassures her. "Nah. We're just following up on some rumors we heard. You know we care about this town. Ozzy won't allow anyone coming in here trying to pull anything."

"Honey, I've been around a long time. I remember that business at the clubhouse years ago and what happened to that girlfriend he had. I know Trick took care of it and kept us all safe. I don't care what anyone says about you boys. You've all done right by this town."

"Thank you, Betsy. That means a lot to us."

She nods as a couple customers walk into the place and turns her attention to them.

"We going to the motel?" Wyatt asks when we walk out of the coffee shop.

"Yeah, let's go check it out," I reply, putting the scones in my saddle bag.

The drive out only takes a few minutes. We loop around the parking lot, but I don't spot any cars or trucks with Nevada license plates.

"Hey, Gus," Linc calls when we walk into the office.

"Boys," he greets, standing from his chair behind the long check-in desk. "What can I do for you?"

"We heard you had a couple guys from Nevada staying here. They still around?" I ask.

"Nope, checked out last night."

"Hm. Do you mind if we look at their check-in paperwork?"

"Everything okay, boys?" His eyes dart between the three of us.

"Everything's fine." I give him the same little spiel I gave Betsy.

Gus goes to his office and pulls out the paper with their personal information on it.

Wyatt snaps a picture with his phone. "I'll give this to Braxton," he says, putting his phone back in his pocket.

"Did they ask about anyone?"

"Yeah, showed me a picture of three guys. I'd never seen them before and told them as much. Said they were the older guys' nephews or something. No one had heard from them for a while."

"Did they ask about a girl?" I ask Gus.

"Nope. Never mentioned anything about a girl."

"Thanks, Gus. How's Mary Catherine been feeling?"

Gus's wife had a bad fall a few months ago and needed a hip replacement. They run this old motel together and couldn't afford to hire anyone until their granddaughter came home from college for the summer. We sent a couple of the girls over to help out with maid service, and Tanya filled their fridge 'til kingdom come with ready-made meals.

"She's much better. It's a long healing process, but having Stephanie home has helped."

I smile at the old man. "I'm glad. If you need any help, call Ozzy, yeah? Or if you see those guys again."

Gus nods, and I reach out to shake his hand.

"Good seeing you."

"You, too. You boys be safe."

I shoot him a wide grin. "Always."

Walking back to our bikes, I think about what everyone we talked to said about Otto and Jasper.

"So, they never mentioned Lucy," Wyatt comments.

"I think Cash was right about them being here for the Bone Breakers. If they wanted to find Lucy or thought she was here, they would have been asking about her, too. Brax never found anything on their phones that would indicate they found her, just talking about finding something and it being a payday," Linc says.

"Yeah, doesn't seem to be any connection," I agree. "I'm going to play it safe for a little while, though."

And Lucy is not going to like it.

Chapter Fifteen
Lucy

A knock on my front door, followed by the alarm being disarmed, wakes me from my nap. After last night and this morning, I'm wrecked. Most of that has to do with a certain British biker, but I slept horribly. Nightmares of being stuck at the compound or trying to hide from a faceless figure chasing me through the desert I haven't been anywhere near in seven years plagued me in my sleep.

I groan and roll over, expecting one of two people.

"Hey, sunshine. What are you doing still in bed," Charlie says, bounding into my room and jumping on the king-sized mattress.

"Long night. Didn't sleep too well."

"Are you feeling better?"

I remember my flimsy excuse to Charlie about why I needed to get home in a hurry.

"Um, yeah," I reply guiltily. God, I hate lying to my best friend.

I completely freaked out yesterday instead of going to her or Jude, which is the exact thing I told her I wouldn't do. And now I'm keeping a secret about Jude and me sleeping together.

"You missed a fun party. Poor Cooper, though. When I got up this morning, he was cleaning the clubhouse and looked ready to throw in the towel on the entire thing. Linc said it's part of being a prospect. You have to do the jobs no one else wants to show them you're up for anything.

"Makes sense."

"Yeah, I guess. But I missed you being there. It's not as much fun at parties when you and Jude aren't around giving each other shit. I'm not interested in watching strippers all night, so you guys are my entertainment."

I let out a bark of laughter. "Sorry to disappoint.

"Jude wasn't there, either. Probably found some girl to take back to his room before we got there."

Well, I suppose now's as good a time as any to spill the rest of my secrets.

"About that. Jude wasn't with a bunny or a random woman last night."

Charlie gives me a cautious look, as if she knows what's about to come out of my mouth but isn't ready to hear it.

"He was with me. Last night. He spent it here."

"Like you guys hung out watching movies, and he slept on your couch here..."

I shoot her a wry look. "No, Charlie, like he came over to check on me, and we fucked all night."

Charlie looks from the bed to me with wide eyes and jumps up.

"Lucy! You let me roll around on the bed you were fucking Jude on all night?"

"I changed the sheets, you fucking weirdo," I say, laughing at the horror on her face.

"Okay, this conversation needs coffee and whiskey. I'm assuming you have both in your kitchen."

She walks out of the room, and I roll my eyes. Jesus, she's being quite the prude over finding out about this new development.

Trudging into the kitchen, I find her pouring a healthy shot of whiskey into the coffee Jude brewed for me before he left.

"Okay. The shock has worn off." She heads over to my couch and sits down with the steaming mug in her hand. "Tell me everything."

I pour my coffee, sans whiskey, and take a seat next to her.

"If you're not in shock, then why did you pour a double in that coffee right there?" I ask, quirking a brow.

"Because I'm hungover. And I have the day off from schoolwork and studying. Figured I'd take advantage of it a little."

"Fair."

Settling back on my oversized couch, I tell her the story from the first night to the daily texts to the scorching kisses every night and him not pushing for more.

"Yesterday, when you and I were in town, I saw Jasper and Elder Otto in town."

Charlie gasps and grabs my hand. "Oh honey, why didn't you say anything? Linc and I would have stayed here instead of going to Cooper's party."

This is the part I feel horrible about because I almost broke a promise to her.

"I freaked out. I didn't have a headache when you took me home. I was going to run, and I wasn't going to come back."

I expected hurt or disappointment to come from Charlie. Instead, she looked at me with love and sympathy in her gaze.

"I can't imagine how that must have felt yesterday seeing those bastards. How scared you were at that moment."

It's so damn typical for Charlie to think about me being scared instead of being angry with me. One of the many reasons I love the slightly drunk girl sitting next to me.

"Linc texted Jude, and he came to check on me and caught me packing a bag. He had... things to say about me leaving."

"Did he say them with his dick?"

I almost spit my coffee all over my new sofa.

"Charlie! I'm cutting you off." We're both laughing to the point of tears streaming down our faces. When I'm finally able to catch my breath, I angle my body toward Charlie.

"He thinks me running is bullshit and he's determined to keep me safe."

A wistful smile passes across Charlie's lips. "How do you feel about that?"

"Wow, you're really sounding like a therapist now. Glad those classes are paying off."

She smacks me in the arm. "Oh, shut it. You know what I mean. Aside from me, you've always fended for yourself. Shit, ever since I've known you, you've always been the one with a plan. You have way more confidence and this"—she waves her hand around—"air of control I've never had."

"What are you talking about? You have that, too."

"Not like you. The five years I spent running, I was scared of my own shadow. You lived life and never backed down from anyone or anything. Especially Jude."

"I had to. I spent my entire life being beaten down and told I was less than because I was a girl. There was no way in hell those assholes would win by me being afraid all the time. But honey, you escaped the fucking mob and lived to tell the tale. Don't ever sell yourself short."

"I guess we're both kind of badass. You just wear it a lot more confidently. To us." She clinks her coffee mug against mine. "Two badass women and the men who love us."

I yank my mug away and pull it to my chest, eyeing her with apprehension.

"I didn't say anything about Jude loving me or vice versa."

This is why I kept whatever was going on between Jude and me close to my chest. As soon as Charlie found out, there was no doubt she was going to have hearts in her eyes.

She smiles behind her whiskey-laced coffee mug.

"We'll see."

A few weeks have passed, and there's been no word on Jasper, Otto, or anyone from the Bone Breakers. Jude's theory that they were here for the three missing bikers was confirmed when they went around asking questions. Ozzy felt confident the story of them going to Boston worked, and we're in the clear. There's no way in hell Jasper and Otto would have left town without trying something if they knew I was here.

This was a close call, and it definitely hit way too close to home for my comfort, but Jude's been true to his word about protecting me. If he's not with me, one of the other brothers or prospects goes everywhere with me. I'd be lying if I said at times, it didn't feel a little suffocating, but all the guys have become like brothers to me in the last few months. They may be stinky brothers that eat all my food, and there have never been sports played on my TV as much as there are now, but it's been nice spending time with everyone away from the clubhouse.

Usually, though, Jude's home with me, and that's been, well, an adjustment. We sometimes spend the night at the clubhouse, but usually, we're at my place. I've never lived with a guy. The only person I've shared space with for any extended amount of time has been Charlie, so I have no frame of reference for what this is supposed to look like. For his part, Jude's actually not bad to have around. He's tall enough to change a light bulb and grab the shit I throw on the top shelf of my cabinets because I hardly use it without having to get a step stool. Not to mention the orgasms. Those most definitely don't hurt.

Maizie and I are working the bar on a Friday night, but it's slower than normal.

"Girl, you can take off. I got this," she says after I've wiped down the bar top and made sure every liquor bottle is facing forward for the fourth time.

"Yeah, that's not a bad idea." I hate being here with nothing to do. "Wyatt, you about ready?"

Jude had some business to take care of, so Wyatt's my guard dog on duty this evening.

"Sure, Lucy." He doesn't sound particularly enthused about the idea of leaving. When his eyes travel to Maizie for the millionth time tonight, I have a sneaking suspicion why. God, for a bunch of bikers who are supposed to be these ridiculous over-the-top alpha males, some of them can't look at a pretty girl and find the balls to ask her out.

The door to the bar opens, and Charlie comes to sit at a stool before I have a chance to clock out.

"Hey, buttercups." She looks around the mostly empty bar. "God, this place is dead for a Friday night."

"Yeah, I was just about to head home. Two of us don't need to be here."

"No, don't go. It's been ages since we've had a chance to hang out," she pleads.

That's true. Since the day at my house a couple weeks ago, she's been busy with work and school, and I've been busy with… things.

"That sounds like an even better plan." I look toward Wyatt. "You mind?" I ask the unusually quiet biker.

"Not at all."

"Maizie, round of shots," I call, coming around the bar to sit next to Charlie and Wyatt.

She pours three and brings them over to us. "One of these better be for you," I tell her.

She looks at Wyatt nervously before her gaze swings back in my direction.

"Oh, come on, Ozzy won't care about one shot. Besides, Wyatt isn't going to tell him, are you?" I squint my eyes at the man sitting next to me.

"What do you take me for? Some kind of snitch?" He pretends to be affronted by my question, but the slight tilt of his lips gives him away.

"Alright, alright." Maizie laughs and grabs another shot for herself. "God, is she always like this?" she jokes, turning to Wyatt.

The man blushes, fucking blushes, under her gaze.

"Pretty much," he replies, shrugging his shoulders.

We raise our glasses for a toast, and I exaggeratedly clear my throat.

"Here's to those who wish us well. All the rest can go to hell."

We clink glasses and slam them on the bar.

"Wyatt, you want another beer?"

"Yeah, thanks Maizie."

"How about you ladies?" she asks, turning to me and Charlie.

"A beer and a whiskey seven, please," I order for both of us. "We don't need Linc coming in here and having to carry you home like he did last time we were drinking together."

"Oh please, I wasn't that bad," Charlie replies, rolling her eyes.

"Charlie, sweetheart, sister of my heart," I say, putting both hands over my chest. "You were going on and on about having his babies and some other weird nonsense about him not being allowed to name them because he comes up with the worst names. Poor man had to haul you over his shoulder to get you to go home."

Maizie is laughing as she comes back with our beers. "Seriously?"

"In my defense, it had been a stressful few weeks. School is kicking my ass. Between working and studying, I needed to let loose and have a little fun. I may have taken it the teeniest, tiniest bit overboard," Charlie defends.

"Hey, sister, I'm not judging," Maizie assures her.

That right there is why I love Maizie. There's never any judgment from her, just a big heart.

The door opens, and a woman walks in by herself. She sits at the bar and lets out a huff of annoyance. Not at anyone in particular, but at life in general, if the way I'm reading her is correct.

"Mia?" Maizie asks, walking over to the woman sitting by herself.

"Maizie. Oh my gosh, it's so good to see you," she replies.

Maizie comes to the other side of the bar and wraps the woman in a big hug.

"I heard you moved back and that you got a job at the high school."

Mia smiles. "Yeah, school librarian. It's so weird being back there." The two women laugh as Maizie walks back behind the bar.

"What can I get you to drink?" Maizie asks.

"I'll take a whiskey and seven, thanks."

"A woman after my own heart," I say to her, raising my glass with the very same drink in it.

"Mia, that's Lucy," Maizie introduces, pointing at me. "And that's Charlie. They both work here."

"Hi, it's nice to meet you," Charlie says. "Come sit with us."

Mia smiles and walks over, shaking both of our hands and taking the seat on the other side of Charlie. "Thanks."

"So, you're from here?" I ask, sipping my cocktail.

"Yup, born and raised. I moved to Arizona for college and stayed for a few years."

"That's a pretty big change. What made you decide to move back?" I can't imagine choosing to live in another desert.

"That's a story for a night when I *don't* have to drive home." Mia laughs and takes a swig of her drink.

"Charlie and Lucy just moved here a few months ago. Charlie is dating Linc Anderson," Maizie supplies.

"I remember Linc. He was a little ahead of me in school. And his brother, Knox." she gets a funny little smile on her face when she mentions the man.

"Oh, did you and Knox have a thing?" I ask. Yes, I'm overstepping. No, I don't care.

Mia blushes at the insinuation. "Oh God, no. I was three years behind him. I have no doubt he didn't even know I existed."

"Don't think twice about that, sweetie. I don't think he paid attention to any of the girls in school." Maizie waves her hand in Mia's direction.

"Did you two go to high school together?" Charlie asks, taking a pull from her beer.

"We did," Mia answers, smiling fondly at Maizie. "We were in band together."

"Then Mia over here decided to move halfway across the country for college, leaving me to waste away in Shine all by my lonesome." Maizie laughs.

"From what my parents told me, you've been pretty busy since I left. I heard you have a little boy," Mia says with a wide smile.

"I do." Maizie's face lights up just like every other time she talks about her son. She grabs her phone, and the two women go through the million pictures she has on there of Colby.

Wyatt watches her with a smile playing on his lips.

"Do you have a thing for the bartender?" I ask quietly so no one overhears.

"What? No. She works for the club, and she has a kid. I'm not about to get tangled up in that."

Yeah, I have a feeling he's already tangled, even if he doesn't realize it yet.

It's rare there are so few people here on a Friday, so I decide to take advantage and put a twenty in the jukebox so we can hear all the music we like for once. Charlie and I pop up from our seats when one of our favorite songs comes on and start dancing around the bar. The whiskey is flowing, thanks to Maizie, and I'm having a blast hanging out with my best friend and the new girl, who I can already tell I'm going to like.

Charlie and I are dancing our asses off and singing totally off key when a strong pair of tattooed arms circle my waist.

"Hey there, Lucifer. You having fun?" a deep British accented voice rumbles in my ear.

It's been a couple of hours since I got off work, and I'm feeling the effects of the cocktails.

"Hi, handsome," I say, turning in Jude's arms and giving him a very inappropriate kiss. "You come here often?"

Jude laughs at my cheesy line and smacks my ass.

"I met a new friend tonight. Come meet her."

Jude smiles down at me and nods. I look over to where Mia is sitting, and low and behold, Knox has taken my seat next to Wyatt, having a conversation. Poor Mia, with her back ramrod straight, doesn't look like she knows what to do with herself being so close to her high school crush. I catch her stealing glances at the giant biker one seat away from her, but otherwise, her body remains still.

"Mia, this is... Jude," I awkwardly introduce after walking over to her. I don't know what to call the man at my side. We haven't discussed what we are to each other. We just... are.

Jude shoots me a wry grin before turning to Mia and holding out his hand.

"Hi, I'm Lucy's boyfriend. Nice to meet you."

Woah. Am I drunker than I feel, or did he just call himself my boyfriend? When Jude looks back at me, he chuckles and puts a finger under my chin, closing my mouth.

"Bound to catch flies, love." He winks and turns to Maizie. "What do the girls owe, Maiz?"

She walks over with our tab, and Jude throws a couple hundreds on the bar.

"Jude, that's way too much," Maizie says, pushing the money back toward him.

"That should cover Mia's tab, too."

"That's still too much."

Jude simply shrugs and turns to me. "Ready, darling?"

Damn him and the way he calls me darling. Usually, I would argue about him coming in and wanting to take me home without asking what I wanted to do first, but Lord help me when he looks at me the way he is now and uses that damn British charm.

"Let me say bye to Charlie."

I turn and spot my best friend making out with Linc as they slow dance on the makeshift dance floor we set up earlier.

"Second thought, I'll call her in the morning."

"Good plan. Now, let's get out of here. My dick has been hard since I walked in and saw you shaking your fine arse all over."

"Such a sweet talker my *boyfriend* is," I reply, emphasizing the word boyfriend.

He smacks me in the ass again on the way out the door.

"Damn straight, love."

Chapter Sixteen
Jude

Lucy wraps her arms around me when she wakes beside me the next morning.

"Morning," she says, nuzzling into my back.

When we got home, I fucked her long and hard. Walking into the bar last night and finding her letting loose and having fun is something I've missed these last few weeks. Though she's played it off well, I can tell there's been a few times when she's still worried that someone from her past is going to jump out of nowhere and take her back to her childhood hell. It's the way she makes sure to clock every car that drives past her house or the way she plays close attention to every license plate she sees when we're on Main Street grabbing a coffee or doing a little lingerie shopping, my personal favorite outing. I don't know if it was the whiskey or the fact no one's been looking for the three assholes we rid the planet of or asked about her, but last night was the first night I'd seen her relax fully in far too long.

"So, about last night," she says, kissing between my shoulder blades.

"Mmm." A low growl rumbles from my chest. "You looking for a repeat this morning?" I reach behind me and pull her tighter into my back. Lucy slaps my lower abs, and I grab her hand. "Careful, Lucifer you're precariously close to a certain appendage that I'd hate to have abused so early this morning."

"You're such an idiot. I was talking about you calling yourself my boyfriend."

I turn around, so both of us are lying on our sides facing each other. My hand brushes her silky black hair from her face, and my gaze meets her tired but bright blue eyes.

"Are you not a fan of labels, or is it that I was the one to use it?" Why the hell am I suddenly feeling insecure? This is why I don't like to have these discussions and never had them in the past. Also, I've never wanted to, nor have I ever laid claim to someone like I did last night.

"It's just that we didn't talk about it. Usually, when you call yourself someone's boyfriend there should be some sort of conversation, don't you think?"

"I wouldn't know. It was a first for me."

Her eyes widen for a brief moment before she schools her expression.

"Jude, I'm sure you've had lots of girlfriends."

It's no secret I've had my fair share of women. Hell, more than my fair share, if we're getting technical. But never once have I been interested in more than a night or two of fun.

"Lucy, I've never wanted to be tied down to one woman. It may make me sound like a right arsehole, but no one has ever held my interest for more than a few hours. Then I met a little spitfire of a woman, and I was hooked. I know we got off to a pretty rocky start, but I couldn't get you out of my damn head. I've never wanted to fight and fuck someone at the same time until you."

She snorts out a short laugh. "You really have a way with words."

A smirk moves across my lips. "I have a way with a lot of things. I'd love to show you some of them."

"I'm beginning to think the only reason you want me to be your girlfriend is so you have easy access to sex."

I roll her onto her back and settle on top of her, propping myself on my elbows, so I don't crush her.

"Darling, I hate to be the one to break it to you—"

Lucy slaps her palm over my mouth and stares me dead in the eye. "Finish that sentence, and my legs will slam shut faster than you can blink."

I lick her palm, and she yanks her hand away with a disgusted look on her face.

"Oh, please, love, I've licked every inch of your delectable body and have had my tongue buried in your delicious pussy. A little lick on the hand is nothing."

She rolls her eyes. "It feels weird. Don't ask me to explain."

"Anyway, as I was going to say..." Lucy quirks a brow, silently asking me if I really want to keep going. It's adorable she thinks she's going to stop me. "There is no wanting you to be my girlfriend. You are my girlfriend. You and I both know this isn't just about sex. As fucking spectacular as it is, there's more here than carnal pleasure or scratching an itch. You know it just as well as I do." I lean down and take her mouth in a deep kiss.

"So, when I tell people I'm your boyfriend, know that it means I want you in my bed." I kiss her again. "In my life." Kiss. "And I have no intention of letting you go." Kiss. "And I won't let you run from this, either."

Lucy looks at me with a gentle smile. "Okay."

"Okay." I wink and roll my hips, causing a gasp to escape from her throat. "Now, about that easy access to sex of which you speak..."

A few hours later, after I've dirtied Lucy up, then washed her in the shower, my phone chimes with a text.

Ozzy: *The Irish want to meet and talk a few new deals. Me, you, Cash, and Linc are going to Boston for the night.*

Goddamnit. I haven't had to leave Lucy for more than a few hours since the whole thing with seeing those guys in town a few weeks ago. But if the Irish want a sit-down, then we can't deny them. Not to mention, I'd never tell my prez no. If he needs me there, then that's that.

Me: *Be there in a bit.*

Lucy is in the kitchen, baking her bacon how she likes it, when I walk in from her bedroom.

"I have to go to Boston for the night, love. I'll have one of the guys stay here with you, or you can come to the clubhouse."

"How about, 'Wow, Lucy, thank you so much for making breakfast' instead of you coming in here demanding I follow orders, hmm?"

Rather than saying anything, I invade her space against the counter, locking her in place with my arms on either side. Her face is clean, and she smells like her jasmine-scented body wash. It's a light floral scent I've become hopelessly addicted to. Nuzzling her neck, I take a deep breath, attempting to get my fill since I won't see her until tomorrow.

"Darling, thank you for making breakfast," I whisper into her ear. "I'm going to enjoy this bacon, then I'm going to express my gratitude on my knees while I eat your sweet cunt." My teeth nip her earlobe, and she inhales a shaky breath. "I'm still learning how to do this relationship thing. I hope you can be patient with me." Pulling back, I meet her heated gaze.

"You're not *too* terrible at it. I just don't particularly like being bossed around." Her eyes dart to my lips, probably imagining all the ways they make her scream.

Lifting one brow, I shoot her a dubious expression.

"Okay, smartass, you know what I mean." She gives me a light kiss on the lips and pushes me back a step so she can take care of the bacon. "You know, not every argument we have is going to be solved with sex and innuendos. Or with you ending each sentence with darling."

That's most likely true, but so far so good.

"I have no doubts we have plenty of fights ahead of us, love, but half the fun is making up." I think about the few fights we've had since we started sleeping together. Or fighting and fucking at the same time. That's awfully fun as well.

"You really can be a complete idiot sometimes."

"But I'm your idiot," I say, opening my mouth for a piece of bacon.

Lucy obliges and lets out a suffering sigh. "Yeah, I suppose you are."

"Nice of you to finally join us, dickhead," Linc grouses when I get off my bike. "You know, just because you have an old lady now doesn't mean you get to laze around all day."

"Shut the hell up, you twat. Do you need me to hold your dick while you piss or something? Ozzy didn't say anything about being in a rush to leave."

"Goddamn, you're cranky today," Linc replies.

"Sorry, mate, I'm a bit out of sorts."

The more I think about having to be away from Lucy for the night, the more I feel this irritating buzz under my skin. It's fucking with my head, and I don't like it.

Smacking Linc on the back, we walk into the clubhouse. A few of the guys are playing pool, and others are sitting on the large sectional couches, watching last night's fights on the tele.

I spot Cooper by the pool table and walk over to him.

"Hey, Coop. You on bar duty tonight?"

The prospect shakes his head. "Not tonight. Why, what's up?"

"I'll be out of town tonight. Lucy isn't interested in staying here without me. I'm going to need you to spend the night on her couch."

I don't love the fact that another man is going to be staying at her house, but Cooper and Lucy have been thrown together on babysitting duty more than once over the last couple of weeks, and she seems to have a soft spot for the kid.

"Of course, Jude. Anything you need."

"Thanks."

Ozzy comes out from his office and sits at the bar, having a midday beer, which isn't like him.

"What's up, Oz?" I ask, making my way over.

My normally unflappable president swipes a hand over his tense face.

"It's this shit with the Irish. They had our backs when Charlie was taken, but heat is ramping up with the Italians. The Irish want to handle them. I get it. Shit, I respect it. Their beef goes back a lot further and is a lot deadlier than ours, but sometimes, I feel like we're sitting ducks here." Ozzy takes a swig of his beer. "The Italians have been too quiet. I expected some blowback, but so far, nothing. The Irish are using it as an opportunity to push guns harder, and they're starting to make a lot of deals with a lot of other organizations. Makes me nervous. Seems like they're raising cash for a war that hasn't started yet. I get wanting to expand, but now they're talking about getting into bed with the Russians. Finnegan needs to slow down. When you push too hard, too fast, people make mistakes that cost lives. I'll be damned if it's any of ours."

"We've never been in the business of playing it safe, Oz," I shrug, not particularly concerned with what has Ozzy knotted up.

"But we've always played it smart. He wants my guys to be the middleman. The Russians aren't exactly known for picking sides and staying true to it. They'll align with whoever they think holds the most power. Right now, it's the Irish. Doesn't mean it's going to stay that way."

"You having second thoughts about continuing to work with them?" That would put a significant dent in our cash flow.

"Not second thoughts. More concerns. I'll talk to Finn and his old man tonight. They want us to meet with the Russians at one of their pubs. Show us a good time and all that shit. Makes me wonder if they're trying to butter me up for something."

"Finn's always been a solid guy."

"Yeah, but we aren't part of the Irish, and they aren't part of the Black Roses. Each of us will always put the interests of our own first. Add in the silence from the Bone Breakers and the Italians, and it's got me a little on edge."

Ozzy has always been a bit wary of anything having to do with the Italians. After everything that went down fifteen years ago, he's tried to maintain somewhat of a truce with them. The Cataldis are slippery-ass motherfuckers who've skated by on many of the charges brought up in Boston, and they somehow always come out smelling like roses. Their last big shake-up was when some lawyer from here got them on a bunch of RICO charges. It rocked their organization for a long time, and there were young capos trying to make a name for themselves. It was a bloody time for the Italians, and the Black Roses got dragged into it. Not something Ozzy wants a repeat of and never talks about.

"So," he says, turning to me with a Cheshire cat grin. "You and Lucy."

"Yup. Me and Lucy."

"Can't say I saw that one coming."

"I doubt she did, either," I reply, thinking of our conversation this morning, then the scene in the kitchen before I left.

"But you did?"

I laugh. “Hell no, mate. That woman is mouthier and more stubborn than any other person I know. And considering who my brother is, that says a lot.”

Ozzy chuckles. “Yeah, Liam is quite a piece of work.”

“He’s a fucking twat, but he’s my brother. Hurting him would break Grandad’s dear old heart.”

Ozzy nods. “Shame.” He takes another sip from his beer. “For what it’s worth, I’m happy about the turn of events. You’re not as much of an asshole these last couple weeks. It’s been… nice.”

“Oh, don’t get too excited. I’m still the same asshole I’ve always been. Just ask Lucy. You haven’t seen me as much, is all.”

“Are you going to be moving out, too? Shack up with your old lady next door to Linc and Charlie.”

Lucy hasn’t brought up moving in together, but we’ve been spending every night together. Sharing an address doesn’t seem like such a foreign concept to me as it would have before I met her. But my girl’s a tricky one. She’ll fight for every last shred of independence, even if she wants to do the opposite.

“Possibly, but not anytime soon. I just got her used to the idea of being my old lady. She’s like a skittish alley cat, that one. She’s as likely to let you pet her as she is to claw your eyes out.” An affectionate smile graces my lips.

Ozzy looks at me with an incredulous look in his eyes. “You like never knowing which it’s going to be?”

“Hell, yeah, I do. Keeps me on my toes.”

He shakes his head. “Then you two are a match made in heaven.”

Or hell, but I decide not to argue the point with him.

All that matters is she’s mine.

Chapter Seventeen
Lucy

"Lucy, you awake?" I hear Charlie call after she lets herself into my house.

"In here," I reply from my bedroom.

"Is it safe?" Charlie stands in front of the doorway with her hands over her eyes.

"You are such a goofball," I laugh out.

"Well, now that you have a boyfriend, I have to worry about walking in on you in a compromising position. Love you and all, but I can live without seeing that much of you or Jude."

"Do you honestly think I would have called you back here if we were in here naked?" I ask, changing the sheets on my bed. "Help me with this." I nod to the other corner, indicating for her to help me put the damn fitted sheet on. Making a king-size bed is a pain in my short ass.

"Listen, I don't know what your kinks are, and I would never judge you for them."

"Well, they aren't having people watch me have sex, so you can rest your pretty little head."

After smoothing out the dark comforter, we throw the ridiculous number of pillows I have to have back on the bed.

"There. All done," I say. "What's up, sister? No school?"

"Nope. Free as a bird. With the menfolk gone, I thought we could have ourselves a little girl day. Pedicures, silly romcoms, and candy."

"Sounds fun."

Charlie is the only person I'd ever do any of that with. She loves all the girly shit. I, on the other hand, would rather go shoot some guns or grapple. Which reminds me, it's been a bit since I've done any sort of training with Jude. My schedule has been all over the place with work, so I haven't had a chance to go back to the women's shelter with him and make him teach me his crazy ninja skills.

"I thought we could call Mia, too. Kind of bring her into the fold. Maizie had nothing but nice things to say about her last night, and she seems like she could use a friend."

"What else?" I ask, sensing Charlie has some ulterior motives.

"Well," she draws out. "Did you see the way she clammed up around Knox?"

I nod, knowing where this is going.

"I just think it would be nice if she starts hanging out with us. Maybe Knox will notice her and take an interest and stop being such a broody loner. Then there would be a little group of us all dating the guys and it would be that much more fun at parties and stuff. I'm tired of not having anyone to hang out with. The bunnies still steer clear, but I still get dirty looks from them every once in a while."

"You want a girl gang?"

"No, that sounds stupid."

"Girl posse," I offer instead.

"Ew. That's even worse."

We both laugh. Both of those are ridiculously dumb.

"Okay, little miss matchmaker, I'll go along with your plan. But all the pedicure stuff is at your house. Plus, I have like no food here, and this day is going to need snacks."

I hear my phone buzz next to me with an incoming text.

Jude: *Cooper's gonna come stay with you until I get back.*

Me: *Oh, he's in for a treat then. I'm hanging out with Mia and Charlie today. We're gonna have a girly girl day.*

Jude: *There better not be any naked pillow fights without me, Lucifer.*

I roll my eyes but smile widely.

Me: *I'll never tell...*

Jude: *Lucy...*

Me: *Oh, for fuck's sake. The only person in danger of being smacked across the head with a pillow while naked is you when you say some stupid shit like you just did.*

Jude: *That's my girl.*

Me: *You're such a weirdo.*

Jude: *But I'm your weirdo.*

I giggle—fucking giggle—at him calling himself mine. Jesus, who am I turning into?

Me: *You better stop now before I rethink this entire thing.*

Jude: *You wouldn't, but I do have to go. Take it easy on the prospect.*

Me: *We'll see.*

Truthfully, I adore Cooper. If I had a younger brother, I'd like to think he'd be like Cooper. Knowing where I grew up, the chances of that would be slim, but Cooper is as sweet as they come.

Pocketing my phone, I head out to the living room and find Charlie on the couch texting who I assume is Mia.

"We all set?" I ask, grabbing my house key.

"Yup, Mia is going to meet us at my place with some stuff from Cool Beans."

"Mmm, I love that place. I thought Cafe Du Monde's beignets were the end all be all, but Betsy is giving them a run for their money with her scones."

I lock up the house just as I see Cooper ride up on his bike.

"Park on the side of Charlie and Linc's place. We're headed there for the day."

Cooper salutes me and rolls into their driveway.

"Jude get ahold of you?" he asks after turning his motor off.

"Yup. You're in for a day of pedicures and chick flicks," I tell him.

"Or I'll just go ahead and be in the garage. Not that I don't enjoy a moving romance, but I need to work on my bike. Shoot." He snaps his fingers and gives me a pathetic pout, totally overacting the disappointment at not being able to join us.

"Suit yourself." I smile at the big goof and head inside.

"Our friend Mia is coming over. You can let her in the side door if you see her," Charlie calls.

"Got it," Coop replies, rolling his bike into the garage.

"Is Linc okay with him using his tools without him here? I know some guys are weird about that."

"He's totally fine with it. Linc said Coop is one of the most talented mechanics he's ever met. I think they're going to put him to work at the bike shop instead of having him at the clubhouse all the time."

"Good for Coop," I say as we walk into Charlie and Linc's house.

"Okay, let me go get all the stuff, and you can pick out a movie." Charlie disappears into her bedroom.

I pull up her streaming service and scan through the selection, settling on a superhero movie.

"Seriously?" she asks, coming out and looking at the TV. "I thought we were going to watch a sappy girly movie that Linc never likes to watch with me."

"What?" I settle back into her couch. "I'm in the mood for a hot guy saving the world from total annihilation."

When she sees the actor come on screen she nods. "You know what? I can get behind that."

I laugh as she busies herself setting up the warm water and bath salts for us to soak our feet in.

There's a knock at her side door, and we turn to see Cooper peeking his head in.

"Mia's here," he says, opening the door to let our new friend in.

"Hey, girl," Charlie greets. "You got here fast."

"I was already at Cool Beans when you texted. I can't stay away from Betsy's baked treats."

"Right," I exclaim, getting up and taking the bags from Mia. "They're the best."

"I grabbed some iced coffees, too. I didn't know what everyone liked, so I got a few different ones." She takes the drinks out of the carrier as I grab plates.

"You're the best. This day is in serious need of more coffee." Grabbing the one with caramel drizzled over the whipped cream, I take a plate with a scone and sit back on the couch.

"Well, it was supposed to be chick flicks and pedis, but Lucy here decided she wanted superheroes."

"Oh, I love this one." Mia stares at the screen for a beat. "God, he's just too pretty to look at."

"I love that you can appreciate the finer qualities of superhero movies with me, Mia," I say. "Between the scones and coffee, you might be my new best friend."

"Hey," Charlie yells from the kitchen. She walks out with a scone and a drink. "I heard that."

"I wasn't trying to be quiet," I throw back.

"Fine, just for that, Mia gets your pedi tub."

I laugh. “Fine by me. I’ll just be over here enjoying my treats and hot guys in tight suits.”

The afternoon passes with lots of laughter, and soon the sun is setting behind the trees.

“We should order some dinner,” I suggest.

“I vote Chinese,” Mia chimes in.

“I love you more and more,” I say and watch Charlie stick her tongue out at me. “We’ll have to be careful and not make my wife over there jealous,” I stage-whisper out of the side of my mouth.

“Just you wait. Mia is going to start hanging out at the clubhouse, and pretty soon Knox is going to sweep her off her feet. Then she’ll be too busy having wild sex with him to hang out with you anymore, and you’ll be stuck with me.”

Mia’s face turns a disturbingly dark shade of crimson.

“Charlie, I think you broke our new friend.”

Mia buries her face in her hands and lets out a groan. “God, I couldn’t even talk to him the other night. Trust me, I don’t think there’s any chance he and I are going to get anywhere near a bed together.”

“I take it this a high school crush you never got over,” Charlie says.

“This is a crush that *started* in high school. When he graduated, I would see him around town on his bike and think there couldn’t possibly be anything hotter. Then I saw him in the bar yesterday, and I was proven so, so wrong. Grown-up Knox blows teenage Knox out of the water.”

"Why didn't you try to talk to him?" I ask.

"Umm, did you see me last night? I was a mess when he sat down. All my teenage fantasies come to life sitting four feet from me. Instead of being the semi-confident twenty-eight-year-old I thought I'd become, the sixteen-year-old shy band girl reared her little head. All of the sudden, words went poof." She throws a hand in the air. "Gone."

"I wish I could give you some advice on how to talk to him, but he hardly talks to anyone except his brothers. I've never even seen him with a bunny," Charlie tells her. "Plus, before Linc, I didn't talk to any guys. I had a high school boyfriend, but that ended pretty terribly."

"Yeah, my mom told me about Linc going to jail for beating up some guy really bad. Was that your ex?" Mia asks.

"Yup. These guys don't mess around when it comes to any man hurting a woman. He didn't even know me at the time, just knew I needed help."

"Linc was always a sweet guy in high school, if not a bit of a player." Mia shoots me an apologetic look. "I'm sorry, you probably don't want to hear that."

Charlie waves Mia's concerns away with a flick of her wrist. "Don't worry about it. Trust me, I know all about his activities before me. You should have seen the bunny drama when Lucy and I showed up at the clubhouse."

The memory of Stacia causes a snicker to escape me. Even though she's gone, the other bunnies haven't warmed up to Charlie or me. I guess we took away their favorite fuck boys.

Oh, well.

"Have you heard from Jude?" Charlie asks.

"I haven't." I realize my phone has been on silent all day, though.

Looking around the couch cushion, I find my phone face down and flip it over to find a notification that popped up a couple minutes ago. My alarm company was trying to reach me. Someone came into my house without disabling the alarm.

I jump up from the couch and peer out the window, looking over at my place. I don't see any cars or bikes. Charlie and Mia look on with concern etched on their faces.

"Lucy, what's going on?" Charlie asks.

"Turn off the lights," I say.

She does as asked, and I continue watching my house looking for anything unusual. If it was Jude coming back early, he would have disabled the alarm. I suppose it could be some sort of malfunction, but my senses are tingling.

"The alarm company sent me a notification. The alarm was tripped and never deactivated."

Charlie runs over to the window to stand next to me, watching to see if anything happens.

Just then, I see what look like flashlights moving from my kitchen window to the back of the house where my bedroom is. And there's more than one.

"What the fuck?" Charlie yells.

"Shh," I hiss. "Go get Cooper and have him come in here, but be fucking quiet."

I don't know if there are more guys outside, and the garage is wide open while Cooper works on his motorcycle.

Cooper and Charlie walk back in moments later.

"How many did you see?" Cooper asks, standing at the window next to me.

"At least two." I still see flashlights in my house, and it's freaking me the hell out.

"Lucy, call your alarm company back and tell them it was a mistake. I don't want the police showing up. Charlie, do you have a gun?"

Charlie nods and runs to her room. We hear the safe click open in the otherwise silent house.

Looking over, I spot Mia on the couch with wide eyes, doing a great impression of a statue.

"Gotta love girl's day," I try to joke. By the look on her face, it's obvious it doesn't land.

Charlie returns with two handguns, handing one to me.

Cooper turns to walk to the door leading into the garage.

"Where the hell do you think you're going?" I ask.

He pulls out his gun from under his cut and checks the clip.

"Call Knox. He's at the clubhouse. I'm going over there."

Charlie nods and lifts her phone to make the call.

“The fuck you are, Cooper,” I say, putting myself between him and the exit. “There’s at least two of them, maybe more. We don’t know who the hell they are, and we don’t know if they’re armed.”

“Lucy, I’m not sitting here waiting for them to run off.”

“So help me God, Cooper, if you walk out that door, I’ll shoot you in the damn foot. You’ve seen me at target practice, you know I can do it.”

Charlie hangs up the phone and looks at Cooper. “They’re on their way. Knox said for you to stay here until they get here.”

Cooper’s tight jaw tells me he doesn’t like it, but when a brother gives a prospect an order, they have to follow.

The three of us go back to the window and watch my house. It’s quiet and dark there now, no flashes of light coming from any window. I’m silent, barely breathing as thoughts rush around. What if I had been home? What if Cooper had been on my couch, and someone came in and shot him? What if, what if, what if. The questions are tumbling around my brain so fast, I can barely keep up. The one thing I know for sure now is they know where I am.

The loud roar of motorcycles breaks me out of the loop of dangerous thoughts, and four bikes come to a halt in front of Charlie and Linc’s house. Knox is in front, charging up the stairs. Charlie opens the door before he has a chance to knock. Shit, from the look on his face, he would have burst right through, leaving a Knox-shaped hole in the damn thing.

Knox's eyes find mine before he looks down and he sees the gun in my hand. He nods his approval. Then his gaze swings to Cooper. "How many?" he asks the prospect.

"I'm not sure. Lucy saw two flashlights inside."

Braxton and Wyatt step inside, leaving one of the other prospects on the porch.

Wyatt comes over to me and takes the gun from my hand. "You're okay, little sis."

It's then I realize I'm shaking like a fucking leaf. Wyatt leads me to the couch to sit next to Mia.

"You good, sweetheart?" he asks my visibly anxious friend.

"Yeah, I think so. I don't even know what's going on."

"And that's what you'll tell anyone if they ask," Knox commands from the other side of the room.

"Knox, Jesus," Charlie admonishes. "Have a little heart. She's just as scared as the rest of us."

It's only been ten minutes or so since I saw the notification from the alarm company on my phone, but it feels more like hours have passed.

Knox nods at Mia. "Sorry." He doesn't sound sorry.

Mia doesn't say anything, just grabs my hand.

"Are you okay?" she whispers.

"No," I reply, shaking my head.

"I'm not going to ask tonight, but I hope you know you can trust me. I'll never say anything about whatever else happens here," she says looking around the room at the tense bikers. It sounds to me like she knows how these things can play out. "I just want you to know, I'm here for you if you ever need to talk."

I give Mia a shaky smile. "And I hope you won't run away screaming."

Mia laughs softly. "It'll take a lot more than a couple bikers holding guns and a little B and E to scare me away."

"Jesus, girl, what *would* it take?"

Mia shrugs but doesn't answer.

"Hey," I say, nudging her in the arm. "That goes both ways. You can talk to me, too."

Knox walks over and stands in front of Wyatt.

"Let's go over there. The prospects are going to stay here while we check out Lucy's place."

Wyatt stands, and he, Braxton and Knox head out the front door, silently walking to my house with their weapons out and down at their sides.

Mia, Charlie, Cooper, and I watch as they enter my house. A few moments pass before I see light shining through the window. Their shadows are visible as they walk around, but there's no yelling or gunshots, so I suppose that's a good sign.

The three of them walk back over to Charlie's and see us all standing, waiting anxiously for a report.

Knox turns to Cooper. "Call Jude and tell him what's going on."

Cooper nods and pulls out his phone.

"Well?" I ask.

"Your place was trashed, but no one was inside. Looks like they picked the lock on your backdoor," Braxton supplies.

"So, it could have been anyone?" Charlie asks.

Knox shakes his head. "Doubtful. This is connected. It's way too much of a coincidence. We need to figure out how."

"Alright, I want to go over there," I say.

"It's a mess, Lucy. Why don't you wait for Jude," Braxton suggests.

"I'm sorry, have we met?" I volley back. "If you think I'm waiting for Jude to hold my hand, you must have forgotten who I was." I stomp past the prospect still standing sentry on Charlie's porch and march across the lawn to my house.

When I walk in, the scene in front of me takes me by surprise. Braxton said the place was trashed, but this is utter destruction. My couch has been ripped apart, and every picture on my fireplace mantle has been thrown on the floor, with shattered glass everywhere. The coffee table is overturned, and all my pillows have been ripped apart, their stuffing strewn around. Jesus, this is the second time my house has been destroyed in about as many weeks. I think it might be time to move.

Walking into my bedroom, it strikes me that whoever broke in left this room alone. That's weird. I see something on the bed, and my blood turns to ice in my veins. Laying there, where Jude and I had spent the night tangled in my sheets, is a photograph. I pick it up, and tears spring to my eyes. It's a familiar face I haven't looked upon in seven years but thought about every single day. My sister.

And scrawled across the photo in red marker are the words, *She misses you. See you soon, Lucinda.*

Chapter Eighteen
Jude

The phone call from Cooper came through twenty minutes ago. When Ozzy saw my face, he didn't care that we were in the middle of a meeting with the Irish and the Russians. He stood up and told Finnegan we had to reschedule. Family emergency. Because that's what Lucy is—family. It doesn't matter she isn't officially my old lady. The deed is as good as done.

The Russians, on the other hand, were obviously offended. When one of their guys said something off color in Russian, I told him to shut his foul mouth before I did it for him in his native tongue. That surprised the hell out of the group. No one suspected any of us spoke Russian. I'm not fluid by any means, but I know enough to get by.

Me and my brothers break every traffic law on the stretch of road between Boston and Shine. Linc and I are desperate to get back to our women. Though it wasn't their house that got broken into, Charlie was way too close to danger for Linc not to be pushing his bike as fast as he can take it. As for my other two brothers, they're just as concerned with the situation unfolding for various reasons. People Ozzy cares about and the club he loves and would lay down his life for are being threatened. Whoever broke into Lucy's house has no idea the hell they're bringing upon themselves, or they're too stupid to care.

The four of us slide to a halt in front of Linc's place. We made it back in almost half the time it took us to get to Boston earlier today.

Jogging to the front door, Linc swings it open with me right behind him.

"Charlie," he calls out.

She jumps off the couch and into his arms.

"I'm fine," she reassures the tightly wound biker who has her wrapped in his arms.

It hasn't been more than a few months since Charlie was abducted and nearly sold to the Italian sex trafficking ring the Irish have been trying to destroy. We wouldn't have found her as fast as we did if it hadn't been for the inside man the Irish have.

"Where is she?" I ask the room.

"Right here," Lucy calls behind me as she walks up the stairs.

I walk over and cup her cheeks in my hands, searching her blue eyes for signs of distress.

"Are you okay, love?"

She lets out a humorless laugh. "No." Her hands cover mine. "But I'm glad you're here."

I pull her into my arms and hold her. Nothing else. No roaming hands, no whispers of dirty promises, I just need to feel her body against mine to reassure myself that she's whole and safe. After a few moments of breathing her in and calming my racing heart, I let one arm fall and face the room, still holding Lucy firmly against my side.

"What the hell happened?" I ask the room.

"I got a notification on my phone that the alarm had been tripped. I looked out the window for your bike, thinking maybe you came home early or something. The house was dark on the inside, except for the flashlights I saw moving."

God, the fear she must have felt. Thoughts begin racing about all the ways this could have gone in an entirely different direction. Lucy must sense the chaos in my head. She squeezes my waist tighter and lays her head under my shoulder.

"I'm okay," she whispers.

I turn and kiss the top of her jasmine-scented head, silently thanking any higher power that might be there.

"Charlie came out to the garage to let me know what was happening," Cooper adds. "When I came back in here, I had her call Knox and grab a couple guns. I wanted to go over there, but Knox told me to wait with the girls."

The kid looks broken up about letting whoever was in her house get away.

"That was the right call," I assure him. "The girls were safe over here, and there was no way of knowing how many people they had with them or what kind of weapons they had."

Cooper seems content with my response, but I can tell it grates on him that they were so close, and he couldn't do anything.

"I'm going next door to check things out," Ozzy says.

"What about Mia?" Lucy asks. "I don't think she needs to stick around now that they left, and everyone's here."

Ozzy peeks his head around the corner. "Hey Mia, long time no see."

Mia looks at him with surprise. "Hey, Ozzy." She gives him a little wave and a tentative smile.

Ozzy looks at Knox. "You follow Mia home, then meet us back at the clubhouse. We won't be long here."

Knox nods and looks at Mia. "You ready."

"Y-Yeah," she stammers out. Mia stands from the couch and heads toward the door.

Lucy steps away from my side and stops her before she reaches the front door. "I'm sorry our night was ruined. Next time, coffee and treats are on me."

Mia leans in and gives Lucy a hug. "I'm holding you to that."

When the girls break apart, Mia slides past the bikers still filling the doorway, and Knox follows. When he passes Brax, he slaps him upside the head.

"Ow, what the hell was that for?" Braxton says, rubbing the back of his head.

"You know exactly what it was for." Knox narrows his eyes before walking to his bike. When Mia pulls away from the curb, Knox is right behind her.

"What did you do?" I ask Brax.

"Nothing. I was just watching her walk to her car."

I raise my brow in his direction.

"And I might have been checking out her ass." He shrugs. "It's a nice one, and I was appreciating it."

I roll my eyes and focus my attention back on my woman. "I want to go to your place, too, and check it out."

Lucy nods. "I went over there before you got here."

That little tidbit irritates me. I would rather she would've waited for me, but I also know Lucy. She waits for no one.

"You good here?" I ask Linc, who's still holding tightly to Charlie.

"Yeah. I think we're going to head to the clubhouse. At least until we can get a few things figured out."

"We'll be there after we go over to Lucy's." I take my woman's hand as we walk to her place.

"They really fucked shit up in there," she warns before I open the door.

Looking around the space, the first thought that hits me is they sure they hell did. The second is this seems personal. No one would go to these lengths if they weren't sending a message.

"I found something in my room. I know who was here." Lucy looks between the destruction and me.

Ozzy is in the house with us and turns to face Lucy.

"Who?" he asks.

"It had to have been someone from the compound." She pulls out a folded picture from her back pocket. "They left my room untouched, but this was on the bed. I think they wanted to make sure I saw it."

Ozzy takes the picture from her and studies it for a few moments. "Who is this?"

"My sister."

Ozzy hands the picture to me. The resemblance is there. While the girl in the picture has softer features, it's obviously a picture of Lucy's sister. The message written on it has me seeing red like the marker it's penned in.

"Fuck that. I'll see them in hell before they get their hands on her," I grit out. Turning to Lucy, the pain in her eyes nearly knocks the wind out of me. Part of me wants to take it away, but the other part, the louder part, is pissed. I had no idea she had a sister.

"Looks as though there's a conversation to be had, Lucifer."

She lets out a long breath. "Yeah."

After Lucy grabs a couple things from her room, she gets in her car, and I follow her back to the clubhouse.

Usually, when we come back from a run of any sort, it's time to relax and have a few beers and shots. Tonight, however, the mood is somber. People we love could have been seriously hurt or worse. That isn't sitting well with any of the brothers. Even the bunnies have made themselves scarce, putting out a tray of sandwiches, then leaving us the hell alone.

"You hungry, love?"

Lucy looks ready to fall asleep standing. Those adrenaline crashes can be brutal.

"I'd rather go lie down. You can stay out here if you want."

"You saying that because you don't want to talk about your sister, or are you pushing me away like you've tried to do twice now?"

"When did you get so damned perceptive?" she huffs out.

"All part of being your man, darling."

Lucy smiles up at me. She doesn't have to say anything. She knows I have her pegged. She may finally be coming around to the idea that I'm not running, and I'll be damned if I let her, either.

We head back to my room, and I put Lucy's bag next to my dresser, noticing the way she's eyeing it.

"That bag is staying in this room, Lucifer. I don't care what threat we're facing, you aren't going anywhere."

"I know. That bag and I have a long history," she says, pointing to it.

I sit on the edge of the bed next to her. "Why don't you tell me about it."

She lets out a breath and lies down. I do the same, so we're facing each other, and put a reassuring hand on her hip.

"I was seventeen when I ran. I took that bag and threw a few things in and tried to get my sister to go. She was always the sweet one, the one my parents didn't want me corrupting. That's why they were marrying me off to Jasper." A shudder runs through her body. "He was one of the elder's sons. The way he looked at me made my skin crawl. I knew if he tied himself to me, he would use me in any way he pleased. And if I ever fell short of his expectations... I have no doubt he would punish me the way his father liked to."

I want to gut them. All of them.

My hand tightens on Lucy's hip as I battle to keep my breathing normal. The thoughts of what a sick fuck like that would have done to a defenseless girl roll around in my head.

"My parents never protected us." She lets out a humorless laugh. "Hell, my father knew what they did to the girls who disobeyed. I'm sure he even had a hand in it. My mother did whatever my dad told her to. I don't know if she ever tried to stand up for herself or us, but there were times we would hear her crying in her room and hear him beating the hell out of her. Then there were the nights when it was different sounds. Those would make me sick. He'd recite bible verses about her being an obedient wife and yielding to her husband." Lucy closes her eyes tightly.

"Hey, love. You're safe. No one here is going to make you do anything you don't want to. That will never happen."

She knows all this, but judging by the look on her pinched face, she could use the reminder.

"There was a girl who ran once," she says, opening her eyes and looking into mine. "They found her and beat her brutally all through the night. In their eyes, she was a traitor to God and a traitor to the church. My friend saw them carry her body out of the church. My father was there helping them." A tear spills over her lashes. "We never saw her again. They beat her to death for sinning against them. Leaving was the ultimate sin for a woman and wouldn't be tolerated."

"They used fear to keep you there," I comment.

"It can be a pretty powerful tool when that's what you're raised with. The night I left, I kind of snapped. The walls were closing in on me, and for the first time in my life, I thought taking the chance and at least trying to get away was better than staying. At that point, I honestly didn't care if they found me and killed me. I had to try."

"But your sister?"

"Cece. She wouldn't go. The fear was still ruling her life. I knew she could tell them she was sleeping when I left and didn't hear me, and they'd believe her. She wasn't a liar by nature and did everything asked of her. Quiet, meek, and so, so beautiful." More tears fall from Lucy's eyes. "Every single day, I'm torn between not staying and trying to protect her from whatever horrid man I'm sure the elders chose for her and being so fucking thankful for the life I get to have because I left."

"It's hard to imagine you were ever a meek girl like that."

"Oh God, no. That's why I was the one being punished all the time. There was this fire, this raging inferno of anger inside me when I finally got away." Lucy rubs the center of her chest as though she can still feel it there. "I wore like a second skin. I'm shocked I ever got hired anywhere. Not that the places I found jobs in were any sort of reputable establishments."

"How did you get from Nevada to New Orleans?"

"I snuck in the back of a truck the Bone Breakers were using to get off the compound. When they stopped for food in Colorado, I snuck out again. I was homeless for about a week. Then, one day, a woman saw me panhandling and asked if I wanted a job cleaning tables. I was hungry, and she could tell I wasn't made out for living on the streets. She took me to a dingy little pool hall she owned, and I started working for her that day." Lucy's eyes shine with gratitude as she remembers the woman.

"That's where you learned to play pool like you do?"

"Yup. I seem to have a natural affinity for anything that takes hand-eye coordination. Learned how to play a ruthless dart game, too."

"I should send that woman a fruit basket," I comment dryly, rolling my eyes, and Lucy laughs.

"I don't know if they allow that in jail. She got raided for operating an illegal gambling facility. Marge was cleaning house with backroom card games. Had a whole little casino set up. When she got raided, I ran again. This time, I had some cash in my pocket, so I made it to New Orleans and found a place similar to Marge's, somewhere no one was going to ask for ID."

"That's where you met Charlie?"

A warm smile covers her face.

"Yeah, about a year after I got there. When I first landed there, I worked in a total shithole. That's where I met a guy who did great fake IDs. One day, Charlie came in looking for a job." She lets out a small huff of amusement. "She was so not prepared for the shit I knew she'd have to deal with. I kind of assigned myself the role of big sister."

"Since you couldn't protect yours anymore," I supply.

"Yeah," Lucy breathes out. "I hooked her up with my ID guy, and we got the hell out of that place. Management wasn't too keen on following sexual harassment policy. One of the bouncers decided grabbing Charlie's ass was a good idea. The broken nose I gave him said otherwise. Ted, the owner, felt I was in the wrong, so I flipped him off, and we found another place. We were there for a few years, too."

"Then Charlie got scared when she saw Cillian and wanted to leave New Orleans," I supply, remembering why they made their way to Texas.

"There was no way in hell I was going to let her go by herself and start all over again alone."

"Of course, you wouldn't, love. That's not who you are."

"How can you say that, knowing I left my sister in one of the worst imaginable places?"

I gather Lucy closer to me. Her tears dampen my shit as I hold her, guilt overwhelming her for what she sees as abandoning her sister.

"Lucy, there was no way you were going to be able to change anything for you or Cece if you'd stayed. Those elder fucks set it up that way. The only thing you could do was run. You couldn't force her to leave with you, and if you had tried, you most likely would've been caught. No one can blame you for saving yourself."

"It doesn't make the guilt go away. That's why I don't ever talk about my sister or tell people I have one. It would bring up too many questions about why she's not with me or why I can't talk to her."

"You could have told me, love."

"I was afraid you would judge me for leaving her there or something. I judge myself for it every day."

"I will never think of you as anything other than the strong woman you are for getting yourself out of an impossible situation. None of my brothers would feel any differently about you, either."

Lucy looks at me with tired, watery eyes. "Thank you," she whispers before laying her head on my chest.

There's nothing more I can say that's going to make her feel better about any of this. Instead of trying, I simply hold her in my arms until her tears dry and her breathing evens out.

"Lucy," I whisper.

When she doesn't stir, finally allowing her body to shut down and take the break it needs, I gently untangle her from my arms.

Looking at the woman in my bed who spent her life running from demons, I decide then and there, it's going to stop. Maybe she thinks she can't do anything about it, but I know for damn sure I can.

I grab my phone and quietly close the door behind me, heading into the main room of the clubhouse. Ozzy and Braxton are out there having a beer, with Cooper serving behind the bar.

"Is Lucy okay?" Coop asks.

"Yeah," I reply, heading to the door. "I need some fresh air."

Stepping outside, I take a deep breath, inhaling the chilled night air. Fuck, since getting the call a few hours ago from Cooper, it feels as though this is the first time I've been able to breathe and center my thoughts.

After hitting the name in my contacts, I hold the phone to my ear. He picks up after the second ring.

"Little brother," Liam greets.

"I need you to find some information for me," I tell him, not wasting time on pleasantries. There's no telling when Lucy could wake up, and I don't want her to be alone.

"Well, hello to you, too," he scoffs through the line.

"Sorry, it's been... a rough night."

"Fine, fine. What is it you need and who is it that needs it?"

"There's a sort of religious doomsday cult in the Nevada desert. They have ties to the Bone Breakers MC out there. I want everything you can find on the compound... who runs it, who know about it, all that stuff. If you can get aerial photos as well, that would be great."

"Sounds like you're planning some sort of mission, little brother. Is Ozzy on board with this?"

"After tonight, I wouldn't give a fuck either way."

Chapter Nineteen
Lucy

The relief I feel from unloading my past to Jude comes as a surprise. For so long, I've played it close to the vest, never letting anyone in. Even Charlie didn't know my story. She knew I had a past I didn't want to talk about, but being the good friend she is, she never pushed. Jude didn't push, either, per se, but a couple days ago after the break-in at my house, it was very apparent he expected something more than I was raised in a cult and they're crazy.

The way he held me when I confessed my guilty feelings about leaving my sister changed something in me. Sure, he'd already told me he was going to protect me no matter what, but he didn't have the entire story. He didn't know about my sister, and after finding out, he didn't look at me as though I was a selfish monster. That thought was what scared me the most.

Then I fell asleep in his arms. There were no wandering hands, no promises of his dick taking the sadness away, which, considering it's Jude I'm talking about, wouldn't have surprised me. What did surprise me was the reverent way he simply held me while I cried, then fell asleep. That has *not* been the MO of our relationship. Anything emotionally charged usually ended up with me or him tearing the other's clothes off. This was... different. Sweet, even. I am wholly unprepared to deal with Jude's sweet side.

"What are you thinking about so hard over there, love," the man himself asks as I study myself in the mirror while brushing my teeth in the little en suite bathroom in his room at the clubhouse.

"Nothing much," I lie. "When do you think I can go back to work?"

Jude looks at me with an incredulous expression.

"Have you lost your mind, woman? You aren't going back to work until these fucks are dealt with."

I sigh in frustration. "Jude, I'm not okay with hiding here. I've given too much of my time and worry to them showing up and doing something. I have you, or any of the brothers with me, at all times. If they come, they come, and we'll handle them and get back to our life. I don't want to live in fear, waiting for the shoe to drop while I'm locked away here like some helpless princess."

The initial fear I felt knowing that Otto and Jasper know where I am has waned. I believe Jude when he tells me he and the brothers will handle whatever comes. Plus, not making any money of my own makes me itchy. When I tried to bring that fact up to Jude yesterday, he assured me it was only temporary, but I've always relied on myself to take care of me. The idea I'm now somehow beholden to anyone, even if it is temporary, makes me incredibly uncomfortable.

"Darling," he says, coming up to stand behind me as I spit the toothpaste from my mouth. "We all know you aren't some damsel in distress. I've seen you fire a gun. I know exactly how lethal you are."

The last couple of days have been filled with target practice and sex. I think the sight of me hitting every target and making it look easy turns him on. He told me the first time he saw how I handled a weapon when Linc was teaching Charlie to shoot, he had to go back to his room and take a long, cold shower to temper his hard-on. The way he's pressing said hard-on into my lower back tells me he's enjoying the memory.

"You can't keep trying to distract me with sex, Jude," I tell him, turning around and leaning against the sink.

The giant of a man cages me in with his tattooed arms and runs the tip of his nose from my shoulder to my ear, inhaling as he goes.

"But it's so fun making you scream while I eat your sweet pussy. I don't consider it a distraction, more like getting my fill of you now that I have you here all to myself."

"Have you had it yet?"

He pulls back and meets my eyes with his smoldering gaze.

"Never, darling."

That son of a bitch knows what it does to me when he calls me darling, looking at me the way he is, as if I'm his meal waiting to be devoured. Though I know this in my brain, that's not the part of my body calling the shots right now.

Jude's hand goes to the towel I have tied around my chest.

"I think I should come up with a rule," he says with hunger in his voice as he stares at where his hand rests on the towel.

"Oh, yeah?" I whisper, shivering with anticipation as he skates his fingertip along the edge of the towel.

"No more covering these beauties up when you get out of the shower. I say anytime we're in my room, you should be topless."

"You're such a tits man," I laugh out softly.

"I'm an everything Lucy man," he corrects. His finger dips between the towel and my chest, and with a little tug, the towel falls to the floor. "Fuck. You're perfect."

I'd hardly consider my body perfect by any stretch of the imagination, but Jude's meaningful stare says he believes it.

His head dips to mine, and he takes my mouth in a wet, playful kiss, our tongues tangling and teasing. My fingers skate up his sides, then down his back, leaving a trail of goosebumps in their wake. I love the feel of this man's silken skin, love the feel of his toned muscles underneath. There is nothing about his body I would change. For being a tall-ass biker, somehow, we fit together perfectly.

"I need you," he whispers, breaking the kiss and gazing into my eyes. The look in his eyes sends more shivers through my body. He isn't saying he needs a body, and any would do the trick. His eyes are telling me he needs me—my heart, my fire, all the pieces of me I've never given to another man. And I know, with him, it's safe.

"I'm right here." My hands trail up the back of his neck and through his long, soft hair, letting the strands glide through my fingers. "You have me, Jude."

This time, when he takes my mouth in a kiss, it's deep. This isn't just a kiss—this is a claiming. His hands travel to the back of my thighs, and he lifts me, wrapping my legs around his waist. Jude turns to leave the bathroom and carries me to the bed, never breaking his kiss. He gently lowers me, far more carefully than he ever has before. Jude and I have had sex countless times, and it's always been explosive and volatile, as though we're tearing into each other like we have something to prove. This is different—the way he's kissing me and softly caressing every inch of skin on display, which is all of it.

I attempt to pull him tighter over me to, I don't know, speed it up, but he pulls away and slowly shakes his head from side to side.

"No, love, not this time." Jude leans down and continues to nip and tease my lips and tongue while his hands trail feather-light touches everywhere.

He's trying to open me up, to break me apart, worshiping me with touch and kiss. This man is going to be the death of me, and, at this moment, I'm okay with it.

He lifts himself from my body and stands at the edge of the bed, slowly pulling off the sweatpants he'd thrown on earlier. His hard cock bobs in front of me, and it's simply too mouthwatering to resist. I wrap my hand around the base and slide it up, twisting as I go. When I lick the tip, the taste of his salty precum floods my tongue.

"You look so beautiful with your lips wrapped around me," Jude says, lovingly stroking the side of my face. He pulls away and gently pushes me back on the bed, falling over me. "I want to feel you with nothing between us," he whispers, kissing my cheeks, my chin before looking into my eyes.

That's something I've never done before, but I've never trusted anyone the way I trust the man above me.

"I want that, too," I whisper.

When he enters me, he lets out a hiss.

"Are you okay?" I ask when he stills inside me.

"Yeah, I just didn't think,"—he tentatively pushes in deeper—"it would feel so good."

When he fills me, I feel everything strip away, leaving nothing but need and want in its place. He is—or already has—clawing his way through my walls, and somehow made a place for himself in my heart. Instead of the thought scaring me, I lean into it, relishing in this moment and this man.

His movements are slow but deep, building the fire in my veins and the sweet promise of relief.

"Oh my God, Jude, I'm going to come," I moan.

"I'm here with you, love. Right here."

I wrap my legs tighter around his middle, anchoring myself to him while my hips meet his thrust for thrust.

"Lucy," he breathes out and takes my lips in an open mouth kiss. He swallows my moan as my pussy tightens around his cock, and wave after wave of immeasurable pleasure races through my body. I feel his cock jerk inside me as he comes, pressing his forehead to mine.

We're a mess of sweat and racing hearts as we try to catch our breaths.

"That was..." I have no words for what that was.

"It was, love." He kisses my forehead. "It is."

I know exactly what that was and what he's saying it is. This was Jude laying claim, making a promise.

This is what it feels like to make love to Jude Ashcroft.

I'm looking through the drawer that Jude cleared out for me when we came back to the clubhouse a few days ago.

"Goddamnit, I have no clean underwear or my yoga pants."

"I'd much prefer you didn't wear underwear, love. One less thing for me to have to strip off you," Jude comments from where he's sprawled out on the bed.

"I am not freeballing in a clubhouse full of bikers or at the women's shelter. Or anywhere, for that matter." He quirks a brow at my use of freeballing. "Shut up. You know what I mean."

"I'll take you to your house, and we'll pick up a few more things," he says, climbing to his feet. He's dressed in joggers and a t-shirt, ready to teach the self-defense class at the shelter today.

"You don't have time. The shelter is in the opposite direction of my house."

"I can skip it for a week or be late," he offers.

"Absolutely not. Those women depend on you. My panty situation isn't as important."

"Any situation involving your panties is important to me," he says, walking up to me and putting his arms around me, kissing the tip of my nose.

"I'll have Cooper take me before his shift at the bar."

Cooper's been covering for me since Charlie is in school, and Maizie can only work so many extra shifts.

Jude looks uncomfortable with the idea of me leaving the clubhouse without him, but I'm not going to argue the point. I need some fucking underwear.

He huffs out a breath. "Fine. But straight there and straight back. And I want both of you armed."

"Yes, *Dad*," I whine obnoxiously like a teenage girl would when dealing with an overbearing boar, kind of like the one standing in front of me.

"Hmm, I didn't think you had a daddy kink, love. We can play around with that."

"You're a dumbass," I laugh out, smacking him in the chest. "Okay, you need to go to your class, and I need to get to my house and back, so Coop can get to work."

We walk out to the main room and find Cooper on the couch, watching TV.

"Hey, prospect," Jude calls to him. "Lucy needs to run by her house. You're going with her."

Coop jumps up from the couch, and I shoot Jude an irritated look.

"You could ask, you know. You don't have to be rude."

"Lucifer, this is how it works. We can't be too nice to the prospects, or they get too comfortable."

I roll my eyes. "Whatever."

"Cooper doesn't need you fighting his battles for him. Just be glad Wyatt or Barrett didn't overhear you. They would have tortured the poor kid."

"That's stupid."

"It's life, love," he replies with a shrug.

We head out the door, and I hand Cooper my keys before going around to the passenger side and opening the door. I look at Jude to wave, but he lifts two fingers and beckons me to him. When I reach him, he grabs me around the waist and smashes his mouth to mine with a breath-stealing kiss.

"See you in a couple hours, love," he says after breaking the indecent kiss.

"Ride safe. I lo— I'll see you when you get back."

Oh my God, what did I just almost say?

Jude smiles and kisses the tip of my nose. Stiffly turning toward my car, I hurry to it and slip in the passenger seat, slamming the door.

"Everything okay?" Cooper asks.

"Yup," I rush out. "Peachy. Let's go."

The drive to my house is short, but I'm lost in thought the entire trip there. I was about to tell Jude I loved him. What in the actual fuck? Yes, this morning was different. There was a connection between us we never had before, but that doesn't mean either of us is ready to voice what that means.

Stepping through the front door of my house, I'm taken aback by how empty it looks inside without any furniture.

"Me and a couple brothers came over the day after the break-in and cleaned everything. Jude said not to worry about buying new furniture. Said you two would go shopping."

I guess he wants input on what goes in my house. That makes me wonder if he plans on moving in when all of this is over. That also makes me wonder if I want that. *Yes*, the little voice in my head screams at me. It's the same voice that had me almost telling him I love him. She needs to slow her roll.

I walk back to my room and grab another bag out of my closet. This time, instead of being in a fog of fear, I'm clear-headed and make sure to grab everything I need. Though Jude says he'd rather I not wear panties, I doubt he'll mind the little number I bought when Charlie and I went shopping before my lockdown at the clubhouse. A knowing smile stretches across my mouth, imagining Jude's expression when he sees it on me later tonight. Throwing the lingerie in my bag, I head back to the living room.

"Ready?" I ask Coop, who's standing watch by the front door.

"After you." He holds his arm out, and we head back to my car.

On the drive back, I think about what it would be like to live with Jude. Not at the clubhouse like we are now, but in an actual house, like Charlie and Linc. The thought of living with a boyfriend never crossed my mind, but now the idea sounds exciting, like I could have something real with someone. With him.

The van racing up behind us registers a fraction of a second before it rams into my car, causing us to spin. Tires squeal as Cooper tries to get control of the car, but it's no use. We head off the embankment on the side of the road, landing upside down.

"Cooper," I call frantically.

He gives me a dazed expression but doesn't speak for a moment.

"I think I'm okay. We need to get out of here," he says, fumbling with his seat belt.

I do the same, and the latch releases, causing me to land awkwardly on the roof of the car. I look toward Cooper again and see boots walking to the car. Cooper has given up on trying to get out, instead reaching for the gun strapped to his side. Before he can pull it out, a face comes into view on the other side of Coop's head.

"Hello, Lucinda."

Elder Otto stands up straight and fires a bullet between Cooper's eyes.

"No!" I scream as I look into Cooper's lifeless eyes. "You son of a bitch!"

"Now, now, Lucinda, that's no way for a woman to speak to a man. Don't worry, we'll cleanse you of your wicked, worldly ways soon enough."

Another set of boots comes into view as I try to maneuver my body around and crawl out my broken window. A rough hand grabs me and yanks me hard through the glass, cutting my legs as he drags me from the car.

Jasper smiles that same creepy-as-fuck smile that used to give me nightmares.

"Let me go, you sick fuck," I yell, trying to break free from his grasp.

"No, no, no," he scolds. "It's time you came home, Lucinda. Back where you belong."

He jabs a needle into my neck as tears fill my eyes.

I never got to tell Jude...

Chapter Twenty
Jude

I don't feel great about leaving Lucy. I know she's with Coop, and I trust him with my woman. He'll be patching in sooner rather than later.

When I get to the women's shelter, I see Matilda at the front desk.

"Your boss has you slaving away up here again?" I ask, throwing her a wink.

"Yeah, she's a real bitch." Matilda laughs. "No Lucy today?"

"No. She had a couple things to take care of. She was disappointed not to make it, though," I reply.

"I like her, Jude. Don't fuck it up."

I bark out a loud laugh. "Matilda, one of my favorite things about you is you don't mince words."

"Never have and never will. Who has time for bullshit?"

That's one of the things that struck me about these new feelings I've had toward Lucy. I thought she was too loud when we first met. She was too... *everything.* But I've come to realize it was me who was caught up in the bullshit of having my ego stroked by club bunnies and women who saw me in a bar and wanted to take me for a spin. I'd surrounded myself with things and people who were never going to matter to me, so I wouldn't matter to them.

Lucy, though? She saw through my shit and called me on it every damn chance she got. That's a huge reason it was difficult for me to get past all her ribbing and couldn't *not* rise to the occasion every time. If I didn't, there was no way to hide behind the asshole persona I'd carefully crafted. Not saying I've changed completely. The asshole is still in there, but with Lucy, it's different. I'm different. How's that for a mind fuck?

"I'm sure she'll be here next week. And don't worry, I have no intention of fucking anything up." I give Matilda a wide smile, and she waves me off.

After finishing class and stepping into the warm afternoon air, it's all I can do not to race home and see my girl. Just the few hours without her make me antsy.

Fuck, I've got it bad.

Checking my phone, there's no text from Lucy. I'd assumed she would've let me know when she got back to the clubhouse, considering I was wary of her going back to her place to get her stuff.

I try calling her, but her phone goes directly to voicemail. Hanging up without leaving a message, I dial Cooper. Again, no answer. That is particularly concerning, being that prospects are supposed to pick up each and every time a brother calls, no matter what.

I dial another number.

Linc picks up on the third ring. "Hey man, what's up?"

"You seen Lucy or Cooper? Neither one is picking up."

Linc laughs. "Maybe she left your grumpy English ass for the nice American."

"Fuck off, twat. Are they back yet?"

"Nah, I haven't seen either of them, but I just got to the clubhouse. I'll try calling Coop."

"Okay. I'm headed back now."

I disconnect the call and get on my bike with a strange feeling in the pit of my stomach. Something isn't right. Granted, maybe Lucy wouldn't have thought to call me and let me know she was safe, a conversation we'll be having when I get back, but Cooper knows better. That guy has been a near perfect prospect since day one. It's not like him to disregard the rules.

Riding out of the parking lot, I decide last minute to swing by Lucy's. Between the clubhouse and her place, I notice tire marks and broken glass all over the pavement that weren't there before. My bike comes to a halt, and I get off, following the tire marks to the embankment off the side of the road. What I see causes my heart to drop to my stomach. Lucy's car is upside down about ten yards off the road.

I run down calling her name, but don't get a reply. Skidding to a stop next to her car, I bend down to look inside. What I see next scares me and enrages me to the point my vision goes hazy around the edges. Cooper's lifeless body is still hanging from his seatbelt, upside down, with a bullet between his eyes.

"Oh, fuck, man," I choke out, wishing like hell I'd never asked him to take her. Shit, if I could turn back time, there's no way either of them would have left the clubhouse today.

I go to the other side and see the passenger window blown out and blood droplets on tiny pieces of glass. It looks like someone dragged their body from the car… or was dragged by someone else. Looking around the car, I attempt to follow where the drag marks went. I call for Lucy over and over, but there's still no answer. My heart is racing as a fear like I've never known overtakes me. She has to be around here somewhere. She had to have gotten away. Suddenly, I hear something crunch under my boot. Looking toward the ground, I move my foot and find a broken syringe.

Motherfucker.

I grab my phone from my pocket and call Ozzy.

"Hey, man—"

"They got her," I rush out. "Those fuckers from Nevada have Lucy and they killed Cooper."

"Woah, woah. Where are you?"

"Right off the highway. It looks like they rammed her car or something, and she flew off the road. Cooper took a bullet to the head, and Lucy's gone. Found a syringe."

"That could have been there from someone else."

"Fuck that, Ozzy. You know it was them. They drugged my woman and are trying to take her back to that piece of shit compound in that filthy fucking dessert!" There has never been a time I yelled at my president. That's all changing today.

"Alright, brother. We're on our way. Sit tight."

"Fuck you, Ozzy. How the hell am I supposed to sit tight while they have my girl?"

"Jude, I'm giving you an order as your president. Stay there. Let us get there and survey the scene, then we'll figure it out. I'm leaving now."

Ozzy hangs up and the urge to throw my phone against the nearest tree is strong. But Lucy may need to get a hold of me if she escapes, and I'll be damned if I don't have a phone and sure as shit don't have time to get a new one.

Not even five minutes later, the silence is broken by the rumbling thunder of motorcycles.

Linc is the first to get to the car and sees Cooper.

"Fucking assholes," he yells, punching the tire in front of him.

Wyatt, Braxton, and Knox are next, followed by Ozzy.

My president walks up to me and clasps both of my shoulders looking me in the eye. "We'll find them, brother, and they will pay for killing Cooper and taking Lucy."

"We need to find her now, Oz. Who the fuck knows how far they're going to take this. They killed Coop for chrissake." My skin feels tight across my entire body, as if I'm about to peel out of it at any moment.

"They aren't going to get away with it, Jude. I promise you that."

I nod because the only thing that could possibly come out of my mouth at the moment is a soul-crushing scream. Losing the plot now won't help Lucy.

"Okay," I eventually croak out.

Cash shows up with a van, and we remove Cooper's body from the wreckage. When he's loaded in the back, I crouch beside his lifeless form, now covered in a sheet.

"I'm so sorry, mate," I say in a broken whisper. "This should never have happened. You would have made a good brother. We'll make them bleed for what they did to you. Fly high, brother." My head hangs to my chest as I say a prayer to a god I'm not convinced is there, then close the doors. When Cash slides behind the wheel, he turns to face me.

"You good?"

"Let's go," I reply, sitting on the bench seat next to Cooper. I'll worry about my bike later. I'll be damned if I leave Cooper back here alone.

We get back to the clubhouse, and Ozzy calls a friend who owns the mortuary and tells them the situation. We don't want paper trails, and Trick has used him in the past, so we can lay a brother to rest without having to deal with police or hospital paperwork.

I grab my phone to call my brother. It's not that I don't have faith in Ozzy and the club's ability to find Lucy, but time is of the essence, and Liam works best against a clock.

"Hello, Jude," he answers on the first ring. "I'm still looking into the information you gave me. These things take time, and I don't appreciate being rushed. You aren't the only case I have going at the moment, you know," he says irritably before I have a chance to speak.

"They took her."

There's silence on the other end of the line for a moment.

"Tell me everything you know. I'm putting you on speaker with Sawyer."

"It looks like they were run off the side of the road. The car had rear damage."

"We're looking for a car, possibly truck with front end damage," Liam tells his hacker.

"I know that" Sawyer says, irritation lacing his tone. "Where did it happen, Jude?"

I tell them the mile marker where the car is.

"Was there any indication of what direction they headed after they took her?" Sawyer asks.

"I couldn't tell. I doubt they would have headed north. That would have taken them through Shine. With a damaged, unknown car someone would have seen them and remembered." These fucks are ballsy as hell for taking my woman, but I'm not sure they're that stupid.

"What's South?"

"Farms, old railroad yards." I think for a few seconds. "There's an abandoned airstrip one of the farms used to have out there. The old man died, and no one wanted to take over. Went to auction, but we've never seen anyone out there."

Liam and Sawyer don't say anything, only the sound of his clacking keyboard comes through the line.

"Got 'em," Sawyer says. "A white sprinter van with a smashed front end was clocked by a traffic camera headed south toward where you said that airstrip is. If that's the place they're using, there won't be any flight logs for me to hack into."

Goddamnit.

"Who the hell is helping these fuckers?" I ask no one in particular. "It's not like they're some huge drug kingpins."

"A lot may have changed since Lucy left, brother. Who knows what these crazy arseholes have gotten into in the last seven years," Liam replies. "Okay, the way I see it is we have a couple options. We pack up and head to Nevada. I can have a team mobilized within the hour, but it will take approximately,"—I hear the clacking of a keyboard again—"forty-two hours in a car." Liam lets out a low whistle. "Or I can see what can be done about getting us a plane. I know a couple people."

"Option two," I reply. "I'm not waiting that long to deal with these fucks."

"That's what I figured you'd say. This may take a few hours still, but we won't be too terribly far behind them."

"You're coming, then?" I ask. Ozzy's going to love that.

"Of course. I doubt Ozzy will object to more manpower, especially considering my team has the training for this type of mission."

I have the same training, courtesy of Her Majesty, but the more the merrier, I say.

"How long?" I ask.

"I need to make a couple calls. I should know within the hour. Keep your phone next to you." Liam hangs up without saying anything else.

I walk back into the main room and see my brothers gathered around the bar and tables.

"Liam thinks they may have taken Lucy on a plane," I tell the group.

"How the hell did they get a plane?" Wyatt asks.

I shrug. "No clue, but I plan to find out who's been helping them. There's no way a bunch of religious kooks could have pulled off something like this by themselves." This question will burn me up later. Right now, I couldn't give a shit who's helping them, I'm getting her back.

"Liam is getting us a plane. He's bringing his team."

Heads nod all around. I look at Ozzy, who hasn't moved from his seat.

"You good with that, Prez?"

"If it means getting Lucy back safe and sound, then yeah, brother, I'm good."

The door of the clubhouse swings open, and Charlie walks in, wild-eyed and searching for someone. When her eyes land on me, she rushes over.

"Jude." Charlie throws her arms around me. I'm stiff as a board for a moment before I tentatively return her embrace. When Charlie was taken, I was the first to find her outside of the warehouse after she shot her ex, then stayed with her while she was at the ER and Linc was in surgery. We formed a sort of bond that day, and I'm grateful Lucy has a friend like her.

"Linc told me," she says, looking up at me with tears in her eyes. "She's going to be okay. We'll find her."

"Of course, she's going to be fine. This is Lucy we're talking about," I try to reassure.

"You will. And when you do, make them pay, Jude."

"Charlie, I can guarantee they're going to wish they never stepped foot in Shine. No one takes what's mine."

Charlie's face lights up with the most blood-thirsty expression I've never seen.

"Make them bleed. No one fucks with our family."

"It's going to be my pleasure."

Chapter Twenty-One
Lucy

It's the jostling that registers first. It's not a feeling of someone shaking me, but whatever car I'm in is going over a bumpy road. I slowly open my eyes and take in my surroundings. I'm not in a car. I'm in a fucking plane. My head tilts to the right to look out the window. What in the actual hell? I close my eyes, trying to remember how I got here. Nothing comes to mind immediately. The only thing registering is the churning of my stomach and the pounding pain behind my eyes. Turning my head to the left, I see two faces close together, having a hushed conversation. Two faces I never wanted to see again.

The memories come rushing back—the van hitting us from behind, losing control and going down the embankment and landing upside down, trying to get out and run, Cooper… Oh my God. I squeeze my eyes shut again, fighting tears and overwhelming nausea. That asshole pulled me out of the car and stuck a needle in my neck after killing Cooper.

I go through a mental checklist of my body while the two psychos sitting across the aisle from me are preoccupied. My head feels like it's splitting open from the drugs, and my stomach is about to lose its contents. My knees feel scraped to shit. I remember Jasper pulling me over the shattered glass from the passenger window, but other than that, I think I'm okay. I feel weak as hell, though, so I don't know how effective I'd be trying to fight my way off the plane. Granted, we're still in the air, so that definitely won't be happening. I tilt my head down and peer at my clothing. Nothing looks out of place. I wouldn't put it past these sickos to have tried something while I was passed out. The look in Jasper's eyes before he jabbed me told me he'd been waiting for his chance.

"She's awake," I hear Otto say.

I turn my gaze toward them, the light sending sharp pangs through my skull.

Jasper turns toward me and gives me a lecherous smile. The memory of him reading from the bible on Sundays passes through my jumbled mind. He was a creepy asshole then. Nice to see some things don't change.

"What the fuck are you smiling at over there?" I grit out. The one thing I can say that's changed with utmost certainty is me. While I used to sit silently and would never dream of disrespecting him or his father, the new me they haven't met yet isn't afraid to speak her mind.

Jasper's smile fades, and he looks at me with revulsion in his eyes.

"You've got a lot to relearn, Lucinda. You've been out in the world too long, and it seems you've picked up a few bad habits." He looks pointedly at the shorts I'm wearing.

"Oh, you mean the backbone I grew or the jeans I'm wearing? Or maybe it's because I'm not afraid to call you a sleazy fucking slimeball now."

If it was any other situation, I would laugh at his pasty complexion turning the color of the bright red tomatoes my mama used to grow in her sad little garden.

"You need to learn your place, girl," he responds in a low, sinister tone.

"Don't worry, son." His father pats his arm. "We'll be landing soon enough. She'll be properly retrained when we get her back in the hands of the church."

"Will that be the same hands that killed Bea all those years ago, Otto?"

"You will refer to me as Elder Otto, Lucinda,"

"I'll refer to you as anything I damn well please."

All this back and forth isn't helping my head or my stomach. It could also be this tiny plane that seems to bounce through the sky making me sicker after being drugged. Not that I have much experience being *fucking drugged.*

"Where did you get the plane?" I ask. "You didn't have it when I lived at the compound."

"Several things have changed since you abandoned the flock," Jasper says.

My eye roll is unavoidable.

"The meth business must be doing well then."

"We've had several fruitful partnerships in the last several years. Seems your new associates have a few enemies. They were more than happy to give us what we needed to return our lost lamb to her family." I want to slap the smug smile of Jasper's face.

That makes sense, though. I don't know who these "new partnerships" include, but there was no way anyone at the compound would have been able to fund a plane like this.

"Do my parents know that you left the compound to kidnap me?"

"It wasn't a kidnapping," Otto interjects. "We are saving your eternal soul. Your father understands that and is perfectly willing to do whatever is necessary to rid the demon from your body."

I always questioned if the members of the congregation believed all the shit these people spewed for years, and if the elders believed it themselves. My answer is staring me right in the face. These people believe everything they say. They believe they are the chosen ones, and their god has deemed it so. They truly believe women are to be kept under the thumbs of the church, their fathers, and later, their husbands. They even believe that doing business with who they deemed as sinners too far gone to save is perfectly acceptable if it's for the church's greater good.

"I need to see my sister when we get back."

Cece may have stayed when I left the first time, but I'll be damned if it happens again. I'm getting the hell out of there the first chance I get. It doesn't matter if it takes months of planning and playing along with their stupid rules to make them believe I've "seen the light." I'll do whatever it takes to get the hell away from them, and this time, Cece is coming with me, even if I have to knock her ass out to do it. The only silver lining is getting to redo the biggest mistake of my life when I left without her the first time.

Otto and Jasper give each other a brief look, but I can't quite decipher what it means, which makes me even more uneasy.

"What is it? Did something happen to Cece?"

"No, no. Your sister is fine. In fact, she was married five years ago."

The rage of being kidnapped and watching my friend die in front of me had my blood hotter than molten lava, but the look on Otto's face has turned it into ice running through my veins.

"To who?"

"Me," Otto says, a wide smile stretching across his pale face. "Unfortunately, the Lord hasn't blessed her with being able to carry my child yet, but I'm sure, in time, it will happen."

I stare at the man sitting across the aisle from me with only his son between us, and fury like I've never known explodes from me.

"You sick son of a bitch!" I scream, jumping from my seat and throwing myself at him. "She was a child."

My nails scratch down the side of his face, causing him to cry out in pain. Jasper picks me up and slams me back into the seat, holding my wrists to the armrests. There's only one thing to do, so naturally, I head-butt him right in his nose. The action sends pain shooting through my already excruciating head, but the blood that runs down his face is oh-so-satisfying.

Jasper delivers a blow to the side of my head which causes my vision to go blurry.

"You little bitch," he grits out, his blood pouring onto my shirt. "You'll pay for that."

"Yeah, you and what army, dick weasel?"

Taunting the already unhinged bleeding man in front of me isn't the best move, but fuck it if I can find my sense right now. The only thing I can think of is that horrid man putting his hands on my sweet sister.

"I assure you, Lucinda, Cecilia is quite content in her place as an elder's wife," Otto says, dabbing the blood from the side of his face with a handkerchief.

"I'll just bet," I scoff. "What happened to your wife? Or does the church suddenly condone polygamy?"

"I'm afraid Jasper's mother fell ill, and nothing could be done. She went peacefully in her sleep."

Yeah right. It's interesting that when a woman outlived her usefulness on the compound—be it she couldn't bear children or got old and couldn't work in the gardens or the labs—she would suddenly die peacefully in her sleep. Now this man tied himself to Cece. That fate will not befall my sister. No way in hell.

Jasper pulls out two pairs of handcuffs. Where he got them from, I have no idea. I was too busy staring daggers at Otto. He circles one around each wrist, then connects the other end to the armrest. Looking me dead in the eye, he tightens the cuff around each wrist, nearly crushing my bones.

"There," he says with a satisfied smirk. Looking at his handiwork, he raises his eyes to meet mine again. "I like the look of you in cuffs."

Fucking gross.

"I like the look of blood pouring from your nose," I reply with a saccharine smile.

That earns me a slap across my face. Sticking my tongue out, I feel the skin that's opened on my lip and a copper tang fills my mouth.

Jasper goes back to his seat, and soon, the pilot comes on the speaker to announce our descent. I look out the window, and the familiar view of the desert I grew up in—and hated every minute of—greets me through the window.

"Home sweet home, Lucinda," Otto says.

I'll be watching it burn soon enough.

When it's time for us to deplane, Jasper unlocks the handcuffs from the arm rests of my seat and cuffs me with my hands in front of my body.

Fucking idiot.

The pilot emerges from the cockpit, and I don't recognize him.

"Are you new to the church? You good with them abducting women?" I ask the stranger.

His sneer tells me he doesn't mind one bit. "Rifiuti di motociclisti."

"Is that Italian?"

He gives me another disgusted look and returns to the plane.

Interesting.

An old truck takes us from the airstrip, which is nothing more than a flat dirt road outside of the compound, to the gates leading inside the barbed wire fence.

Home sweet home indeed.

Faces peek from the windows of the resident's homes, trying to get a glimpse of the commotion. God only knows what's been said about me since I've been gone, or if any of these people knew Jasper and Otto had planned to bring me back.

It wasn't often Otto or any of the other elders left the compound. When they'd leave for more than just getting supplies, they would tell us that God needed them to go on some sort of pilgrimage, and they would come back with new rules or some supposed vision they had while away. I have a feeling they were actually out meeting with new suppliers or something of the sort. Being the steadfast believers that everyone here was, they had no problem swallowing the lies being fed to them.

"How did you find me?" The question has been plaguing me since the car accident.

Otto chuckles. "We saw you walking with one of your friends. Dumb luck, really, considering we were there looking for the missing Bone Breakers. We saw you get into a truck and followed you home. You should have been more careful, Lucinda."

"It was God's will," Jasper chimes in.

It's fucking always "God's will" when they decide to commit crimes against women.

Out of the corner of my eye, a blonde head catches my attention. It's brief, but I would know that willowy frame anywhere. Cece. Craning my neck, I try to get a better look at the sister I haven't seen in over seven years, but she ducks around a corner before I have a chance. Tears well in my eyes for the life she's had to endure, and the painful pit in my stomach that's always there, always missing her, is becoming unbearable.

We finally pull up to the church that's the scene of so many horrible memories. This is where I was taken for punishment any time I stepped outside the rigid lines I was forced to stay in throughout my childhood. It never ceased to amaze me the blood that would cover the floor but be washed away by the time Sunday rolled around, like nothing ever happened.

Three men are standing in front of the doors leading inside to what's sure to be my torture chamber. I recognize the one to the left immediately. It's my father.

"Lucinda," he says when I'm hauled from the truck. He nods in acknowledgment, but the look of disgust and irritation is stamped across the hard lines of his face. What strikes me, other than the fact the years he's been working on the compound or in the meth lab haven't been kind to him, is the gold cross hanging around his neck. It's the same one all the elders of the church are gifted.

"Father," I reply coldly. "I see you have some new jewelry." I tilt my head to the same type of cross I saw waving in front of my face when I was receiving punishment. "Did you get that as a reward for selling off your youngest daughter?"

His face bears no emotion as he walks up and slaps me across the face. The same side Jasper had hit only an hour before. The cut on my lip reopens with the force, and I spit the blood that's pooled in my mouth at his feet.

"Insolent child. You never knew when to keep your mouth shut. Your years away will do you no favors here, girl."

Little does he know my years away and everything I've learned will get me and my sister the hell out of here.

I stretch my lips into a wide, bloody smile. "I just love family reunions."

My father raises his hand to hit me again, but Jasper stops him.

"She'll receive her punishment in due time. Right now, we have more important matters to attend to."

Lowering his fist, my father gives me an ominous look but backs away.

Jasper leads me up the stairs to the church and unceremoniously shoves me inside the empty building.

"I'll have someone bring you food and water while we're gone." He looks at my outfit and sneers. "And more appropriate attire." His hand goes into his pocket and pulls out the keys to the cuffs around my wrists.

"Great." Sarcasm laces my tone as he removes the handcuffs and I rub the tender flesh, trying to get blood flow back into my hands. "What do you plan on doing to me? Why bring me back after all these years, Jasper?"

He cocks his head to the side. "We were to be married before you left. That plan hasn't changed. Maybe put on pause for a bit, but I still intend to make you my wife, Lucinda."

"You've got to be kidding me?" The man has lost his fucking marbles. Not that he had many in the first place. "Why would you lower yourself to bed a worldly whore?"

That's how they used to refer to the women who lived outside the compound or anyone who dared to show some ankle.

"Seeing you again made me realize that I'd deviated from God's plan when I married my late wife. God rest her soul." He bows his head as if showing respect to his dead wife. "When she couldn't bear children, God obviously saw fit to call her home so she could be reborn with a body that worked the way He intended."

I audibly swallow. Is every man on this compound certifiable? I don't even know why I'm asking that. The answer is unequivocally yes.

"What happened to her?"

"An unfortunate accident with one of my rifles."

He doesn't try to hide the menacing smile creeping across his mouth.

"Next time you tell that story, you might not want to smile at the end like a fucking creep, Jasper. It would make it more believable."

His dark chuckle sends a shiver through me.

"No one is going to question me. Just like no one would question my father. If a woman can't do what she was put on this earth to do, the best thing for her is to no longer suffer in her mortal toil."

"You're going to burn in hell. You, your sicko father, and all the elders." My gaze sears into his eyes, not showing an ounce of fear.

"We will be exalted, Lucinda. We're the Lord's Chosen." He holds his head high with pride. "After you've had something to eat and clean yourself up, we'll be back to begin your exorcism."

"I'm not possessed, you dumb fuck. I just think you're a piece of shit."

"Your demon has such a hold on you, you poor girl," he says, feigning concern. "Don't worry, we'll rid the beast from you, then you'll see your purpose and revel in being the wife of such a godly man." With that, he spins on his heel and exits the church.

I sit in one of the pews and stare at the altar in front of me.

"Listen, I don't know if you exist up there." My head tilts to the ceiling. "But on behalf of all mankind I'd like to formally apologize for all the shit these people do in your name. Amen."

Chapter Twenty-Two
Jude

The silence is killing me. I want to call my brother and hound him again, but he's already called me an impatient twat and told me to fuck off, and he'll call when the plane was ready… after the eleventh time I'd called.

The only thing left to do is wait. All of us have checked and rechecked our weapons, packed bags with extra ammo, and stared at each other like a bunch of ninnies.

Sitting in my room, the overall feeling is the same I used to have just before being sent out on a mission. My cold eyes stare back at me in the reflection of the mirror above my dresser. There is no fear or uncertainty on my face or in my eyes, just a fierce determination to get my woman back safely and not lose another brother. There is no other way for this to end.

We're planning an all-out tactical assault, but the waiting and anticipation is eating a hole inside me. Never has any mission been as important to me as the one we're about to go on. All my brothers are risking their lives for Lucy. And me.

Standing from my bed, I stomp into my bathroom and pull out my clippers. I always wore my hair short when I was in the service, so there were no distractions and nothing to give the enemy an advantage.

Clean and tight, my commander used to tell us.

I turn the clippers on and place them against my scalp, running the guard through my hair. The long blond strands fall into the sink. I go to the section next to it, then the next, and the next. When all my hair is scattered in the sink, counter, and floor, I rub a hand over my shaved head.

"Clean and tight, asshole."

Throwing the clippers in the sink I return to my room and change into a black t-shirt and tighten my shoulder holsters over it. I check my gun for the hundredth time and count my extra clips again before shrugging into my cut. As far as I'm concerned, there's no such thing as being over prepared, not in this situation.

Walking out to the main room of the clubhouse, Linc is the first to spot me. He says nothing, simply sends me a tight smile.

"Heard from Liam?" he asks.

"Not yet."

Cash, a former military man himself, comes from the kitchen. He nods and sits at the bar. Cash knows what it takes to prepare for a military op. This is no different in my eyes, except the outcome has much more important ramifications for me. I can't lose her to those fucks. I refuse.

A loud whirring sound comes from in front of the clubhouse. It sounds like a helicopter. Assuming it will pass, I don't think much of it. We don't get many helicopters passing over, but it isn't unheard of. Instead of getting quieter, the noise intensifies. Ozzy comes charging out of his office and looks around.

"What the fuck is going on?" he asks, walking to the window and peering between the blinds. "You've got to be shitting me," he turns to me. "Your fucking brother just landed a chopper in my parking lot."

Fucking Liam always has to make an entrance.

Walking to where Ozzy is standing, I raise the blinds and watch Liam and three other men get out. They start hauling case after case from the chopper.

"And looks like he's brought some extra firepower," I point out. "I'll gladly take it." I head to the front door and open it, walking outside to greet the newcomers.

"Brother," Liam says, looking me over. "Like the new hairdo, very circa two thousand ten."

Ozzy follows after me, and Liam opens his arms wide as if the gruff MC president is going to give him a hug. Ozzy simply stares at my brother, completely nonplussed.

"Not a hugger," Liam comments, dropping his arms. "Noted."

"We try to keep a low profile out here, Ashcroft," Ozzy says, waving his arm toward the aircraft. "This is not that."

"Not really my style." Liam shrugs, unbothered by the irritation in Ozzy's tone. "Jude needed me, and this was the quickest way to get here. I don't give a shit about your profile, to be honest."

The ease with which he basically tells my prez to fuck off is quite impressive, if not a little irresponsible. Men simply don't talk to Ozzy that way.

"Let me introduce you to my team," Liam says before Ozzy can reply. "This is Sawyer, my hacker extraordinaire." Sawyer looks up from his phone and gives the crowd that's gathered a two-finger salute. "Abel, he's a wiz at recon." The man comes to stand next to Liam and gives us a nod. "Kingston, who I believe you all met after the incident at my cabin." Liam quirks a brow at Ozzy. "Don't think I haven't forgotten you had my favorite safe house compromised, Oz."

"Ozzy," my prez replies. "And that was out of our control. I didn't exactly invite that fuckwad over for a beer."

Liam waves a hand dismissively in Ozzy's direction. "To-may-toe, to-mah-toe."

If Liam isn't careful, he might be the recipient of not-so-friendly fire.

"Lastly, this is Hendrix." The giant of a man doesn't say anything. Just raises his head from one of the boxes, looks around the crowd, then gets back to whatever he was doing.

Normally, I would be offended at the disrespect, but I'm so fucking grateful for my brother and his team being here, I let it slide.

"Where's the plane, Liam?" I ask after introductions are concluded.

"That little airstrip we figure the weirdo zealots used..."

I nod.

"It will be there within the hour. Which gives us just enough time to go over the plan."

If there's one thing I remember about these types of operations, it's you can have every detail down pat, but something always goes haywire. My brother is a master at accounting for every possible contingency, so I trust the whole thing won't go tits up.

We walk into the clubhouse, and one of the prospects brings us all coffee as Sawyer lays what looks to be satellite images across the wooden bar top.

"Where did you get these?" I ask.

Sawyer shoots me a look that conveys if I think he's going to tell me anything, I'm fucked in the head.

"This is the compound your girl grew up on. From what you've told Liam, I've tried to establish which building is which. Obviously, there's the church." He points to a grainy image. "And there are a few large barns scattered throughout. With the amount of artillery they could possess, being a crazy fucking cult, it's safe to assume this is where the bulk of it is stored. If you notice, each barn has several houses surrounding it, which would make for quick access to the weapons if whatever apocalyptic war they think is going to break out happens." Sawyer points to the out houses dotted throughout the images. "These look like run-of-the-mill meth labs. Nothing extraordinary about those except they're fucking tinderboxes waiting to explode. Let's try to steer clear of those or figure out a way to use them to our advantage." He tips his head back and forth, thinking about it. "We'll see. Jude," he says, looking at me. "Liam said your girl talked about the elders doling out punishment in the church, correct?"

My jaw tightens. "Yes," I grit out.

"It's safe to assume that's where they're keeping her, then." His finger lands on the church. "Getting to the church is our primary objective."

Ozzy leans over the images and stares at one in particular. Squinting his eyes, he points to a small blip in the photo. "What's this?" he asks Sawyer.

Sawyer has a look. "That's a plane. My guess would be the same one they used to get Lucy to the compound."

Ozzy stands straight and looks at Liam. "I want any information you can get me on that plane. There's no way some desert rats who cook meth could afford something like that. I want to know who else had a hand in this."

Liam nods. "Gonna cost you another favor."

"I don't give a shit. If it means keeping my brothers safe, I'll fucking do it."

Liam turns to Sawyer. “When all is said and done, do you think you could get the info?”

“Possibly. It’s grainy as hell, but maybe my friend could get me a clearer image.”

Liam turns back to Ozzy. “Consider it done.”

The fact that Ozzy is willing to be further indebted to my brother warms that organ in my chest that hasn’t beaten right since Lucy was taken.

“Now, let’s talk about a plan. We have twelve people, correct?” I ask.

“Thirteen. A friend from Philadelphia is flying the plane.”

“What friend?” I ask. My brother doesn’t have friends.

“Aiden Clarke. We served together,” Liam replies.

I vaguely remember meeting the man, but I do remember my brother saying he was always calm under pressure.

“Better keep him away from the meth labs. He has a particular history with things blowing up around him,” Sawyer jokes.

All of my brother’s men chuckle, even Hendrix, a sight that’s oddly terrifying.

“Okay. I want two men on each barn. If that’s where they keep most of their artillery, we don’t want them getting access to it. Three men should approach the church from here.” I point to one side of the property. “And three from here.” I point to the opposite end.

The men all around nod in understanding before my brother's phone chimes with an incoming text. He glances at his screen, then pockets his phone.

"Load it up, boys. Our ride's here."

The clubhouse goes into a flurry of activity. Bags are looked through once more, and my brothers start carrying things out to the vans we have parked. I stand in the middle of the chaos, not moving. I take in a deep, centering breath through my nostrils and let it out slowly through my mouth. When we get back, Lucy will be with me, and she'll be safe. This nightmare she's been running from will be over.

"You good, brother?" Linc asks, clasping my shoulder.

"Right as rain."

We get in the vans and head to the tiny airstrip those bastards used right under our noses. A man is standing outside the aircraft and waves when we approach.

"Jude, good to see you," he says when I exit the van.

"Aiden, thank you for coming," I reply, gripping his outstretched hand. "How did my brother rope you into this?"

"Hey, there was no roping. A simple request was all it took," Liam says, walking up behind us with a large black duffle in his hand.

Aiden shoots my brother a withering look. "Same old song and dance. He has guys tied up and needed someone who knew how to fly a plane."

"You weren't a pilot."

"No, but my fiancé wanted to take lessons. There's something about being in the air that calms her. It's something exciting she can do away from people. There was no way I was going to let her do it on her own."

"Congrats on the upcoming nuptials."

He smiles. "Thanks, mate. Now let's get down to business and get your girl back, so she and her family can drive you crazy with wedding plans."

I look around and think about what a wedding to Lucy would look like. She doesn't have family aside from the crazy assholes we're about to rain hell upon. But she has us. She has Charlie and every single one of my brothers. And if she wants a big-ass, loud-as-hell biker wedding with the family we've both chosen, then so be it. I'll give my woman anything she wants or needs, so long as there's breath in my body.

Aiden and I help load the plane with the packs and cases from the vans and strap in. It takes less than ten minutes once everything is said and done before we're airborne.

There's a certain relief in getting things underway and anticipation for what's to come at this point in a mission. I'm envisioning myself walking the dirt streets of the compound up to the church and picturing what I'll find when I open the doors. I'm thinking of the blank faces of the men I'm going to put in their graves tonight. I imagine Lucy being next to me as we fly home. It's all playing in my head on repeat.

"We've got this, brother." Ozzy sits next to me, pulling me out of the fantasy of slitting throats and letting dead bodies fall at my feet.

"I know. We don't have any other option."

"Where did your brother get a plane like this on such short notice," Wyatt asks, sitting across from us.

"A politician from South America. We rescued his daughter a while back," Abel answers. "When Liam called to ask for the favor, he was more than happy to get his plane to us."

The fact my brother, the one who everyone owes favors to, was willing to give one away says something. Liam didn't have to come. He didn't have to bring his men, but he did because he wasn't going to let me do this without him. Goddamn, I love the shit out of him, even if he drives me up the fucking wall.

"That's where Aiden had a little run-in with a hollowed-out car and explosives. It was insane. These fuckers rigged old cars all through their property with explosives. Must have seen us on camera and started blowing them up. Aiden was close to one when he was running with the little girl. Almost took them both out, but his body protected her from the blast," Abel explains. "He was lucky as shit, man. To this day, Liam talks about watching him fly through the air, thinking this was it. He was going to have to tell a senator that he got his security specialist killed and watch all our contracts dry up." He shakes his head. "His girl's friend calls him Captain America since he's apparently indestructible."

"But he's British," Wyatt comments.

"You try telling a feisty ass redhead she's wrong." Abel laughs. "If she wasn't so damn in love with her boyfriend, I'd take a shot at that. I love a redhead."

"Boy, Abigail Barnes would chew you up and spit you out before you uttered a single word," Liam says, coming to sit next to Ozzy.

"We're close to our rendezvous point," my brother says, looking at me. "Head on straight?"

"As an arrow," I reply.

The plane lands, and several trucks are parked on the makeshift airstrip.

"Friends of yours?" I ask Liam when I see three men standing beside one of the vehicles.

"I use them to procure certain things from time to time. They won't be going with us, though."

I nod, and we all exit the plane.

Liam walks up to the older of the two and shakes his hand. "Sampson, nice to see you," he says, using his other hand to reach into his pocket and pull out a thick envelope, handing it to Sampson.

"Liam, pleasure doing business with you." Sampson takes the envelope and hands it to one of the younger men standing next to him.

"Any word about these guys?" Liam asks, pointing in the direction of the compound.

"From what I heard around town, they're crazy as shit. Keep to themselves mostly, but whenever they send their women to town, it's like watching zombies walking around, not looking anyone in the eye. Everyone gets a real creepy feeling about them, ya know? They don't appreciate some of the people they do business with, either. Seems there's a biker gang that doesn't know how to act when they head out this way. Caused a lot of problems at the local watering hole on their trips."

"Thanks for the info, Sampson. Tell the wife I said hello."

"I'll do no such thing. She thinks I'm delivering car parts a couple hours from here. You know she hates your ass."

Liam chuckles. "She's not the only wife I tend to piss off."

They clasp hands, then Sampson and the other two get in their own truck and drive away.

We load up and gather around, a tense feeling thick in the night air.

"Aiden should stay with the plane," my brother says. "We don't know what kind of shape Lucy will be in or if anyone is going to be following us."

"As far as I'm concerned, the only souls safe on that compound are the women and children. Every other person in that place meets their maker tonight," I tell the group. I look at Liam and his men, then at my brothers. None of them blink an eye.

"The only thing I ask is save Otto and his fuck of a son for me if you can," I grit out. "I want to deliver them to hell myself."

Chapter Twenty-Three
Lucy

It's maybe an hour before anyone comes into the church. I've made one of the pews a makeshift bed, meaning I'm just lying on the hard surface, trying to come up with some sort of plan but still dealing with whatever that asshole shot me up with. When I was a girl, I used to sit here and wonder what it would be like to live a different life, one where I didn't see bruises on women and wasn't told because of what was between my legs, I was less than.

The door to the small church creaks open.

"Lu?" a familiar voice squeaks.

Tears spring to my eyes as I shoot straight up out of the pew, covering my mouth with my hand in shock at finally seeing her again.

"Cece."

Running toward her, she drops the items in her arms before I launch myself at her, throwing my arms around her slight frame.

"Cece," I say again, choking on her name.

Her thin arms encircle me, and we stand there for what could be seconds or minutes. I don't know and don't care; I'm hugging my sister. When we pull apart, my hands cup her cheeks, wiping away the tears that pour down them.

"I thought I saw you earlier on my way through town."

"You did," she says softly. "I didn't want Otto to see me, though. If he thinks I'm excited to see you, he'll become suspicious."

"Oh, Cece." My arms wrap around her again. "I'm so sorry they married you off to that man. I'm so sorry I left and couldn't protect you."

"Shh, now, sister." Her hands move up and down my back in a comforting motion. "It wasn't your fault. You know as well as I do there was nothing you would have been able to do to stop it." She breaks the embrace, grabbing me by the upper arms, intently locking her gaze on mine. "I'm glad you got out. Don't take this the wrong way, but I never wanted to see you here again. It would have meant you'd been captured and brought back. Imagining you in the world living a life of your choosing brought me peace."

Cece looks to the pile on the floor and bends to pick up a brown sack.

"Here, I brought you some food and water."

I take the bag from her and pull out a sandwich and water bottle. Unwrapping the sandwich and taking a bite of the fresh homemade bread causes me to smile around my mouthful.

"You always had a talent for baking, Cece. It's just as delicious as I remember."

"The elders thought seeing a familiar face would temper your resistance to being here." She shoots me a wry smile. "Of course, I had to act like I wasn't chomping at the bit to come here. I told them I'd help you see the error of your ways, and you would be more open to hearing it from me than them."

"I'm shocked they agreed with your plan."

"I've played the obedient elder's wife for a few years now."

The sandwich turns to thick ash in my mouth. The last thing I want to hear is everything she's had to endure since I've been gone, but I need to. It may break both of our hearts, but I need to know what she's gone through.

"How did you end up becoming his wife?"

Cece takes a breath and closes her eyes.

"When his first wife died unexpectedly, he began coming for dinner more often and sending little gifts to me. At first, I thought it was on Jasper's behalf, but then Jasper's marriage was announced to one of the other girls, so I was a little confused. About a month after their wedding, Otto came to the house and had a meeting with Father. I was called in and told I was to marry Otto, and Father was going to be elevated to an elder."

"What did Mama say?"

Cece's eyes widen. "They didn't tell you?"

My brows pull together tightly. "Tell me what?"

"Oh, Lu... Mama passed... not long after you left. She fell ill, and her fever raged out of control. There was nothing anyone could do, and Father refused to let her go to a hospital."

My head falls forward, and more tears pour from my eyes. My mother was never the affectionate type. She let Father punish us how he saw fit, which was often brutal and unyielding, without ever attempting to stop him or assuage his anger. But to hear she died in what had to be such a painful way does something to me. Anger... that's the emotion that's forefront. Anger for her and the countless other women and children who have died here because it was "God's will."

"Do you know," I begin, swallowing hard around my words. "Are you certain it was natural causes?"

"It was. I would have been suspicious if Father had remarried right after, but several members of the church fell ill around the same time. Even the men. Father never remarried. Even after I was married off and he didn't have anyone to cook or clean for him." She rolls her eyes. "Of course, it still falls on me to help take care of him and the house and my own house."

It's so strange to hear Cece talking as an adult with the responsibilities the older women in the compound always had. Now she's one of those women, and it fucking breaks my heart.

"Has it been terrible for you?" I ask.

"You know, at first, I tried. I tried to be a good member of the church and tried to be who they always expect us to be, truly believing I was doing right by God, but I don't know, something changed. I thought about all the ways I was made to feel inferior. The ways they would preach one thing from the pulpit, but we were making drugs that killed people. Then trading those drugs to gangs and whoever else would supply the elders with weapons. The more I thought about it, the more I started seeing the cracks. Does that make sense?"

I nod, thinking back to the day I left. "Perfect sense, Cece."

"I wish I would have come to the realization so much sooner, Lu. I should never have let you leave on your own."

Telling her I feel the same isn't going to make any part of her life since I left better. Instead of uttering a word, I wrap her in an awkward embrace over the food she brought me.

"You know I have to try to get out of here, right? There's no way I'm staying and putting up with any of this."

I'm positive Jude knows I'm missing by now, and I'm sure he's going absolutely crazy trying to find me. The problem with a compound like this is it's in the middle of a very vast desert. Aside from going to the Bone Breakers and getting the location, I don't know how long it's going to take him to find me, but I'm sure as hell not going to be waiting around. He'll do everything in his power to get me, but the truth is, there's no telling how long it's going to take or how long I have. The elders may decide to make an example of me like they did Bea.

"I know, Lu. And I'm going with you this time. I can't live like this anymore. Otto has been relentlessly badgering me about having a child. I'm just thankful it hasn't happened yet. No child should be raised in a place like this."

"If anyone sees you or asks you about seeing me, you need to play the part of the disappointed sister. And you have to be convincing, Cece. The less suspicion anyone has about your motives for visiting me, the better the chance we'll have of getting out of here. They won't suspect you of being a traitor."

"You can't betray a cause that's done nothing but betray you since birth," she says.

That awful feeling I had when my mother said nothing about me being married off to Jasper comes rushing back. No one stood up for me, just like there was no one to stand up for Cece in the last seven years.

"Where will we go?" Cece asks.

"There's a little town in Massachusetts called Shine. I've been living there with my best friend who I met in New Orleans when I lived there for a while. There're men there who treat women with kindness and respect." I get choked up thinking of all the brothers and Cooper. "They would lay down their lives to protect their family."

"You love them," Cece states with a smile on her face.

I nod. "They're my family." I reach for her hand. "And they'll be yours, too."

"They must be so worried."

Jude's face comes to mind. "If I know anything about them, they're looking for me as we speak."

We don't get a chance to say much more before Otto and my father walk in the church. Cece immediately stands and gives me a reproachful look.

"She ate her food. I've been reciting scripture to her to show her the error of her worldly ways."

Wow, Cece has turned into quite the little actress during my time away.

"I know you've done everything you could for her, wife. We'll take it from here."

Cece turns to leave.

"No, Cecilia. You need to stay and witness this," Otto commands.

She silently takes a seat in the pew while my father grabs my arm roughly and hauls me to the altar.

"Time for your punishment, daughter."

He takes the leather belt from his pants and hangs it ominously in front of my face, nodding at Otto.

Otto begins reciting some Old Testament bullshit. After every verse, a loud thwack sounds through the tiny church as my father hits my back with his belt.

A sharp cry erupts from my throat—the first is always a shock to the system—but I grit my teeth and successfully keep silent with the subsequent lashes. Fuck them if they think this is going to break me.

"Do you repent?" My father asks.

I remain silent.

Thwack.

"Do you repent?"

"Fuck you."

That earns me a blow to the face, courtesy of his fist.

"Do you repent?" he screams at me, spittle flying from his mouth.

No words leave my mouth as blood dribbles down my chin to the floor, which has seen much of my blood throughout my childhood.

My father huffs and resumes his position behind me.

I turn my head slightly and see Cece watching the horror show in front of her. Her face is an icy mask of indifference, but when I meet her gaze, the pain within them is clear as day.

Otto resumes reciting scripture, and my father resumes with his lashes. What can only be a few minutes, but feels closer to a few hours, passes slowly. Sweat is beading on my brow with the effort it's taking to stay silent and upright as my father continues to deliver blow after blow. My back and legs must have welts covering them by this point. It's a good thing I didn't change into the clothes Cece brought for me. It wasn't uncommon for them to lift our skirts and beat our bare thighs for whatever transgression we committed, then beat us further for tempting them with our naked flesh, saying that we wanted them to see our bare skin.

The door opens suddenly, and two men I recognize from the congregation hurry up the aisle.

"Elder Otto. We're under attack. The Great War is upon us," the first man says excitedly. These dumbasses have been waiting to be attacked since I can remember.

Otto looks at me with fury in his gaze.

I smile and return his hateful look with one of my own. "Seems the Great War was a little earlier than expected."

Otto and my father stand still for a moment as the two men who interrupted my punishment await orders.

"Get to the barn and gather the weapons. We'll meet you there," Otto commands.

"You two are staying here." He points to Cece, then to me. Otto leans over my kneeling form and grabs my chin, wrenching my head back. "If you think they're going to get you back, you're wrong. The devil won't win today, Lucinda."

"You're right. He won't."

Otto narrows his eyes, clearly understanding what I'm telling him. If he thinks he has a chance in hell of making it through the night, he's crazier than I gave him credit for.

He and my father stomp out of the church, and I slump to the floor. I wasn't about to show any weakness in front of them, but damn, my back is on fire.

Cece runs over to me, cautious consideration marring her features. "I don't know where to touch you," she says when I wince from her light touch.

"Here, take my hand." I reach out, and she helps me stand. The desire to fall to the floor in a heap and not move is strong, but I know exactly who showed up to this hellhole.

"Do you think it's your family?" Cece asks.

"I'd bet my left tit, sister." A small chuckle mixed with a groan escapes my throat. "There's something you should know about the men that came to help... they're bikers."

Cece's eyes go wide.

"They're nothing like the Bone Breakers or any of the other disgusting clubs the elders did business with. These are good guys, I promise," I'm quick to reassure.

Cece still isn't convinced. "I'm not going to lie, Lu, that scares me."

"Do you honestly think I would leave one hell to get tangled in another? I promise, no harm will ever come to you at their hand."

Gunfire is getting louder as we stand in the church. Until I see who's firing, there's no way my sister or I are going out there. Leave it to one of the members of the church to "accidentally" shoot me between the eyes.

"No! Sto—" I hear through the weathered doors of the church. A second later, blood is seeping inside from under the door. Just more stains to add to this disgrace of a congregation. Before I have a chance to take another breath, the door is kicked in and nearly falls from the old frame.

"There you are, love."

Chapter Twenty-Four
Jude

The heat of the desert is stifling, even though the sun went down hours ago. We took the trucks as far as we thought safe. No one wanted anyone on the compound alerted to our presence. There's something eerie as hell about traipsing through the open desert at night. Every once in a while, a sound that's similar to bacon frying is audible. Someone walked too close to a rattlesnake. I hope like fuck no one steps on one. Though we're all wearing military-grade night vision goggles, accidents can happen.

The compound is dark when we approach the fence line. There's no patrol in sight, but from what Lucy's said, they're there. However, she wasn't certain how many patrolled the fence, plus that could have changed in her time away.

It may have made more sense to stake it out and see for ourselves if we could determine a pattern, but like hell am I going to wait. Shit, if it had been up to me when I saw Cooper's dead body on the side of the road, I would've stormed the compound my damn self and killed anyone who got in the way of me getting to Lucy. Luckily, my brother and Ozzy talked me out of that plan.

The twelve of us gather around when we reach the fence.

"Once we're inside, chances are high that we'll be spotted. There likely isn't a way for us to go about this quietly with the amount of information we don't have," Liam says.

Not one of my brothers blink an eye at his statement. Though my brother likes a plan and all possible variables to be accounted for, even if his plans go off the rails from time to time, he understands that's not how things work in my world. Sometimes, you simply don't have time to formulate a strategic attack, and brute force will have to do. My brothers and me? That's an area we thrive in.

When no one raises any concerns, Liam nods.

"Alright. We'll enter here. Ozzy and Brax, you cover the barn on the south end. Linc and Wyatt, you'll take north. Barrett and Hendrix, you have the east. Sawyer, Abel, and I will loop around and head to the church from here." He points at the crude map he drew. "Knox, Cash, and Jude will approach from here. Keep them out of those barns, boys, but don't be surprised if they have other weapons at the ready."

None of us are sure how much artillery these people have, but what we have and they don't is training and experience. Lucy told me that all the kids on the compound are trained in weapons from an early age, but no one has real-world experience. How could they? They've been training for a war that isn't going to happen.

Tonight, though, we're bringing hell to their doorstep.

Abel cuts a hole in the fence, and all of us silently move through. After a few hundred feet, we break apart into our groups, each heading to our designated location.

The three of us hide in the shadows, keeping a low profile. Hopefully, we blend into the background enough not to be spotted by someone passing by an open window. The dirt streets are dotted with tiny, rundown houses. It strikes me how sad everything looks. I know there are children who live here, but not one bike or playset is in front of a single house. White paint is peeling from just about every house so badly, it's noticeable even in the dark. These people are poor as dirt, living on promises from a cult leader and hardly anything else.

I point to the steeple of a church about a hundred yards up ahead of our group, peeking over the tops of the houses. Knox and Cash nod in acknowledgment, and we continue our journey.

Suddenly, three shots ring out in the distance, followed by several more random pops of gunfire. Shit.

"Here we go, boys," Cash says with his gun raised and ready to fire.

Now that they know we're here, there's not much point in trying to keep quiet. The three of us start jogging through the streets, scanning each yard quickly as we pass, not wanting to be taken by surprise. As I'm passing a house closer to the church, a tiny face peeks from between the curtains. A little girl with wide, terrified eyes stares at us. This is why we're here tonight. I think of Lucy at that age and how afraid she would have been seeing three large men strapped with guns running down her street. Then I think of what that little girl would grow up believing about herself and about the world. It becomes clear to me we can't leave these women and children here. No man is safe as far as I'm concerned, but the kids? The women who are forced to live a life of servitude? They need an out as badly as my woman. We'll be giving it to them tonight.

The church doors are in view, but I don't see Liam's group yet. They may very well have been the ones firing. Two men franticly run up the stairs and into the church. As we approach, they come back down the stairs and head in the direction of the closest barn, still too far away to make out their faces, but now there are two more with them. Another man stands in front of the doors as though he's guarding anyone from going in or making sure no one gets out.

We approach from the side, keeping to the shadows. I remove my blade from its sheath before launching myself onto the porch of the church. The guard catches the movement from the corner of his eye.

"No. Sto—" Before he has a chance to react any further, I slide behind him, slicing the razor-sharp knife across his throat. He drops to the floor in front of the double doors, and his blood pools around him. There's a certain satisfaction that comes with wiping a piece of shit from the planet. The thought occurs to me that most people would consider me a monster for feeling that way, then I remember that I don't give a shit.

I try to open the door to the church as Knox and Cash face the street, keeping a lookout. The damn thing's locked. I could go through the pockets of the dead man in front of me to try to find the key, or I could kick it in. Option two it is.

The door flies open, nearly ripping off the old hinges, and in front of me, standing tall and brave, is Lucy.

"There you are, love," I say with a slight smirk ghosting my lips. Fuck, but is she a sight. My gaze zeros in on her as I stomp up the aisle with Knox and Cash guarding my six and take her face in my hands. "Let's not do this again, yeah?"

Tears pour from her eyes as she stares into mine. I lean down and smash my lips against hers, barely registering the thin woman next to her but immediately recognizing her from her picture—Cece.

Lucy whimpers, but it isn't one of pleasure. Breaking the kiss, I notice her cut lip. They'll pay for that. My gaze leaves her eyes and travels down the rest of her body, noting every injury and speck of blood on her.

These fuckers will pay for all of it.

"Where else?" I ask gruffly.

"What happened to your hair," Lucy asks, jolting out of her surprise.

"Jesus, Lucifer, that's what you want to know right now?"

"Well, it's a little shocking to see you storm in here without your long hair." She shrugs. Fucking shrugs like her reaction is completely reasonable.

"Come here, woman." I wrap my arms around her and pull her tightly into my body. Lucy lets out a cry of pain the second my arms touch her back.

"Turn around," I demand. Thankfully, she doesn't argue with me for once. When I get a look at her back, there's blood soaking into her light-colored tank top.

"Motherfucker." I gently raise her shirt up, exposing the welts and cuts on her back.

"It's not that bad," she tells me before pulling away from my touch.

If this isn't that bad, I hate to think what she's gone through that she *would* consider bad.

"Jude," she says, turning back around. "This is my sister, Cece."

My attention turns to the tall blonde who looks much younger than the age I know her to be.

"Hello, little bit," I greet, offering her a small smile.

Shots ring out closer to the church before she has a chance to respond.

"Give me a gun," Lucy demands.

I grab the pistol out of one of my holsters, and she takes it, checking the clip and cocking it. Fuck, that's insanely hot.

Lucy looks at me and notices my appreciative gaze.

"Not the time," she says, rolling her eyes.

Shots are fired into the church, but they go wide, thankfully missing us.

"These are the people you learned to shoot from?" I ask Lucy while ducking behind a pew next to her. She pops up and fires two rounds. We hear a scream of pain from outside, and she ducks back down.

"I was always a better shot than my teachers."

"Thank fuck for that," I tell her.

I stand and shoot, hearing another cry of pain.

"Not so bad yourself," she remarks.

"High praise coming from you, Lucifer."

Knox and Cash peek their heads out the door and disappear for a moment. When they come back inside the church, they're hauling two men inside, one bleeding from the leg, the other from the shoulder.

"Who are they?" I ask Lucy.

"Jasper and Otto. They're the ones who took me and killed Cooper."

I nod at the door, signaling for one of my brothers to close it. I want to take my time with these two and don't want to be interrupted. The men are hauled to where Lucy and I are standing in front of the altar and forced to their knees.

"How dare you attack God's chosen disciples," Jasper spits at us.

A sinister smile spreads across my face. "Big words for such a little man. Did you think you could kill my brother, take my woman, and live to tell the tale?"

"She was mine first."

"I was never yours, you sick son of a bitch," Lucy says before walking up to him and punching him square in the face. "That was for the plane, asshole."

"Cecilia, how could you turn your back on the Lord? On your husband?" Otto says, looking toward Lucy's sister.

"No," Lucy says, his attention swinging back to her. "You don't talk to her or look at her."

"She's my wife to do with as I please."

"Consider yourself divorced, areshole," I tell the powerless man.

"How dare you defile our holy sanctuary," is heard from behind me.

From the corner of the church, a man walks in with his gun raised to Cece's head.

"Father, put the gun down," Lucy says, turning to face the man who has the barrel of his gun pressed firmly to the back of Cece's head.

"You think you can tell me what to do?" he asks angrily. "A whore has no right to speak to a man of God."

Cece is crying silently as the man, who was supposed to raise and protect her, is pointing a gun at her head.

"You aren't going to get away with this," Lucy tells her father.

"Maybe I die today, but I'll be welcomed into the kingdom of heaven, whereas you, daughter, you'll be going straight to—"

A shot rings out, and Lucy's father crumples to the floor, missing the side of his skull.

"If I had to hear one more word from that man's mouth, I was liable to turn the gun on myself," Liam says, walking nonchalantly from the shadows.

Cece starts to wobble on her feet, but my brother grabs her around the waist before she can fall.

"Shh, now. I've got you."

He leads her to a pew and sits her down gently.

"Who do we have here?" Liam asks, walking over and standing next to us. From the corner of my eye, I see Sawyer and Abel enter from where Liam emerged.

"Elder Otto and his son, Jasper. The ones responsible for Cooper," I inform him.

Liam nods. "Alright then, brother. I'll let you and yours handle this."

Sawyer and Abel stand at the back entrance of the church to make sure there are no more surprise guests.

I walk up to Jasper. "Look at my woman over there, Jas. She's beautiful, yeah?" My gun waves in Lucy's direction.

He nods stiffly but doesn't speak.

"You tried to take what was mine to love and protect. And for what? To turn her into a mindless shell of a woman who was only good for breeding and cleaning." I look at Lucy, watching the man on his knees with hate in her eyes. "Nah, mate. A woman like this was never going to bend to a boy like you. She needs a man who can handle her fire, and you?" I point my gun at his head. "You need to die."

I pull the trigger, and he falls to the floor, a bullet right between his eyes like they did to Coop.

My body shifts toward Otto. "And then there was one."

Lucy walks up behind me, shaking with rage as she eyes the man on his knees.

"How many times?" she asks.

"What are you talking about?" Otto sneers.

"How many times did you rape my sister as she cried out silently, praying to your god to make it stop? How many girls did you give away to disgusting men like yourself to be used and thrown away?" Lucy stands next to me and holds out her hand. "Give me your knife."

Placing the blade in her hand, I watch with fascination as the vengeful goddess next to me invokes an almost tangible fear in the man who once did the same to her.

"It was God's will. You have no right to interfere with that." Otto eyes the knife with terrified desperation, finally realizing he has no hope of making it out of this church alive.

"You had no right to bring me here against my will or commit any number of horrific crimes you did in the name of God, yet here we are."

Lucy takes a few steps and plants her feet in front of his trembling body.

"You'll burn in the pits of hell for this, Lucinda. Mark my words."

She pretends to ponder his statement tilting her head back and forth and looking toward the ceiling. When her eyes meet his once again, they're hard as steel and just as unforgiving.

"I suppose I'll see you there, then."

Lucy holds my knife in a tight fist and slashes it across his throat. She watches as the blood pours from his wound, a look of shock on his rapidly paling face. It's only moments before his life is over. Knox releases him from his grip, and Otto falls, his eyes stare blankly at the altar of his church.

Lucy turns to me and hands me the blade. "We can't leave all these women and children here, Jude."

I smile softly at my little demon. Leave it to her to take a man's life in one breath, then worry about the welfare of the other women with the next.

"I know, love." After we settle things here, Matilda will be getting a call from me and a large donation to cover the costs of her new residents.

The night has turned quiet as I open the door to the church. Looking out, there are dead bodies littered throughout the town. Men who believed a corrupt elder and followed his teachings are nothing more than corpses in the dirt.

Cece, Liam, and my brothers come to stand in the middle of the small road with me and Lucy.

Ozzy and the rest of my brothers walk toward us, along with the rest of Liam's men.

"I think every man on this compound is dead," Sawyer says. "It was fucking freaky as hell. Some of them ran toward us with their rifles, wielding them like a fucking club because they were out of ammo."

"It was like those nightmares I used to have as a kid," Wyatt says. "No matter what, the vampires kept coming at you."

Liam chuckles. "Too many horror movies before bed?"

"Yeah, man." Wyatt lets out an exaggerated shiver. "Fucking vampire movies still scare the shit out of me."

Cece, who's standing next to Lucy, looks around the group. "What are we going to do with their families?" she asks as doors and windows creak open.

"Do they trust you?" I ask.

She shrugs. "Probably more than you at this point."

I see a little of the fire her sister has in her. Good, she's going to need it.

Lucy and Cece go around to all the houses and tell the women we're here to save them. Since Cece was an elder's wife, they're inclined to believe her, even though they gather around with suspicion and trepidation in their eyes. I catch sight of the little girl who saw us through her window. She stares at me when I send her a finger wave, smiling at her. Her head immediately turns to her mother's chest, and she hides her face. That's okay. As long as she grows up knowing she isn't a second-class citizen doomed to live under a man's harsh and unforgiving thumb, then my job is done.

"I need to get a bigger plane," my brother comments from next to me. He takes his phone from his pocket and walks away. "Senator," he greets when whoever is on the other end picks up.

My brothers and I collect the bodies scattered around the tiny town and haul them into the church.

"You know we could have left them out for coyote food," Barret says.

"No, I have a better plan," Lucy says, holding her sister's hand.

She and her sister walk to one of the barns and return moments later with a petrol can in each hand. Silently, they pour the fuel around the perimeter of the building before coming back to stand with us.

Lucy looks up at me with a smile on her face. "Love and protect, huh?" she says, repeating the words I spoke to Jasper.

"I love you," I burst out on a breath.

She lifts her brow, taken aback by my abrupt admission. "Why did you say it like that? All rushed or whatever."

I smile. "I didn't want you to say it first. I figured, after everything, you could let me beat you to something."

"You are fucking ridiculous, Jude Ashcroft. Only you would turn the first I love you into a contest to see who could say it first. Jesus, sometimes I wonder why I—"

Slamming my mouth to hers, I cut of her rant the best way I know how. I pull back and hold my finger over her lips.

"I think the words you meant to say were, I love you, too."

She purses her lips and rolls her eyes.

"I love you, too, asshole." Then she bites my finger.

A loud laugh booms from me as I take her mouth in another kiss, this one sweeter than the last. Lucy breaks the kiss and turns to her sister.

"Ready?" she asks, and Cece nods.

Pulling matches from my pocket, I hand them to Lucy. She shoots me a small smile before lighting one, then the rest in the book. Holding her sister's hand, Lucy drops the fiery book of matches onto the trail of petrol leading up to the church. We watch as fire licks up the outside of the dry wooden structure, quickly engulfing everything in a fiery inferno.

I turn around and watch the women's faces as they take in the scene before them. Some of them are crying—tears of relief or sadness, I can't be sure. Some of them are looking stoically at the flames, no emotion on their faces. The rest, like Cece, are wearing triumphant smiles. Those are the women who will take the others under their wings and, one by one, hopefully erase the years of programming and abuse every other woman here has endured.

Liam walks back over and pockets his phone. "We have another plane on the way." He looks down at Cece as she continues to be transfixed by the fire. "You know, I've never had a little sister. I'm rather looking forward to it. Especially seeing as she's a little pyromaniac like you used to be."

"Jesus, brother," I say. "It was one small garden fire. And it was an accident."

"Keep sticking to that story, little brother."

I let out an irritated huff as Lucy wraps her arms around my middle.

"Ready to go home?" she asks, the light from the flames dancing in her eyes.

Lucy calling Shine her home eases something in me. Without anyone chasing her, she's free to settle anywhere she wants, but what she wants is Shine. And me.

"Music to my ears, darling."

Epilogue

Jude

I hold on to the headboard to try to keep it from slamming into the wall as Lucy rides me, her glorious tits bouncing up and down with her movements.

"That's it, darling. Fuck, you feel so good," I praise, using my other hand to rub her swollen clit.

"Oh God, I'm going to come," she cries out softly.

"Give it to me, love. I want to feel you squeezing me."

Her tight core flutters around my cock before she opens her mouth and lets out a silent scream, her walls clamping down hard on my dick. I release the headboard and grab her hips, pistoning up into her as I empty inside her slick heat, trying to stifle my feral moan.

When the aftershocks of her orgasm subside, she raises off me and flops down on the bed by my side.

"Good morning," she purrs, brushing her fingertips over my damp chest.

"Yes, it is, love."

This is how we spend most mornings, and evenings, and sometimes afternoons. I can't get enough of my woman, and she's just as insatiable. I call that a fucking win.

My phone vibrates from the bedside table, and I look over at the screen. Liam's name flashes, eliciting a groan from me.

"That's the second time he's called," Lucy says. "It must be important."

"Not as important as making my woman come. I'll call him back in a bit."

I get up from the comfortable bed—good on me for picking out a king-size mattress all those months ago—and walk into the bathroom to grab a washcloth.

When I return to the bedroom, Lucy is sprawled on the mattress, looking delightfully fucked and heart-stoppingly beautiful.

"Oh no, you don't," she says when I bite my lip staring at her delectable curves.

I'm just about ready for round two.

"We have shit to do today, and you need to call your brother back."

Leave it to Liam to cock block.

Lucy's decided to go to college. Since she didn't have any school records or even an actual birth certificate to prove who she was, Sawyer did whatever magic he does and got her a social security number, an ID, and somehow made it appear as though she had graduated high school in the little town next to the compound. He's actually been doing that for many of the women we rescued from Lucy's childhood home/nightmare. Her fake was good, and even Liam was impressed, but to get into college, you need some sort of educational background, which Sawyer was happy and able to supply.

"Fine," I gripe. "I'll go make coffee."

Turning to open the door, Lucy calls to me from the bed.

"Umm, I think you're forgetting something," she says, pointing at my naked form.

Ah yes, we have to be clothed every time we leave the bedroom now. Cece is living with us, and unbeknownst to me when she moved in, she's an early riser. The screech she let out, and the days of not being able to meet my eyes after she got a full view of my naked arse one morning isn't something any of us need to relive.

I pick up some sweats and pull them on, grabbing my phone from the nightstand to ring my brother. Lucy rises from the mattress, and I smack her fantastic backside on my way out the door.

"I'll be right out," she laughs as I toss a wink over my shoulder.

I hit my brother's name on my call log and start the coffee.

"Finally," he answers, "I thought I was going to have to send out a search party."

"Hello to you too, arsehole. Why have you been ringing me all morning?"

"I need you to get in touch with Ozzy for me. He won't answer my calls."

"You sent him a bill for the usage of the planes that Silva and Hayes let you borrow for free. He's a bit miffed," I reply, rolling my eyes.

"It was a joke," Liam exclaims. "The man needs to lighten up."

"I'll be sure to pass that along," I say, sitting at the kitchen table, waiting for the coffee to brew. "What do you need?"

Liam explains the situation as Lucy comes out of her bedroom and takes a seat on my lap. Her small frame nuzzles into my body, and I kiss the top of her dark hair.

"Fine. I'll go over in a few after I've had my coffee," I tell my brother.

"This is important, Jude. And I think it will help solve the Italian problem that keeps popping up for you and your friends." By friends, Liam is referring to the Irish.

"Fine, fine." I hang up and wrap both arms around Lucy.

"I love it when you're sweet like this," I say, rubbing a hand over her back.

"I love it when you wake me with orgasms, then coffee," Lucy replies.

"I'll happily supply both every day, darling."

She wiggles on my lap, causing my dick to stir in my sweats.

"You know, I could use more of both."

"You said we didn't have time," I reply, peering down at her seductive smile.

"I can spare a few minutes."

"Hell, yes, you can," I say before pinching the arse I love so much.

Lucy squeals and jumps off my lap, shedding her shirt as she makes for our room with me hot on her heels.

Fucking love this woman.

I knock on Ozzy's closed office door after arriving at the compound an hour later. Poking my head in, I spot my prez at his desk, going over paperwork. Poor guy. This is why I would make a terrible MC president. Way too much damn paperwork.

"Got a minute, Oz?"

"Yeah. I'm just about seeing double at this point." He opens his desk drawer and pulls out a bottle of Irish Whiskey. "Want one? We have a shitton."

It's only late morning, but fuck it. If Ozzy's drinking this early, he must need it, and I'm never one to make a brother drink alone. He hands me a glass and sips his own as some of the tension in his shoulders ease. The Irish have fantastic taste in whiskey.

"What's up, Jude?" he asks.

"My brother called earlier. He needs some help."

Ozzy blows out a breath, likely still irritated at Liam's "joke."

"What is it?" he asks.

"There's a girl—"

“There always is.” Ozzy shakes his head, and a little chuckle escapes. Hope the whiskey isn’t going to his head already.

“She’s pissed off some dangerous people. People we’ve had dealings with.”

The fucking Italians have been a thorn in our side for too long now.

My prez groans and looks me in the eye. “Don’t tell me.”

“The Cataldis,” I reply.

“Fuck. Okay, what does he need?” The tension that seemed to release a few moments ago is starting to creep back in.

“He said he’s stretched thin at the moment, and this girl needs a safe place to lie low for a while until some shit gets sorted. That’s all he told me.”

“Did he say anything about who the girl is or what the shit is?”

“She’s some lawyer in Boston who’s been working on putting the high-ranking capos behind bars. She has some pretty hard evidence, and they want it back and want her gone. They’ve already tried to get to her once. Seems she has some friends in Philly who hooked her up with my brother.” It was Senator Hayes’ wife, actually. Apparently, they went to college together.

“Fucking great,” he says, sounding as though he means the exact opposite. “Are we protection for hire now or some shit?”

Shit, we should be. That might bring in a nice little penny.

"Liam said she grew up here, and you, Linc, and Knox all went to school together."

Ozzy cocks his head to the side, a bit more interested now in whom I might be talking about.

"Yeah? What's her name?" he asks.

"Freya Campbell."

I watch Ozzy's jaw tighten to the point I'm afraid he's going to break a molar. The tension that was creeping back has now ratcheted up tenfold. I've never seen my president look this stressed in all the time I've known him.

Who the hell is Freya Campbell?

The End.

Thank you so much for reading Jude and Lucy's story! I hope you loved them as much as I loved writing them. The rest of the brothers will be getting their books very soon!

If you enjoyed their story I would be forever grateful if you left a review. You can do that by visiting Jude's book page. Reviews are so incredibly helpful for us authors, and a great way to help us spread the word about our stories.

Do you want to know what it was like for a few of my guys growing up in Shine? Join my newsletter by going to my website www.katerandallauthor.com or by scanning the QR code to get a free prequel, **Rose Colored Glasses**, when you subscribe. It's an angsty first-love novella featuring Ozzy and Freya. Don't worry, you'll get to know more about them soon!

<u>Stalk me on my socials!</u>

TikTok

Facebook

Instagram

Goodreads

BookBub

Scan the QR code below for a link to all my socials and to sign up for my newsletter!

Also By Kate

The Ones Series

The Good One

The Fragile One

The Other One

The Black Roses MC

Linc

Jude

Ozzy

And more...

Acknowledgements

Where to start? First off, I want to thank YOU for going on Jude and Lucy's journey. The fact that you took the time and read my words means the absolute world to me!

Thank you Kiki, Megan, Colleen and Anna with Next Step PR. You keep me on top of all the "other stuff." I'd be lost in this author world without you all. Who knew there was more to being an author than just writing the words? LOL. I appreciate your reminders and support more than I can possibly say!

Molls, my sister from another mister and part time therapist. You keep me sane when I'm ready to lose it and remind me that this is what I was meant to do when I doubt myself. I love you, sister!

And last, but never least, Matt, the best husband the universe could have possibly given me. You gave me the courage to write and publish with three words... "Sounds good, babe." Even when I'm on crazy deadlines that I set for myself then cry about, your support and understanding never falters. I love you to the moon and back times infinity.

About Kate

Kate is a lover of all things books. It doesn't matter what sub-genre, as long as there's a HEA, she's in. She started reading romance in high school and would hide novels in textbooks to read during class. Becoming an author was always a dream she had and finally decided to put pen to paper (or finger to keyboard) and write what she loves. She grew up in the beautiful upper peninsula of Michigan then became a West Coast girl where she lives with her amazing husband and hilarious son. She would love to hear from readers so check out all her socials and sign up for her newsletter so she can keep you up to date on her books and whatever other ramblings come to mind.

Made in the USA
Columbia, SC
08 March 2024

32281486R00202